The Heatstroke Line

EDWARD L. RUBIN

Mechanicsburg, PA USA

Published by Sunbury Press, Inc.
50 West Main Street
Mechanicsburg, Pennsylvania 17055

www.sunburypress.com

NOTE: This is a work of fiction. Names, characters, places and incidents are the product of the author's imagination or are used fictitiously, and any resemblance to actual persons, living or dead, business establishments, events or locales is entirely coincidental.

Copyright © 2015 by Edward L. Rubin.
Cover Copyright © 2015 by Sunbury Press, Inc.

Sunbury Press supports copyright. Copyright fuels creativity, encourages diverse voices, promotes free speech, and creates a vibrant culture. Thank you for buying an authorized edition of this book and for complying with copyright laws by not reproducing, scanning, or distributing any part of it in any form without permission. You are supporting writers and allowing Sunbury Press to continue to publish books for every reader. For information contact Sunbury Press, Inc., Subsidiary Rights Dept., 50 W. Main St., Mechanicsburg, PA 17011 USA or legal@sunburypress.com.

For information about special discounts for bulk purchases, please contact Sunbury Press Orders Dept. at (855) 338-8359 or orders@sunburypress.com.

To request one of our authors for speaking engagements or book signings, please contact Sunbury Press Publicity Dept. at publicity@sunburypress.com.

ISBN: 978-1-62006-626-3 (Trade Paperback)
ISBN: 978-1-62006-627-0 (Mobipocket)

Library of Congress Control Number: 2015951590

FIRST SUNBURY PRESS EDITION: September 2015

Product of the United States of America
0 1 1 2 3 5 8 13 21 34 55

Set in Bookman Old Style
Designed by Crystal Devine
Cover design by Lawrence Knorr
Cover art by Emma Podietz
Edited by Celeste Helman

Continue the Enlightenment!

To my family and Planet Earth

CHAPTER 1

Daniel Danten didn't really want to have a family. What he wanted was to be a scientist, to teach at a university and produce original research. But this seemed so unlikely, given the state of things in Mountain America, that he decided to hedge his bets or he'd have nothing to show for his life. So he married a woman he convinced himself he was in love with and had three children. As it turned out, somewhat to his own surprise, he achieved his original goal, probably because he switched fields from astronomy to entomology, a subject of enormous practical concern these days. And now, with a secure position at one of Mountain America's leading universities, his own lab, and a substantial list of publications to his credit, he spent most of his time worrying about his family. His wife, Garenika, was depressed, his ten year old son Michael was suffering from one of the many mysterious ailments that were appearing without warning or explanation, and his fourteen year old daughter Senly was hooked on Phantasie and running wild. Worst of all, his sixteen year old, Joshua, who had always been such a reliable, level-headed and generally gratifying son, had become an American Patriot.

On a blazing, early September afternoon, with the outdoor temperature spiking at 130 degrees Fahrenheit, he was sitting with Garenika in the waiting room at Denver Diagnostic Clinic while Michael was being examined by still one more doctor. Garenika thought they would get some sort of answer this time, but Dan was convinced that the doctor would come out of the examining room and say that she really couldn't tell them what the problem is. Senly was spending a rare evening at home and Joshua was just returning from his field trip to the Enamel, an expedition that, Dan felt sure, was designed to make the participants angry, rather than providing them with information. The doctor appeared and Garenika jumped to her feet.

"Well," the doctor said, "I really can't tell you what the problem is."

"Why not?" Garenika asked, her voice tinged with its increasingly frequent sense of panic. "Why can't you find an answer for us? Look at him—he's losing weight, his skin keeps getting blotchier, and he's exhausted all the time."

"I'm sorry. As you probably know, we're pretty sure that we're seeing all these new diseases because the climate change has wiped out a lot of the beneficial bacteria that we used to have in our bodies. Commensals, they're called. But we've never really figured out how they work, so it's hard to compensate for their disappearance."

"Okay," said Dan. "So what can we do for Michael?"

"Keep him comfortable and give it time. Put cold compresses on any area where there's a rash. Try to get him to eat, lots of small meals if he can't tolerate a large one. We're expecting some new medicines from Canada that may relieve the symptoms. Michael's getting dressed; he'll be out a few minutes."

When Michael came out, they went back down to the clinic carport. Dan set the car for Return Home and sat in the rear with Michael, letting Garenika sit alone up front. They were quiet on the drive back home. Dan kept watching his discolored, fragile little boy, trying to think of something reassuring to say, but nothing came to mind. So when they arrived at the house, where Senly was waiting for them, he just gave Michael a long hug and told him to take a nap.

"Be quiet when you go into the room" Senly said to Michael. "Josh got back a few hours ago and he's sleeping." She turned to Dan and Garenika. "He was really tired out from the trip, so he decided to rest up. But he's looking forward to having dinner with you."

"Wonderful," said Dan, "we'll all be together."

"Well, actually," Senly answered, "I figured you'd be occupied with all the news from Josh, so I made plans to go out. Anyway, the kitchen might break if we have to program another meal for tonight. It hasn't been working very well."

"That was our decision to make, Senly, not yours," said Garenika.

"I was just trying to be considerate. Remember, you told me that you wanted me to take other people's feelings into account without being asked. So that's what I did. I even took the kitchen's feelings into account."

Dan couldn't suppress a grin. Senly got up to leave. "You can reach me on my wristlink. I'll just be having a quiet dinner with Ranity and Sharana."

As soon as she was out of the room, Garenika turned to Dan with a troubled, overwhelmed expression on her face. "You did it again. You smiled at her for her smart-ass comeback. You seem to think that anything she does is okay, as long as she acts clever."

Garenika was right. Dan knew that he valued intelligence too much. Somehow, he thought Senly's good mind and quick wits would make up for her surly irresponsibility, and that she would turn out well in the end. But it was his job as a parent to exercise more control over her, to keep her from getting into some kind of trouble she couldn't get out of, and maybe even to teach her some sense of morality.

"You need to be more careful, Dan. You have a career, but these three children are all I've got."

In fact, Garenika was a food inspector for the government, but she hated her job.

Josh appeared in the multi-purpose room promptly at 7:15, just as the servo-robot was putting out the plates for dinner. He looked completely refreshed and as handsome as ever. After announcing that he was glad to be home, asking where Senly was, and telling Michael that he was looking better, he launched into his account of the trip by using his wristlink to project images onto the wall.

"I couldn't send anything from the Enamel, of course, but that's what it looks like. I know you've seen it Dad, but Mom and Michael haven't. Isn't it awful?"

A scene appeared of wide, flat land, part brown rock and part dark clay, with scattered pools of water, jumbled piles of brick and stone, and a few stunted, scrawny bushes. Josh had taken the footage on an overcast day to heighten the effect.

"This used to be the richest farmland on Earth," he continued. "Until the Canadians raped it. You know where the term Enamel comes from, don't you?"

"Yes," said Dan. "NML—No Man's Land."

"I didn't know that," said Michael.

"They called it that because it's supposed to be a buffer between us and the UFA, didn't they?" Garenika asked.

"That what I thought, particularly because of the Canadian communications blackout there," said Josh, "but Stuart told us that the Canadians would actually have been glad if we kept fighting with the UFA. American netnews writers named it No Man's Land because no one could live there after the Canadians got through with it. Stuart really knows a lot about it."

"I should hope so," said Dan, "he's probably the leading American history professor at the University of Mountain America."

"He's really nice. And he ran a great trip."

"If he hadn't been running it, dear, we wouldn't have let you go," said Garenika.

"There are the train tracks," said Joshua, switching scenes. "You can't really get a good sense of them from a picture, but it's horrible to see them in real life. There are three sets, each twenty feet wide and running straight into Canada. Did you see them Dad?"

"No, I went to the Enamel to find insects. I never got that far east."

"Maybe if you'd seen the tracks you would feel different about the whole thing. Stuart said it took three years for them to transport all that topsoil up to Canada, even with those giant trains. Just think, three years ripping the surface off seven states."

"Well, we did drop nuclear bombs on their two largest cities," Dan replied.

"We were justified. They were supposed to let our citizens move into the Arctic, instead of taking in all those Aussies, Brits and Frenchies. They just let us die from the heat. What were we supposed to do!?"

"Not that. Even the Russians didn't do that when China conquered East Siberia."

"But both sides used nuclear weapons."

"Just tactical ones, on the battlefield. The United States was the only country that ever used them against civilian targets."

"Are you two going to start arguing again?" said Garenika. "I thought we were just hearing about Josh's trip."

"Well, the purpose of Josh's trip was to get him revved up so he'd argue with me."

"The purpose of my trip was to provide me with information so I can explain to you why it's so important to be a Patriot. We were the most powerful nation on Earth before the Second Civil War. And we could be powerful again if the three Successor States united. Just think, we'd have almost as many people as Canada."

"How do you figure that?" said Dan.

Josh was obviously waiting for that question. "Mountain America has 24 million people, the UFA has 25 or 26 million, and Pacifica has 12 or 13."

"Well, that's a little over 60 million by my math. Canada has 150 million."

"Yeah, but five million of them are in New England, and another 20 are in Alaska. Those used to be part of the United States. If you subtract 25 million people from Canada and add them to us, the difference gets a lot smaller."

"But why would all those people want to leave a richer, stronger country with a decent climate to join three smaller, overheated ones?"

"Because they used to be part of the greatest nation on Earth."

"Not the people in Alaska. They came from Australia, Britain and France, as you just mentioned."

"Only some of them. There are plenty of Patriots in Alaska. Plus another five million people in the Confederacies, and almost all of them are Patriots."

"They may be Patriots," said Dan, "but according to the last count, there's only about three million of them."

"That information comes from a Canadian satellite survey, and they falsify the data to make the Patriots look weak."

"Did Stuart tell you that?"

Josh was getting rattled, but he held his ground. "No, Noah told us that."

"Noah!" Dan exclaimed, with a snort.

"Noah knows a lot."

"Noah's a nut case," said Dan. "A Revivalist nut case." He was about to add that Josh would be a nut case too if he kept listening to people like that, but he caught Garenika's eye and restrained himself.

"I'm tired," said Michael. "Can I go back to bed?" Dan noticed that he had barely touched his food.

"Of course, darling," said Garenika. "I'll come in to say goodnight in a few minutes."

"Actually," Dan continued, trying to be slightly less contentious, "even three million people is impressive. Most of the areas below the Heatstroke Line are completely uninhabited these days."

"That's American ingenuity for you," Joshua said.

"And that's just a Patriot slogan."

"Dad, if all the Successor States were unified, we could repopulate the South. Crops grow there, so there's no reason it couldn't hold more people."

"That's impossible, Josh. I'd be surprised if they can even sustain the present population very long."

"Why exactly is that?" Garenika asked. "You can live below the Heatstroke Line if you have air conditioning. I mean, I'm a nutritionist, not an h-vac engineer, but the Halcyon units are really good. Ours can handle 150 degree weather easily."

"So it would seem," said Dan, "but it never works. It's a matter of social organization, not engineering. You've got to keep a power plant going all the time. As soon as it breaks down, or the fuel supply is interrupted, or one of your enemies blows it up, you die. Then there are the biter bugs. You've got to give everyone a stun gun or life is just intolerable. Even with the guns, it's pretty damn unpleasant. You're always on edge."

"But everyone in the Confederacies does have a stun gun" Josh responded. "And the power plant situation isn't as bad as you say, because they're not so far south. You can survive in winter without air conditioning, so it's only a little more than half the year that a power failure actually kills you."

"Well, that was the idea behind President Garcia's program of repopulating West Oklahoma, Central Texas and New Mexico," said Dan, "but the problem in that case is that there's no water. It's a lost cause."

"The problem," said Josh, "is that it created an unnecessary conflict with the Confederacies in Arkansas, East Oklahoma and East Texas. We need to start working together, not competing for little bits of extra territory. The Canadians never could have invaded us if it hadn't been for the Second Civil War."

"Well then," said Dan, "you should be an enthusiastic supporter of President Simonson."

"Simonson's a lot better than Carletta Garcia. At least he's trying to establish better relations with the Confederacies. But he's not a Patriot. He has no vision. One day we'll elect a real Patriot and start putting this country back together."

"One day," said Dan, "you'll go back to fantasizing about being a medieval knight, or hunting dinosaurs, or something else that's more realistic than the lost cause you've got for yourself now."

When Dan and Garenika were lying in bed that night, she told him that he was being much too hard on Josh. Dan was tempted to respond that he was just following the advice she had given him about Senly, but he realized that would be a smart-ass, Senly-type remark and stopped himself.

"You know," he said instead, "what Josh is doing can be dangerous, maybe more dangerous than Senly's Phantasie parties with those so-called friends of hers. I trust Stuart, but when they were looking at the train tracks, they were pretty close to territory claimed by the UFA. And American Patriotism is a criminal offense there; they could all have been arrested."

"But it's legal here. And at least he's using his mind and doing something constructive." She paused. "Oh hell, you're right. I'm worried about him too. I'm worried about all of them."

CHAPTER 2

Dan went into his lab at the University a bit early the next day, but he had trouble concentrating. He certainly had plenty of things to do. He had just received a new government grant to investigate the reason why the coffee being grown in Idaho had started tasting like potatoes. The Department of Agriculture's explanation was that potatoes had been the major crop in Idaho before the climate change. But when someone mentioned the problem to Dan, he realized that this explanation, like most of the Department's explanations, didn't make sense. He then recalled some research from early in the twenty-first century that attributed potato taste in coffee to an insect infestation and had applied for the grant. A more important project was a paper for a conference at the University of South Baffin Island on the connection between the climate change and accelerated insect evolution. Most people would have regarded this subject as important because of the biter bugs, but Dan was interested in the underlying theory, and was flattered to have been invited to present a paper at such a prestigious university. He began by working on the evolution paper, but when he found that he was having difficulty concentrating he tried switching to the coffee project. That didn't work either; all he could think about in any sustained way was his children.

Yesterday had been a disturbing day. He realized that a great deal of his upset stemmed from a lack of control. He couldn't control Michael's health, he couldn't control Senly's behavior, and he couldn't control Josh's beliefs. But something else was bothering him about last night's conversation. He felt he hadn't framed his arguments very well, that he should have been able to refute Josh's assertions more effectively. But it seemed ridiculous to be competing with his own child. Was he just indulging his old desire to assert his intellectual superiority in any circumstance, as Garenika had pointed out to him on many occasions? Or was

THE HEATSTROKE LINE

he beginning to wonder whether Josh was really right, that there was something about Patriotism that made more sense than he was willing to admit?

By 11:30, he decided to give up and go down to the cafeteria for an early lunch. His weekly meeting at the Department of Agriculture was at 2:00, so if he chatted with two or three people, he could use up the extra time and then head off to the meeting. At 1:30, after chatting with seven or eight people, he went downstairs to the carport and set his car for the Government Center. He had to drive because the Brighton Avenue mag-lev had fallen into disrepair under the Garcia Administration and hadn't been repaired by President Simonson, despite his campaign promise. As usual, there was a lot of traffic, and about two miles short of the Center, the car came to a complete halt. Dan looked up from the article he had been reading on the car's link screen. The sun was streaming directly through the side window and he could feel its power, although the inside of the car was still comfortably cool. The external temperature, according to the thermo-indicator, was at the fatality level. Dan felt a sudden sense of vulnerability. All that stood between him and the brutal, suffocating heat was a bubble-shaped piece of metal and plastic machinery. As a practical matter, he could easily reach one of the buildings along the avenue if his car broke down, and most drivers would take in someone who was out in the heat—he had done that himself on several occasions. But the sense of being in a hostile environment, of depending so heavily on a potentially vulnerable machine, awakened a sort of primordial terror in him.

His wristlink buzzed. It was Retiba Walters, the Research Director for the Department of Agriculture, asking him if he was going to be on time for the meeting. This seemed odd. The weekly meetings were generally rather casual and no one could be expecting him to report about the coffee project since he'd gotten the grant just a few weeks ago. In any case, he told her he was stuck in traffic two miles away and would do his best to arrive as close to 2:00 as he could.

A few minutes later, the traffic began to clear and, to his surprise, he was only five minutes late. The meeting hadn't started yet. In fact, everyone was sitting around the table in silence, which was also surprising. Besides the usual participants, Soronia Hernandez, from East Montana University, was there. Dan nodded to her. He figured that she was in Denver for some other purpose since these meetings were generally attended only by the

9

Agriculture staff and the few local academic researchers. Being late, Dan didn't want to ask why the meeting hadn't begun, but after another five minutes, his curiosity got the best of him.

"We're waiting for someone," said Retiba, unhelpfully. More time went by. Suddenly, the door swung open. Two large men and an equally large woman came into the room and stood on either side of the entrance. Then Temarden Goldberg, the Secretary of Agriculture came in, followed by a familiar-looking black woman whom Dan couldn't place, and then by President Simonson. Dan had never met the President in person. Simonson was taller than he had expected, but looked older; Dan wondered whether his image on the net was being real-time edited whenever it appeared. All three of the new arrivals took seats around the table and Simonson nodded to Goldberg, who began speaking.

"Everything you are about to hear is to be kept in the utmost secrecy," he said, in his usual, sententious tone. "You will understand the reason momentarily. Unauthorized disclosure of any information from this meeting constitutes an act of treason. Do you all understand?" Dan had never particularly liked the man. When Goldberg was the Department of Agriculture's Research Director he had tried to involve Dan in two projects using bio-chemical toxins to control agricultural insect infestations, in violation of the Canadian import standards, and Dan had distrusted him ever since. But he nodded along with the other people around the table. Goldberg paused for a moment, then continued.

"There has been an outbreak of biter bugs in East Montana. It happened yesterday morning, in the fruit growing country about twenty miles south of Glendive. We immediately sent a control team in, quarantined the inhabitants and burned approximately ten thousand acres of land. Hopefully, we got all the bugs. We have managed to keep the outbreak off the net so far, but obviously, it is going to become public very quickly. That means we may need to deal with a general panic. So the first thing we need from you"—here he waved his hand toward the far end of the table, where the scientists were sitting—"is an assessment of the situation. Why don't you start, Saronia, since this happened in your neighborhood. Could this be a natural occurrence?"

"I'll start by saying that I'm not really an expert on biter bugs," she said. This was a veiled reference to Mark Granowski, who had been Mountain America's leading authority on the subject. He had been dismissed from the Department of Agriculture when

THE HEATSTROKE LINE

Simonson became President, on the ground that the government didn't need him now that it was abandoning the previous administration's effort to re-occupy West Oklahoma, Central Texas and New Mexico. Saronia's gumption in beginning that way was admirable, Dan thought. She continued: "But as far as I know, there's no way it's natural. Biter bugs just don't spread like that. They move incrementally, never more than a few miles each season, and they don't skip intervening territory. So even if we're dealing with a cold-resistant variety of the bugs—which would obviously be a nightmare—it's not likely that they got there on their own."

"Dan, what do you think?" Goldberg asked, continuing down the table from Saronia.

"Well, I'm not an expert on biter bugs either," said Dan, feeling honor-bound to support Saronia. "But from what I know about insects generally, I agree. So far, the biter bugs only live below the Heatstroke Line, which is about a thousand miles from where you're telling us this outbreak occurred. There used to be an insect called a monarch butterfly, which in some cases migrated nearly two thousand miles. But biters, although they're not a true bug, are a kind of beetle, and beetles just don't travel like that. As Saronia said, they extend their territory only by short distances in a given generation. Besides, the monarchs always migrated to the same place each year. They didn't show up in places that they'd never been before, or—"

"Okay, we got it, Dan. You're next Janaly."

Janaly Francesca was the entomologist at Colorado Technical, the other university in Denver. She was quite young, but Dan thought she was very good.

"I have nothing to add. I think Saronia and Dan are completely right."

"David?"

Unlike Janaly, David Hardaway wasn't very good at all. He was the entomologist at the University of Colorado down in Boulder, which, having survived both the Second Civil War and the UFA-Mountain America War intact, was the oldest and most prestigious university in Mountain America. Dan admired its elegant brick buildings and gracious landscaping, but he thought most of its faculty was overrated and owed their positions to political influence. That was certainly true for David, who had managed to get a number of lucrative grants. Although he wasn't based in Denver, he made sure to attend all the Department meetings.

"Before I concur with my colleagues, I would need more empirical evidence," he began. "It's hard to say right now whether—"

"But right now is when we need your opinion, David," said Goldberg, who may have been devious and bureaucratic, but certainly wasn't stupid.

"Then, as a provisional matter, I'll go along with the others."

"Okay," said Goldberg. "You've all confirmed what we've concluded. You see, we found some puddles of aircraft fuel right where the outbreak started."

Dan was annoyed at being tested, rather than being told all the information right away, but restrained himself. "What kind of aircraft?" he asked.

"It is difficult to say, given how many aircraft are patched together and re-conditioned these days. But it certainly looks like the bugs were brought in from somewhere else." He stopped talking and looked at the President, perhaps in response to some signal Dan had missed.

"Thanks Temarden. So the question is, who brought the bugs into Mountain America, and why. I've asked Liz to look into this question, so let's hear from her next." He turned to the woman next to him, whom Dan now recognized as Lizabetta Smith, the Assistant Secretary for Successor State Affairs.

"We think this is the work of the UFA. We can't be sure, but several things point in that direction. First, they've shown a fair amount of hostility to our new administration, probably because of our efforts to avoid conflict with the Confederacies. Second, we know they've built a new lab to study biter bugs and they've hired Mark Granowski, who several of you have just made implicit reference to, as the head of the lab. Third, as you probably know, they're facing a succession problem. Hanary Carson has no children, and since Cantara Carson's daughter died from one of these mysterious diseases, she only has her son left, who everyone regards as a moron. So it's possible they want to engineer a crisis in order to test some new people, since the twins are getting old and Cantara may be ill."

"Thanks, Liz," said Simonson. "We've contacted the UFA, and they've agreed to meet with us—on their territory, as usual. Liz will head our delegation. In addition to our diplomatic and military representatives, we want you four entomologists along so that we can make an immediate assessment of their response. You'll be leaving in a few days." He paused. "I can't emphasize to you how important it is to keep this conversation completely confidential, even after the news about the bugs hits the net. The bugs themselves will cause enough panic. We don't need to add war hysteria to it."

He nodded to Goldberg, who began speaking immediately. "The code name for this mission is 'Repulsion.' You will each be getting a link message from me under that designation with a time and place to report. When you do, you must be ready to leave immediately and be prepared to stay at least three days. And let me underscore what the President has said about secrecy. You are not to discuss this matter among yourselves, or with anyone else, including your family. Identify your reason for leaving as 'government business.' "

Dan drove back to the University of Mountain America with a sense of unreality. The possibility of war with the UFA, after nearly 40 years of a stable, if uneasy truce, was terrifying, and the possibility that the biter bugs would infest Mountain America even more so. He had been worrying about his wife and children, but at least he had been able to deal with their problems on his own terms, without having large, external forces impinging on him. Was that about to change? Was the life he had created for himself about to be invaded by forces beyond his control? He tried to feel flattered about being chosen to be part of what was obviously an important mission, but even the assignment felt threatening. He hadn't been given a choice about it, and he disliked that intensely. He was tempted to refuse and wondered what would happen if he did.

As soon as he reached the University, he went to Stuart McPherson's office. Fortunately, Stuart was there, surrounded by three screens of documents that cast oddly lighted patterns on his elfin face and slender frame.

"Hey Stuart. How are you? Listen, I want to thank you for taking such good care of Josh on the Enamel trip."

"You're welcome. He's a great kid. I thought you'd be mad at me about the trip, though. I know you're not a big fan of American Patriotism."

"Well, you're not the one who got him into it. Tell me, though, do you really believe all that stuff?"

"I don't think the Successor States are going to get together and conquer Canada, or that we're going to get Alaska back, if that's what you mean. But it would be nice if we could cooperate with each other. If we were able to reconstitute the United States, we could be one of the major powers, just like Canada, Europe, Russia or China."

"Yeah, but how do we do that? I wouldn't want to be part of the UFA."

"Neither would I. But you know, the twins are getting pretty old, and it's not clear there's anyone to succeed them. So there could be an opportunity in the next few years."

Dan's sense of uncertainty about his own beliefs returned. Stuart was one of the few people whom he was reluctant to argue with. Besides, he had something more urgent to talk about.

"Actually, that leads me to why I'm here. I have a question for you. I've just been assigned to go on a sort of diplomatic mission to the UFA. I can't give you any details—it's all confidential, on pain of death and that sort of thing. But it's over a pretty confrontational issue, and I was just wondering whether you thought it would be safe."

"Confrontational? Sounds like there's some kind of crisis."

"Yes, but I really can't tell you any more about it. I'm not even supposed to say as much as I have. But I wanted your advice."

"Can you tell me who gave you the assignment?"

"Nope."

"Okay. I can guess it was a high-ranking government official. I'm surprised I haven't heard anything about it."

Dan realized that Stuart was annoyed that he hadn't been consulted. He was, after all, one of Mountain's America's leading experts on American relations. Dan thought about saying that the issue involved his own area of specialty, but he realized that would give away the nature of the crisis, assuming Stuart hadn't figured it out already.

"Anyway, you want to know if it's safe to go on a diplomatic mission to the UFA. I should think so. Why not?"

"Well, as I recall, they executed some diplomats a while back."

"Yes, but that was under the old man. The twins don't do that sort of stuff. That's not to say that they're not aggressive. But at least they're rational. Why, were you looking for an excuse to say no? You don't like being ordered around, do you?"

"I guess not," said Dan, feeling a little queasy about having told his observant friend as much as he had.

"See, this is the sort of thing that concerns me," Stuart continued. "Do you have any memory of the UFA-Mountain America War?"

THE HEATSTROKE LINE

"No, I was a toddler. And I grew up in Utah, which wasn't directly affected."

"That's right, I'm several years older than you. I remember the UFA troops advancing across the Enamel. And we were living here in Denver so I remember taking shelter in the bunkers and hearing the bombs falling before Canada imposed the truce. It was awful."

"I'm sure it was."

"So when you go on your mission," Stuart said with a wry smile, "do your best to prevent us from going to war again."

"Absolutely. And I'll see if I can get the twins to resign and merge the UFA into Mountain America."

CHAPTER 3

The message from Temarden Goldberg came early the next day. Dan had assumed he would simply drive to Denver Airport, which adjoined the Government Center, but the message said that a car would come by to pick him up in forty minutes. Despite Stuart's reassurance that the UFA wouldn't kill him, he felt his heart pounding and he broke out into a sweat. He was already packed, and he had already discussed practical arrangements with Garenika, but felt compelled to go back into their bedroom to review things with her one more time.

"Remember, Michael has his middle school orientation tomorrow. The auto-bus will come for him at eight. Be sure he's had his medicine, OK?" She nodded. "If the kitchen breaks, or even the servo-robot, just go to a restaurant. It's not that expensive. I'll arrange for the repairs when I get back." He turned to leave, then stopped. "You'll be all right, won't you?"

"I'll be okay, Dan. I'm just worried about the kids, but so are you."

"I know. But they'll be fine. Try to relax a little." Garenika gave him a dubious look and Dan, not knowing what to say, got his suitcase, looked into the multi-purpose room to tell Josh and Senly that he was leaving on "government business" he had already mentioned to them, and went into the entryway to wait for the car. Then, on a sudden impulse, he went back.

"Josh, can I talk to you for a moment?" They sat down into one corner of the room. "Listen," Dan said quietly, "I'm sorry if I was hard on you the other night. As you know, I'm not a big fan of Patriotism, but I talked to Stuart and I realize that it makes more sense than I've been willing to admit. I wanted you to know that."

"Thanks, Dad, I appreciate it. I just don't want to live my life the way we've been living up to now. Things could be so much better for us."

"You'll have a great life regardless, Josh. You're a great kid."

He patted Josh on the back and turned to Senly.

"Uh-oh," she said, "now I bet you want to talk to me."

"I do."

"I'm not such a great kid, am I?" she said. She had obviously overheard at least part of his conversation with Josh.

"Yes, you are. You're really smart, and you're a nice person."

"Some of the time."

"No, all the time. I don't like a lot of the stuff you're doing, but that's because I want things to work out well for you. I'm sorry if I've been harsh. It comes from concern, Senly. I'm not trying to make you miserable."

"Are you about to ask me for some kind of promise?"

"No, I'm not, other than being nice to your mom while I'm away. I just wanted to tell you how much I care about you."

Not knowing what else to say, Dan looked into the bedroom Michael shared with Josh. Michael was still asleep, and Dan decided it would be overly melodramatic to wake him up, so he went back into the entryway to wait.

A big blue military car pulled up, with the official Mountain America insignia on its side and a human driver, a stolid man in uniform. Dan got in, thinking that if the government was really so concerned about secrecy, they wouldn't have sent a vehicle like this down a residential street. The driver nodded to him but said nothing. They didn't drive to Denver Airport, as Dan had expected, but to the military airfield a few miles to the south. The driver, still without speaking, directed him to a small, squat building alongside one of the runways. Dan went in to what was clearly a briefing room, with about 50 folding chairs arranged in rows facing a large screen in the front of the room. Temarden Goldberg was there, sitting on one of the seats at the front of the room and talking in hushed tones to David Hardaway. Dan sat two rows back, feeling excluded and vaguely uncomfortable. A few minutes later, Saronia and Janaly came into the room and sat beside him. Goldberg broke off his conversation and addressed all four of them.

"Okay, let me update you. We have arranged a meeting with the UFA State Department. We're hoping Jesse Davis will be in charge, but they refuse to say for sure or to inform us about the exact time of the meeting. It will probably be tomorrow morning, but it might be today, depending on whether and when Davis is available. Obviously, they are being difficult, so we are going to confront them. One thing we want is to inspect that new insect lab they have established, the one that Mark Granowski has been placed in charge of. That's where you come in, or at least one place where we need you. We may also need you to determine whether what they tell us at the meeting makes sense. But don't say anything on your own. I will inform you if we want you to talk." Saronia looked at Dan and rolled her eyes. "There's a car outside that will take us to the plane. So collect your luggage and proceed at once."

The plane, as Dan expected by now, was a military aircraft, with the three snow-capped peaks of the Mountain America insignia on its side. Lizabetta Smith was already inside, talking to several other people who Dan didn't recognize. Retiba Walters, the Research Director for the Department of Agriculture who Dan regularly dealt with, wasn't there, however, and neither, of course, was Stuart, although his expertise regarding inter-American relations would have been useful. A few more people got on, two in military uniform, and with no further announcements, they took off.

Dan tried to think of something conversational to say, at least to his fellow entomologists, but nothing came to mind. He realized he should have brought a reader pad so he could read a novel from his wristlink; since he hadn't, he moved to a seat next to the window and looked out. It was a clear day, with harsh sunlight pouring out of an adamantine blue sky. The Denver suburbs sprawled across the flat land to the east, the grey cryoplastic houses punctuated by a few blue swimming pools that occasionally flashed golden in the morning light. Then they were out over the plantations of East Colorado. Dan could easily recognize the circular coffee fields, irrigated by their giant pivots— concentric circles of squat, dark green shrubs separated by thin strips of brown earth. The corn and soybeans, which needed less water, grew in rectilinear strips, scarred here and there by irregular tornado tracks, while the fruit trees were planted in smaller patches and separated by wide paths to allow for the passage of mechanical equipment. It was easy to distinguish the palm oil trees, with their dense, spiky clusters of fronds that joined into a continuous mat of greenery. The orange and grapefruit trees grew separately, each one a dot of green against the brown earth, and Dan could tell them apart as well, the grass-green leaves of the grapefruit trees contrasting with the deep green of the oranges.

In less than an hour, they had reached North Platte, the capital of Nebraska. It was smaller than Denver, but still covered

THE HEATSTROKE LINE

a large expanse of dead-flat land, with the Platte River curving sinuously across it. The plantations became more widely spaced; then the plane crossed the eastern border of Mountain America at the 100 degree West longitude line and they were over the Enamel. In some places, it consisted of bare rock which glinted in the sun and seemed to justify its mistaken name, while in others enough soil remained to support a sparse growth of creosote or sagebrush. The land was punctuated by irregular ponds of greenish water and by ruined towns that had somehow acquired the colors of the surrounding landscape.

Dan tried to summon his son's sense of anger about the removal of the topsoil from what had been such rich farmland, but he found himself unmoved. The United States, after all, had killed six million Canadians in the nuclear attacks, so one could hardly blame Canada for retaliating. Besides, Dan had always seen himself as a citizen of Mountain America, not some larger nation. It wasn't possible to be an academic researcher anywhere in Mountain America—or in any of the Successor States, for that matter—unless one got funding from government grants. The Mountain American government had consistently funded Dan's work, through four different presidential administrations, and that was where his sense of loyalty resided. Any merger of Mountain America into a larger entity—even if that was a real possibility— would only endanger his position, and Garenika's as well. Josh was obviously a victim of youthful idealism and would presumably grow out of it when he had to start earning a living. On the other hand, there was nothing flighty or irresponsible about his son. Maybe, Dan thought as he looked out over the relentlessly bleak landscape, Josh—and Stuart—were making sense. Maybe some of America's former prosperity could be restored, and life could be better for everyone, if the three Successor States and twenty five odd Confederacies could be re-united.

In another hour, they had crossed the Enamel, and then the Mississippi River. Now they were over the UFA territory and the plantations began again, in this case all at once and densely spaced. Clouds appeared and soon joined together into their characteristic pseudo-snowfield, ironically, Dan thought, given the blazing heat at this time of year. When they landed at Columbus Airport, the sky was grey and a light rain was falling. But this failed to relieve the heat, which wrapped itself around their group with a suffocating intensity on their short walk from the terminal to a waiting bus, an official vehicle with the UFA thunderbolt emblazoned on its side. Once they were all seated in the bus, Lizabetta announced that she had received a link message from the government, and that they were being taken directly to their meeting.

Dan had only been to the UFA once before, for a conference at the University of Michigan, and he had been so concerned about his presentation—it was while he was a junior professor—that he had barely noticed his surroundings. Now he watched attentively as the bus drove itself into the city. At first, they were on a freeway, which looked the same as any freeway in Mountain America, but when they exited and drove through a residential neighborhood, the difference was immediately apparent. Unlike Mountain America, many of the homes were pre-war structures made of brick and stone, with modern cryoplastic buildings scattered in between. The older homes were enormous; most were two stories, and Dan guessed they each had as many as eight, ten or even twelve rooms. He was surprised to see that a number of these buildings were empty, boarded up or falling into ruin, but, on reflection, it made sense. Unlike Mountain America, which had accepted at least some of the refugees from the coastal cities, the UFA had many fewer people now than it did before the Second Civil War. The abandoned buildings made the streets seem dreary, but the occupied structures looked prosperous, and Dan was additionally surprised to see that some of the streets were lined with trees in large, but evidently movable containers. That was one way to preserve some urban planting despite the tornadoes, Dan reflected.

The downtown skyline was significantly larger than Denver's and had several glass and steel buildings from the pre-war era as well as modern cryoplastic ones. Again, no reason to be surprised, Dan thought; Mountain American hadn't bombed Columbus or any other UFA cities during their war over Oklahoma. Just short of downtown, the bus turned off the road, went through an electronic gate, and pulled up to the entrance of a long, three or four story white building. As soon as they got out, they were shepherded by uniformed guards through a mercifully cool hallway and found themselves in a conference room, with a large rectangular table running down the center and a gleaming metal model of the UFA thunderbolt at one end. The UFA representatives were already seated on one side of the table. There were at least as many as in the Mountain America entourage, and they were all in uniform. Jesse Davis, whom Dan would have recognized from his ubiquitous image on the net, wasn't there. As soon as their group was seated, a young blond man, tall and notably thin, stood up to begin the meeting. Dan prepared himself for the formalities that he assumed would initiate a high-level diplomatic event. All the people at the table would be asked to introduce themselves, he thought, and he starting rehearsing in his mind the version of his title he would use, and whether he should refer to himself as Dan or Daniel.

"We hear there's been an outbreak of biter bugs in Mountain America and that you're accusing us of having caused it," the man said, in a harsh, accusatory tone. "We categorically refuse to respond in any way. What we want you to understand is that the United Federation of America is a sovereign nation, and we will not stand for any such accusations."

The man stopped abruptly and stared at Lizabetta. She responded in a quiet, steady voice.

"No, Saul, we're just asking for information. If the UFA isn't behind this outbreak, all you need to do is tell us. If it is, then I would remind you that we're a sovereign nation as well."

To Dan's surprise, the man started shouting in response. Dan felt himself cringe, as if he were a child being reprimanded by a teacher.

"That is an accusation, and I want you to know that it's an act of war. Do you hear me? An act of war. We will not tolerate it under any circumstances."

"That's not true," said Lizabetta in her same calm, steady voice, "but introducing biter bugs into another nation is an act of war, don't you think?"

"We refuse to respond to any demand for information, so you have no way of knowing whether we've done that or not. But we know for sure that you've accused us, and that's an act of war. We've informed Canada that we are mobilizing against you. You have chosen this course of action, and you will have to live with its consequences."

"Seriously, Saul, do you really think . . ."

"This meeting is over. You will be taken back to your plane, under instruction to return to Mountain America immediately. If you remain in the United Federation of America for any reason, or speak with any other person, you will be arrested and executed."

Five minutes later, they were back on the bus, an hour later they were on the plane, and by late afternoon they were back in Denver.

CHAPTER 4

By the time Dan got home that evening, news about the biter bug outbreak was all over the net. There were visuals of the area in East Montana that had been burned to kill the biter bugs, background stories on the bugs, and a few speculations that Canada or the UFA was responsible for the outbreak. Next morning, the speculations were rampant and largely focused on the UFA. News about the diplomatic mission had gotten out despite the attempts to keep it secret, and many of the commentators and link mongers were talking about war. Footage of the UFA-Mountain America War from thirty-seven years ago, particularly the land battles in the Enamel and the bombing of Denver, was being accessed with obsessive frequency. People were demanding statements from the government and, by 9 AM, there was an announcement that President Simonson would address the nation over the net that afternoon.

Since his mission had been so abbreviated, Dan was able to take charge of getting Michael ready for his middle school orientation. They waited together in the entryway. Dan talked about the coming year, making a conscious effort to ignore the possibility that Michael might be too ill to finish school. The bus was a bit late, and the rest of the family was having breakfast by the time he came back into the multi-purpose room. They had all figured out that Dan's "government business" was the diplomatic mission to the UFA and they wanted to know what had happened. Dan protested that everything was supposed to be secret, mainly because Garenika seemed hurt that he hadn't previously told her what the mission was, but he quickly concluded that all the secrecy was mere play-acting and launched into a full, detailed account of the previous day's events.

"See, that's what I mean," said Josh. "Our main problem is that we can't get along with each other. If the UFA dropped those bugs in East Montana, it was an idiotic stunt. And if they didn't, they should have said so instead of trying to act tough."

"Is there going to be a war, Dan?" Garenika asked.

"I don't know. On the plane ride back, one of the military people was saying that there definitely would be, that they've been seeing troop movements in the UFA for the last two months. But someone else said that the UFA is always moving troops around, and Goldberg was sure that the Canadians wouldn't allow the UFA to go to war with us, even though they didn't seem to mind us fighting in the past."

"What did Lizabetta Smith say?" Josh asked.

"Good question. As far as I could tell—"

The tornado warning blared. Garenika gasped and Senly said "Oh, shit." Dan immediately activated the floor hatch and the four of them trooped down the narrow stairs into the basement shelter. A bolted cryoplastic house like theirs would survive even in the direct path of a tornado, but there was always the danger that some object would come flying through the roof or one of the claroplastic windows, so it was essential to take cover.

As soon as they entered, the screen that occupied one entire wall of the small room switched on and began projecting numerical estimates and a location map. The tornado had touched down to the east and was headed toward them. It was of standard size, a mile wide with 200 mile per hour winds. If it persisted and continued in the same direction, it would reach them in an hour. The map showed the tornado's location as a black cross, moving slowly but steadily across East Colorado.

"What about Michael?" Garenika asked, breathlessly. "Isn't he on the bus?"

"Well, he's probably at school by now, or he'll be there in a few minutes. Don't worry, all the schools have excellent shelters."

But Garenika's gasping became more severe, and her eyes were filled with tears.

"Oh, calm down Mom," said Senly.

Dan knew this was not a setting where he could suggest that Garenika use Jiangtan, so he got out one of the tranquilizer pills that he kept in the shelter and gave it to his wife with some water. "It'll start working in a minute or two," he said.

"Phantasie works faster," said Senly.

"Shut it Senly," Josh answered.

"Let's all stay calm," said Dan. "We should all be used to these things by now."

The wall screen switched to footage of the tornado itself, taken from a drone-camera which had been launched to fly a mile or so in front. With the sun behind it, the funnel was a dark grey, boiling mass, towering up into the clouds. It was chewing up the agricultural land in its path and tossing objects of different shapes and sizes to its sides as it advanced. There was no sound, which somehow made the storm's implacable approach more threatening.

"I planted roses this spring," said Garenika, catching her breath. "I wanted something beautiful around this house. My family's old home in Houston had a rose garden. I guess I told you that. It was right next to the veranda, and you could smell them when you sat outside in the summertime."

"Wasn't that house sucked up in a tornado?" Senly asked.

"No dummy," said Josh, "it's under water. Listen Mom, I can help you plant flowers again if we lose them. They'll do better in the winter, anyway, when it's not so hot."

The tornado advanced toward them in nearly a straight line, veered off to the side when it was about five miles away, then turned back and hit them. As it did, they lost the visual on the screen, and then they heard the wind, a dull, deep-throated roar that seemed to reach down the stairs into their small, now darkened shelter. A few minutes later, the screen flashed on again and then the all-clear signal sounded. As always, they followed the irresistible impulse to go outside to see the storm's effects.

On the next block, a delivery truck had been thrown onto one of the houses and had smashed in an entire side. Dan watched a dazed young couple emerge from the house and stare wordlessly at the wreckage. There was an overturned car in the middle of the street, and a neighborhood kid came running toward them, shouting that the people in the car were dead. By strict public regulation, all the houses on the block were one-story cryoplastic structures, so they had survived intact and without sending fragments flying through the air. But the street exhibited the disheveled look that was the invariable aftermath of a tornado. While the dirt, concrete or plastic grass front yards showed few signs of damage, the real grass or other foliage that some people had managed to plant was all torn up, and clumps of soil, bushes and leaves were scattered over the street, together with children's toys, a few twisted bicycles, scraps of paper and masses of multi-colored garbage. Amidst the debris, there was the body of a cat with its hind legs torn off. The roses that Garenika had planted in front of their house, in a little square that Dan had cleared by cutting away the plastic grass, were gone without a trace.

Dan turned to Garenika. "I should have set up an indoor garden for you, Garenika. You know, I thought about it, and then I figured that you'd enjoy seeing something green and colorful outside the window."

"I did enjoy it."

"But it didn't work out so well, did it."

"It's not your fault Dan."

"Somehow, I think it is."

"But it's not. You tried—it just one of those things you can't control."

They lived for the next month under the looming threat of war, a war whose scope and consequences were as uncertain as its arrival seemed inevitable. Angry messages passed back and forth between Mountain America and the UFA, mixed with offers to negotiate, demands for pre-conditions, and rejections of those pre-conditions accompanied by accusations of bad faith. The UFA advanced ground troops to the midpoint of the Enamel, an act which it announced as an assertion of sovereignty but clearly intended as a threat. Mountain American troops were mobilized in response, but remained west of the 100 degree West longitude line. Canada, which Mountain America hoped to enlist on its behalf by staying out of the Enamel, remained strangely silent.

Meanwhile, there was nothing for Dan's family to do but proceed with daily life. Three more tornados came through the neighborhood, but two missed their street entirely, and the third had lost most of its force by the time it hit. Josh, as always, performed brilliantly in school, although his enthusiasm for American Patriotism didn't slacken. Senly performed just as well on her exams as Josh, but she rarely turned in her homework, despite bribes, threats and heart-to-heart talks. Michael's health showed no improvement. Garenika, who stayed home with him for one week when he suffered a sustained attack of nausea, and another week when she had a series of migraine headaches, received an official reprimand from her supervisor for excessive absence. With all these sources of stress, Dan was astonished that he was able to get any work done, but in addition to teaching his introductory bio class and making progress on the coffee project, he finished his paper for the University of South Baffin Island and sent it to the conference coordinator on time. His main worry about the political situation—somewhat absurdly, he realized—was that it would prevent him from attending the conference. But mid-October arrived without any cancellation from the University or disruption of commercial flights to Canada. He felt uncomfortable leaving Garenika alone with the children, but by skipping the second day of the conference and scheduling early morning flights to Hectorville and back, he was able to limit his absence to three days and two evenings.

The flight to Hectorville left Denver at 6 AM on the day before the conference. Dan had planned to start reading Dickens' *Little Dorrit* on the plane, but he had never flown in this direction before and he found himself fascinated by the landscape. Through the scattered clouds, he watched it move below the airplane window at its magisterial pace—the plantations of Mountain America, the vast grain fields of central Canada, the autumn dappled woods and thriving vegetable farms surrounding Hudson's Bay, nourished by the topsoil that had been transported from the Enamel. Then, quickly crossing the strait between the mainland and Baffin Island, the plane flew into Hectorville Airport. To his surprise, Jarrel Lucan, the University of South Baffin's leading entomologist, and one of the best-known scientists in all of Canada, was waiting for him at the airport.

"We've got a few hours until the dinner starts, so I thought I'd show you around Hectorville. Have you ever been to Canada, aside from the conference in Anchorage where we met?"

"Just one other time, for a conference in Calgary."

"Well, Hectorville's different from either Anchorage or Calgary. It's a planned city. We knew Baffin Island was going to become habitable well in advance, so the whole city was laid out before anyone actually moved here. I'll show you."

Their first stop was the city center. It consisted of a large grassy plaza surrounded on three sides by the tall buildings that formed the city's skyline. The plaza's fourth side looked out over Hectorville Bay, a long narrow inlet of the ocean, framed by slopes that were covered with single family houses and apartment buildings set among the autumn-colored trees. Flower gardens and groves of willows were placed at even intervals across the plaza, and the whole area was filled with people, some strolling, some sitting on benches, and some walking dogs. The dogs attracted Dan's particular attention. It was possible to have a house cat in Mountain America, but dogs need to go outside and couldn't stand the heat.

"The big statue in the center of the plaza is Cornelia Hector, naturally," said Jarrel. "I hope you're not offended."

Hector was the Prime Minister of Canada who had led the invasion of the Successor States during the Second Civil War.

"No, not at all," Dan said immediately, but on reflection he was not quite sure, and not sure how he should respond. "How many people does this city have?" he asked, struck by the central plaza's grandeur.

"Three million. The University is on the north side of town. I'll show you two residential neighborhoods on our way."

The first neighborhood was built on a sloping hill that faced the Bay. Most of the homes had their entrance hall and garage at the top, and then descended three or four floors down the hillside. Jarrel took him into one home that was empty because it was on the market. It was large, with a separate living room, dining room and family room, and nearly every room had a magnificent view out onto the Bay. The next neighborhood was further back, on a level plateau surrounded by the craggy hills. The curving streets were lined with trees and there were more trees on the spacious plots of land that surrounded each of the homes. Dan had seen footage of trees with autumn colors many times, but the images had failed to convey the astonishing intensity of the reds, oranges and yellows, especially as they contrasted with the bright green lawns. Jarrel had obviously shown him two of the more prosperous neighborhoods in Hectorville, Dan reflected, as the car took them further north to the University campus, but he was nonetheless impressed.

The pre-conference dinner at the University Club was enjoyable. Dan saw a number of people he had met at previous conferences or over live net links and was introduced to the other invitees. Many people said they were glad to meet him and seemed familiar with his research, something that never failed to flatter him no matter how often he told himself that it was mere politeness on their part. By the time he lay down on the aero-bed in his hotel room, he was exhausted and somewhat tipsy. He cautioned himself that he had to be rested for his presentation the next day, but he couldn't get to sleep. He had forgotten to close the window louvers, and the occasionally passing cars were casting striped, rapidly changing trapezoids of light onto the ceiling. For some reason, Dan didn't want to reach over to the control panel and close the louvers. Then he remembered watching these same ceiling patterns during the first nights in his family's new home in Arches Park City, when he was seven and had gotten his own room for the first time. The memory was profoundly sweet, and Dan watched the patterns for what seemed like a long time, finally falling asleep with the light still flickering across the ceiling.

He was tired the next day and—feeling a bit unprepared—kept rehearsing his talk in his mind as the Dean of Arts and Science welcomed everyone to the conference and the first two presenters gave their papers. Dan was next, the last paper before lunch, and he was surprised how nervous he felt when he was being introduced. He started with a pleasantry about seeing autumn colors, which fell flat, but the presentation itself went well. Dan's paper challenged the common view that elevated temperatures around the world had accelerated the pace of evolution. That was mysticism, he argued; the proliferation of insect and bacterial species was simply a predictable response to the environmental changes. In the case of insects, and specifically necrophagi like the biter bugs, Dan used a mathematical model to demonstrate that the new species had arisen to take advantage of the tremendous number of unattended bovine, porcine and human corpses that had collected below the Heatstroke Line during the previous century. Despite the ungainly size of the biter bugs, their hard shell had enabled them to compete effectively with smaller carrion eaters such as mottled blowflies and skin beetles. Once the carrion had been consumed, many of these new species had become extinct, but the biter bugs, a form of silphinae, had made use of their adaptation to feed on the flesh of live animals, specifically the remaining humans, pigs and lizards. Dan fielded the questions from the audience easily, particularly a challenge from an elderly biologist who insisted that evolution was accelerating. To the predictable inquiry about whether the biter bugs could possibly evolve into a form that could survive above the Heatstroke Line, Dan simply responded that he had no way of knowing, and neither did anyone else.

As the conference participants headed into the dining hall for lunch, several people came up to Dan to compliment him on the paper. When Jarrel approached him, Dan found himself expecting, or hoping for, another compliment, but instead Jarrel told him to eat quickly so he could get a tour of the University laboratories. Once more, and again to Dan's surprise, Jarrel took Dan around himself. The labs were lavish by Mountain American standards, with state of the art equipment, generous workspaces, and graceful furnishings that contrasted with the functionalism to which Dan had become accustomed. As they reached the end, Jarrel said that the Dean would like to meet him.

"Isn't the conference starting again?" Dan asked, recalling, with a sense of embarrassment, that he didn't remember a word of what she had said at the beginning of the conference.

"Oh, I guess, but the first paper is by Martinson, and he's an idiot."

The Dean was an older woman named Bredetta Horace. Dan had never seen a faculty office like hers. One entire wall was glass, not claroplastic, and provided a perfectly clear view out on an ocean inlet—the one north of Hectorville Bay, Dan realized. It was in an almost pristine state, with brightly colored trees lining its sloping sides, punctuated by rocky outcroppings and an occasional stone or cryoplastic structure. The sun, just beginning its westward descent, filled the inlet with a golden glow and awoke bright sparkles on the dimpled surface of the water. As they entered, Dean Horace, who was seated at a long, polished wood desk that faced out onto the view, turned to greet them and motioned them to take seats in cushioned chairs opposite her desk.

"How did you like our labs?" she asked.

"They're wonderful," Dan responded, with enthusiasm. "And let me say that this whole conference has been a real pleasure so far. Jarrel and the other organizers have done a great job. I'm enormously impressed."

She smiled. "I'm glad to hear it. As it happens, we're impressed with you. We think your research is absolutely first-rate. And that brings me to the reason for this meeting. How would you like to join our faculty? I can't extend an official offer until the Biology Department votes it, but I'm sure they will if you tell us you're interested." Dan was genuinely surprised. He realized that he should have been expecting this because of Jarrel's various ministrations, and he felt naïve, but he was also very flattered.

"I'm very flattered," he replied.

"We all like your work, Dan," Jarrel answered. "We'd love to have you join us."

"Well, frankly, I haven't thought about the possibility of moving. Mountain America's been good to me. I've gotten a steady series of grants, and I have a good relationship—pretty good, I guess—with the Department of Agriculture. And my family's settled there, of course." He realized he was simply thinking aloud at this point, that the compliments had overwhelmed his ability to plan his responses.

"I understand your wife's a food inspector," said Dean Horace. "I'm sure we could find employment for her. And your children would be able to attend better schools. I realize that you and your family are settled in Mountain America. But it's not a very promising place to live at this point. You'd have a better future here."

"Are you referring to the fact that we might be going to war with the UFA?"

"In part. I can't promise you that Canada won't have conflicts with Europe, given how close Greenland is to us, or with Russia and China about navigation in the Arctic Ocean. Even if we do, I would guess that they'll have less of an impact on people's lives. Bigger countries absorb these things more easily. But I was also thinking about something else. Our meteorology people think that the climate is beginning to get warmer again."

"I thought it was stable."

"We thought so too. Now we're not so sure."

"But how can that be? There were five billion people on Earth when the warming began, and ten billion at its peak. Now there are, what 700 million?"

"That's about right," said Jarrel. "But they have to run air conditioning almost all the time, and most people are living up north where we need to keep the lights on in the winter."

"I guess we'll meet with the other major powers to see if we can slow it down," Dean Horace added. "Given the political tensions, though, I wouldn't be optimistic, at least in the short run. So, the bottom line is, I think you and your family would be better off here."

"Well, as I said, this is really unexpected. It's flattering, very flattering—I guess I already said that—but unexpected. Can you give me some time to think about it?"

"Certainly. You really don't have to decide until March, when we set the teaching and research schedule for the next academic year. Talk it over with your family and stay in touch with us."

As she said this, Dan thought of his family huddled in their shelter, watching the tornado on the wall screen. The sun was directly behind Dean Horace now, shining on the hillsides, and the autumn colors of the trees were glowing in response.

CHAPTER 5

an had never considered leaving Mountain America before, but an offer of the sort he had received was impossible to ignore. The day after his return, he talked to each member of his family separately, except for Michael, carefully planning what he would say in advance. None of them reacted quite the way he had expected. He thought Garenika would find the possibility of moving stressful, but she was pleased for Dan and surprisingly positive about what she called "a change of scene." Senly saw the whole thing as a plot to get her away from her friends, and then informed Dan that she was in contact with a lot of Canadian kids through the net, and that they used thought-enhancing drugs just as much as kids in the Successor States. Josh, whose reaction Dan was most concerned about, questioned him closely about whether the move would really be good for his career, and whether he would feel guilty about leaving Mountain America. Those were the questions Dan was asking himself. He was impressed with his son's emotional maturity in asking them, but —for that very reason—found the questions even more troubling than they had seemed when he himself had thought of them.

A week after his return from Canada, Dan received the "Repulsion" signal on his link for the next morning. The routine was the same as it had been the first time: he was picked up by a military car with a human driver, brought to the airfield where he joined Temarden Goldberg and the other three entomologists in the briefing room, then taken to a military airplane which flew them to Columbus. After landing, they were put on a UFA bus, and Lizabetta Smith informed them once again that they were being taken directly to their meeting. They were ushered into the same conference room and took seats along the same side of the lengthy table. This time there was no one on the other side, but as soon as they were settled, Jesse Davis came into the room. Dan recognized him immediately, a tall black man with white hair, but he seemed much heavier than he looked on the net and his face was badly pock-marked; clearly, his net image was being real-time edited. He was breathing audibly and perspiring, and he moved with a ponderous, ungainly stride indicating, in Dan's view, that he was ill. But any negative impression that these physical defects might have produced was counteracted by his lively eyes, open expression, and broad smile. Instead of taking a seat, Davis went up to Lizabetta Smith and then Temarden Goldberg, greeting them warmly and asking about their families. By the time he went around to the other side of the table, Mark Granowski had come into the room. Davis waved to him, and the two of them sat down next to each other.

"Welcome to the UFA," said Davis, in a steady, mellifluous voice. "I'm delighted to see you here. I believe most of you know Mark Granowski, who I've asked to join me for our talk this morning. Why don't all of you introduce yourselves, and then we can begin."

Davis paused after the introductions and flashed his smile. "Excellent. Now, first of all, I believe I can safely say that neither of our nations wants a war. There may have been some misunderstandings between us, but I'm confident that when you asked us about the origins of your biter bug outbreak, you were simply requesting any information we might have available, rather than accusing us of having caused the outbreak."

"That's exactly right, Jesse," Lizabetta said smoothly.

"Excellent. In that case, Presidents Hanary and Cantara Carson don't see any need for demonstrations of hostility, so the UFA is unilaterally standing down. We still claim our half of the Enamel, needless to say, but we'll withdraw our combat forces to the east bank of the Mississippi."

Although no one on the other side of the table actually sighed with relief, a sense of having done so seemed to emerge from them as a group.

"Now I know some of you have been curious about our biter bug research," Davis continued, "particularly since we've hired your leading researcher on the subject after you told him you no longer needed his services." He smiled once again. "If I tell you that we've asked Mark to explore the possibility of containing the bugs, you might—just perhaps—be dubious, since there are no bugs in the UFA. So let me disclose one of our diplomatic secrets to you, which you must promise to keep confidential." He paused, and flashed another smile. "As you may know, much of Kentucky

THE HEATSTROKE LINE

is only just below the Heatstroke Line. Temperatures there reach fatal levels for only half the year. The UFA needs space—we have as many people as you do in little more than one third of the area —so we'd like to move some of our people into Kentucky. We've been in negotiations with the three Confederacies there and they're willing to establish an alliance with us and take some of our people. After all, they're under-populated and they'd benefit from the UFA's support. The problem is that they've got biter bugs. As long as they do, no one in the UFA is going to move there. So our plan to establish a mutually beneficial alliance with the Kentucky Confederacies depends on finding some way of at least containing the bugs. I'm sure you'll agree that there is no one more qualified to lead such an effort than Mark, and that it made perfect sense for Presidents Carson to hire him when he became available."

There was a short silence and then Goldberg, a bit slower on the uptake than Lizabetta, said, "I agree, that certainly does make sense."

"Excellent. To show you our good faith, we invite the four entomologists that you've included in your delegation to tour the laboratory we've built for Mark and his team and see the sort of research that they're doing there. We understand that this isn't definitive proof that we don't have a different lab somewhere else, but it seems to me that building an entire lab just for show would be an extraordinarily elaborate—and expensive—fraud. Why would a nation that was bent on war bother with something like that? As I said at the beginning, we have no desire to start a war. So I suggest that we diplomats proceed to our dining hall for a beautifully prepared, reconciliatory lunch, while the scientists grab a cold sandwich and enjoy themselves by examining Mark's lab." He smiled merrily at the scientists.

"We'd like nothing better, Jesse" Lizabetta answered.

"Excellent. Any further questions?'

"I have one," said Lizabetta.

Davis smiled again. "You want to know if we have any idea where your biter bugs came from, since they didn't come from us."

"Yes."

"In fact, we do. We think they came from the Confederacies. They're the ones with the bugs, after all."

"But why would the Confederacies attack Mountain America now, under President Simonson's administration. He's reached out to establish friendly relations with them and he's abandoned

33

President Garcia's plan to establish colonies in Central Texas and West Oklahoma. It doesn't make sense."

"I hardly need to tell you, Lizabetta, that what happens in the Confederacies doesn't always make sense. In any case, we don't know. Our information comes from Jacksonia."

"They can't be behind something like this," said one of the Mountain American military people.

Dan recalled that Jacksonia was a small principality on the east side of Mississippi Bay, centered on the old city of Jackson, Mississippi. The least impoverished of the Confederacies, it derived its income by unloading ships coming down the Ohio River from the UFA and down the Missouri from Mountain America, sending the goods overland to the Confederacies located east of the Bay, and shipping the goods that these places produced, mainly rice and bananas, back to the UFA and Mountain America. Its economy was thus entirely dependent on continued peace between the Confederacies and the Successor States.

"No," Davis answered, "but that's not what I said. I said they gave us the information. That suggests that they want to be cooperative, which is what you'd expect. But the information came from back channels and we didn't pursue it because, to put it bluntly, we weren't attacked. So it's up to you to get in touch with them and see what they know, or at least what they're willing to tell. Ready for lunch?"

After being driven to a nearby building, Granowski and the four Mountain American entomologists in fact had a pleasant, if quick lunch in the employee cafeteria and then went for a tour of the UFA lab. Mark, largely ignoring Janaly Francesca because she was junior and David Hardaway because he was stupid, directed his attention to Saronia and Dan. Despite himself, Dan was flattered and pleased, since he respected Mark and had collegial feelings toward Saronia. As director of Mountain America's biter bug project, Mark had been a fairly high-ranking official at the Department of Agriculture and Dan was astonished that he had been dismissed so quickly by the new administration. Mark was highly knowledgeable about his subject and had always been supportive of Dan's work, even though Dan's practical research focused on agricultural pests, not biter bugs. Dan's collegial feelings for Saronia were based on her intelligence and expertise, but also on the fact that she never competed with him for grants. This was partially due to the influence of her wife—incidentally one of the most beautiful women Dan had ever met in person—

who was a graphic artist with no interest in science. But it was mainly because Saronia was independently wealthy—her family owned one of the largest construction companies in Glendive.

The biter bug lab was new and a substantial amount of money had clearly been spent on it. It couldn't compare to the lab Dan had seen at the University of South Baffin Island, but because the Canadians didn't need to deal with the bugs, this was certainly the largest biter bug research facility in North America. As far as Dan and Saronia could tell—they consulted openly, since that was the purpose of the tour—the lab was exactly as Jesse Davis had described. There was no evidence that it was stockpiling the bugs or trying to breed them. As a test, Dan asked Mark about the one containment strategy that overlapped with breeding bugs, which was to release sterile males into the environment over the course of several successive years in an effort to produce a population crash, something he himself had done to control a particularly resistant strain of West Dakota fruit flies. Mark quickly responded that he had always been dubious about that approach and that, in any case, it was politically impossible to increase the biter bug population, even temporarily.

By the time they arrived back in the conference room, all the other participants were seated around the table and the mood was noticeably more relaxed. Davis asked the entomologists to report on their tour, and Mark turned to Dan and Saronia. Saronia told Dan to proceed, as he knew she would, so Dan addressed the entire group, the first time he had said anything other than his name in either of the meetings. Aware that he was being charmed and flattered by people who were more politically astute than he was, he tried to speak with circumspection. Nothing in the lab gave any evidence that biter bugs were being bred for infestation of new territory, he said. The equipment in the lab was devoted to various containment strategies, including genetic modification, microbial pathogens such as bacteria and viruses, the use of pheromone antagonists as chemical communication inhibitors, and attract-and-kill or push-pull strategies. Another possible technique, which had been used with success for agricultural pests, Dan said, was low-level noise repulsion, but he did not see any evidence that this was being explored. He was about to point out that the release of sterile males was not being explored either when Davis interrupted him.

"Excellent. Thank you for the report. I think your conclusion's clear, and I hope it provides some additional confirmation of our good faith. I'm not going to pretend that there are no sources of conflict between the UFA and Mountain America, but it would certainly be foolish to go to war over our efforts to discover something that can benefit all humanity, don't you think?"

As the Mountain America delegation boarded the airplane to fly back to Denver, Dan was worried that he would be told by the politicians or the military people that he had misspoken. He was clearly out of his depth in dealing with diplomatic issues and other matters that were so much larger than insects. He was reminded of Lucien in Balzac's *Lost Illusions*, surrounded by machinations that he couldn't comprehend. But other than Saronia and Janaly, who complimented him, no one said anything one way or the other. Most of the conversation centered on the UFA's intentions. There seemed to be general agreement that Davis' explanation about the motivation for the biter bug research was unreliable, and that, if there was any truth at all in what he said, the most likely scenario was that the UFA was planning to invade and conquer the three Kentucky confederacies, rather than allying with them. Dan was disappointed that the people weren't feeling more upbeat, as well as being worried that things had happened that he didn't understand.

By the next day, however, his mood had improved. The news about the end of the confrontation with the UFA was all over the net and President Simonson addressed the nation that afternoon in real time. As Dan listened to Simonson speak, he suddenly realized that, for the first time in his life, he had played a role in history. It was a minor role, to be sure, but he had been present at an important event and had influenced its outcome. What pleased him most was Joshua's outright admiration. Being a research scientist and contributing to knowledge had always been Dan's highest aspiration, but he knew that no one in his family really shared that view. They were not exactly embarrassed that he spent his life studying insects, but they were certainly bemused by it. Even Garenika, who was willing to pay attention to his descriptions of his work long after other people stopped listening, never quite understood the appeal of entomological research. But his role, however minor, in ending the recent confrontation was something everyone understood and appreciated.

As Dan sat in his lab the following day, getting the paper he had given in Canada ready for publication, he began thinking about the situation in the Successor States and his own

THE HEATSTROKE LINE

connection to it. He had always thought of himself as having developed and pursued his personal life plan, but now he realized that he had actually been rather passive, writing theoretical papers or applying for the grants that were announced by the Department of Agriculture. Developing his own research project for the coffee problem was about as proactive as he had ever been. Could he play a larger role, he wondered. Could he continue to build on the heady feeling of accomplishment that his participation in the negotiations with the UFA had given him?

The moment he asked himself the question, the obvious answer occurred to him. Of course he could—he could get a grant to do research on ways to control the biter bugs, instead of limiting himself to theoretical models about how they had evolved. Under President Simonson, Mountain America had already reached out to establish better relations with the Confederacies. What could support that effort better than eradicating the pest that made life in the Confederacies more miserable than anything besides the heat? Besides, Dan thought, the UFA had already made a major commitment to this enterprise. When his own research got going, he could suggest that the two countries share their results, and maybe even work together. That would forge a bond between them. Suddenly, the intriguing possibility of reuniting the Successor States took shape before him. The Carson twins were getting old, as Stuart said. Once they were gone, or at least less active, it might be much easier to establish an alliance between the UFA and Mountain America. Joint scientific research could certainly contribute to those relations—working together to solve a common problem was the essence of cooperation. And if they actually solved the problem and got rid of the bugs, the Confederacies, which were really too small to be viable on their own, might be willing to join the alliance.

As a sense of excitement took hold of him, Dan suddenly felt confined in his crowded, windowless laboratory. He left and went striding down the hallway, but his restlessness only increased. The University of Denver consisted of about twenty cryoplastic buildings connected by long, underground hallways that looked the same and lead to nothing but another building and another hallway. The urge Dan felt, he realized, was to go outside so he could walk more rapidly than was considered proper in the busy hallways, and follow a route that he had chosen on his own. Why not? It was late October, and no longer brutally hot. Most of the exits from the hallways lead to the carports, but there were a few that led outside. Dan took the first one he reached and went through the double set of doors designed for thermal insulation. He found himself in a broad, open space between two of the university buildings, paved with concrete and filled with rusted metal machinery. A few workers in heat-reflecting coveralls were disassembling some sort of railroad car, undoubtedly left over from an earlier time. Dan began to feel a bit foolish but he persisted, crossing the open area and heading toward a line of tangled tropical foliage about a hundred yards away. Beyond the university buildings and the junkyard between them was a drainage ditch, too wide to cross unless he took a running leap that would look undignified, so he walked alongside it until he found a board laid across it as a bridge. When he reached the foliage, he realized it was only one narrow, unkempt line of elephant ears and bamboo bushes, with Evans Avenue beyond it. There was a steady stream of traffic on the Avenue, and no sidewalks.

By this point, Dan's enthusiasm for walking had abated and he was starting to sweat. He sat down heavily on a broken block of concrete. Maybe he should be more prudent, he reflected, maybe his sense that he could shape the future was an illusion. He had always tried to plan things, always assumed he could control his situation. But this might be something different, something that was truly beyond his capacities and demanded caution rather than self-confidence. It was an unfamiliar way for him to think, he realized. Maybe he was just tired and overwrought from the events of the past week.

CHAPTER 6

Dan's sense of excitement had returned by the next morning, and he was now ready to do something more practical about it than walking through a junkyard. He called Retiba Walters in her capacity as Research Director for the Department of Agriculture. She was surprised at first; Dan could see it on her face, since they were talking over a live link. Biter bugs, after all were hardly an agricultural pest, there were none in Mountain America, and the Simonson Administration had abandoned its plans to colonize any of the adjoining territory below the Heatstroke Line. The attack in East Montana had rattled everyone however, and she readily understood the value of finding a response. Dan pointed out, moreover, that the project would be an excellent way for Mountain American to reach out to the Confederacies, which were so badly afflicted by the bugs.

"Are you planning to work with anyone on this project?" Retiba asked.

The thought had not occurred to him. "Why," he responded, "do you think I should?"

"Maybe. It's a problem that's been around for a while, and a lot of people have tried to solve it. You might find it easier to get funding if you had a collaborator. It might even be helpful, Dan."

"Well, I'll give it some thought."

"Okay. In the meantime, I'll run it by Temarden and see what he thinks."

"He'll probably think that I should stick to agriculture."

"We'll see. I think he liked being part of a diplomatic effort. This may appeal to him."

So, Dan thought, the mission had made Temarden Goldberg feel special too, even though he was a high ranking official to begin with. Dan felt a little less original than he had before, but the whole idea still appealed to him, and Retiba's reaction had been positive. Now he apparently had to think of someone to collaborate with. His first thought was Saronia Hernandez, but she would probably be unwilling or at least unenthusiastic. Mirbel Rappaport, who had been Dan's teacher, was still at Utah University, but he was far too elderly to begin a new line of research. The universities in West Montana and East Wyoming didn't have an entomologist and Dan didn't think any better of the one at Idaho than he did of David Hardaway, who was obviously out. Then he thought of Janaly Francesca. Despite her lack of experience—she and the new entomologist at West Wyoming were Mountain America's two junior people in the field—Dan thought her work was good and he had found her pleasant to deal with on the two missions. Moreover, she was in Denver, which would make working together more convenient. He texted her and, half an hour later, she contacted him on a live link. She was obviously flattered that he had asked her, understood what Dan was thinking right away, and seemed full of enthusiasm for the project. They agreed to meet at Dan's lab that Friday to start drafting a proposal.

The day before his meeting with Janaly, Dan received a message from Temarden Goldberg. "Your idea sounds interesting," it said. "It lies somewhat outside the Department of Agriculture's jurisdiction, and it will not be inexpensive because you will need some new equipment. I am going to consult with the State Department about obtaining the requisite funding, given the potential connection with the UFA and the relevance of the research to the Confederacies. Please re-contact me when you are ready to submit the proposal."

Janaly was impressed when Dan showed her the message. They sat down next to each other at Dan's computer to start outlining a research plan. The bugs didn't communicate with each other except during reproduction, so using pheromone antagonists didn't seem promising. They had no natural enemies, push-pull was largely ineffective with carnivorous insects and genetic modification would probably be too complicated, given Mountain America's limited resources. Dan wouldn't even consider bio-chemical toxins. The best approach, it seemed, was to focus on microbial pathogens. While the biter bugs' reproductive system had proven to be remarkably robust, their respiratory system had long been thought to be a potential weak point. Like all insects, they breathed through their skin, by diffusion, and insects as large as biter bugs should have difficulty oxygenating the deepest portions of their bodies. Even a minor disruption of their absorption capacities, therefore, might have fatal effects.

Moreover, Dan explained to Janaly, he had a theory that he hadn't mentioned to anyone previously because controlling the biter bugs had been outside his area of research. He had always wondered why the bugs were only found below the Heatstroke Line and was unconvinced by existing theories based on their genetic programming. Everyone knows, however, that hot air diffuses more rapidly than colder air. Perhaps the bugs, being so large, needed the more rapid diffusion rate of heated air to keep the deep parts of their bodies oxygenated. Janaly thought that was a brilliant idea. She remembered an old article, written when the biter bugs first appeared, that might have some information supportive of Dan's theory, and began searching for it on his computer.

As they sat side by side, leaning toward the computer screen, Dan gradually became aware of Janaly. She was wearing brown shorts and a tight, yellow sleeveless top. Her arms and legs were firm and shapely and her skin unusually tan. Her position was neither relaxed nor tense, but poised, as if prepared for action. Janaly wasn't particularly pretty, and certainly didn't have Garenika's delicate features or graceful bearing. Her hair, which was jet black, was cut short, her eyes were brown, she had a wide mouth and slightly crooked teeth. But a kind of animal energy seemed to radiate from her body, a slightly fragrant warmth that Dan felt with increasing intensity. He realized that he knew very little about her, only that she was from Pacifica, where she had been trained, and had moved to Mountain America two years ago to take the position at Denver Technical. He had always thought of her as small and young, probably because she was junior to him, but in fact she was nearly as big as he was, and must be, he reflected, at least thirty years old.

Dan moved back from the computer a bit and looked at her. "Does this seem like something that you want to work on, Janaly? I hope I'm not diverting you from your research plan."

"No, not at all," she answered, turning toward him and touching his arm in a gesture of reassurance. "This is a great opportunity for me."

"Well, I'm not sure it will lead to anything that will help your career. How are you proceeding with that?"

"Thanks for asking. Actually, they've promised me a pretty secure position, since I'd been teaching for three years at Eureka.

And I think the people in the Bio Department like the research I'm doing."

"Well, that must be reassuring."

"Yeah, it is. I felt confident enough to buy a house."

Dan was about to compliment her by saying that she was way ahead of where he was at her age, but somehow didn't want to emphasize the age difference between them, so he just told her that it was impressive.

"I guess so," she said, laughing slightly. "It's a very small house. I live alone, though, so I don't need that much space."

Dan noted this fact, which Janaly seemed to offer rather gratuitously. They continued chatting for a few more minutes, then turned back to the computer and their research plan. Janaly agreed that they should pursue Dan's theory, repeating that she thought it was a brilliant insight. They divided up the literature search between them—Janaly hadn't found the article she was searching for—and agreed to meet at Dan's office at the same time next week to start outlining their proposal. He touched her arm in a friendly gesture when they said goodbye, and although she barely moved, he sensed something responsive in her reaction.

Dan felt buoyant as he sat in his car on the way home. A confused succession of thoughts came to him that he didn't try to sort out, but it seemed to him that his life had moved into a higher gear, that new vistas were opening up in front of him. He had been drifting for a long time, just following the same routine, content that he had fulfilled his wish to become a research scientist. Now he had taken control, he was doing things of real significance. He felt Janaly's admiration, and her vital energy, infusing him with a new sense of himself. It was hard to know how things would turn out, but he felt ready for the challenge.

Garenika was waiting for him when he pulled into the carport at his house, and he could see she was upset. He had a momentary sense of irrational guilt, then thought that Michael must have taken a turn for the worse.

"Senly's been suspended from school for a week," Garenika told him.

"For what?"

"Just what you'd expect. Taking Phantasie in class. I didn't want to disturb you when you were working on your new research proposal, but you need to talk to her. I've already tried to, but you know how difficult she is. She's in her room."

Senly had her own room, unlike Josh and Michael. It was quite small, but she had covered the walls with 3-D posters that gave Dan a vertiginous feeling. She was lying on her aero-bed as he entered, which she had turned up so she was nearly two feet off the surface, her arms and legs hanging limply downward. Dan sat down on her desk chair and turned to face her, which meant that he was also facing the poster from one of the on-line games she played, an image of some two-headed reptilian creature breaking apart as it fell into the depths of space.

"Okay, Senly, tell me what happened."

"I made a mistake, that's all. I was tired, and I lost my Phantasie control. I let myself think that Mr. O'Hara sounded like a duck. Sure enough, he became a duck and I couldn't stop laughing."

"You know you're not supposed to take Phantasie in school."

"I know I would be bored to death by Mr. O'Hara if I didn't."

"Well, I realize that you're ahead of most of the other kids in your class, especially in a quantitative subject like Physics. But your intellect is supposed to enable you to excel, not to get you suspended."

"Okay, I don't want to get suspended. But I don't want to excel either."

"Why not Senly? You need to make a life for yourself, you know. You have the ability to have a wonderful career, and maybe even make a contribution to this world. All you have to do is be more serious."

"I don't want a wonderful career, and I don't want to make a contribution to this world. This world sucks."

"Come on, that's just teenage cynicism. Maybe it impresses your friends, but it doesn't impress me. We're talking about your life and your future, not the state of the world."

"You're the one who brought up the world. I didn't."

Dan was angry enough with Senly so that he wasn't even tempted to smile.

"I meant something different, and you know it. This is the world you've got to live in. Don't you want to have a good career, and maybe help people and leave things a little better than you found them? Do you really want to spend your life playing make believe games on the net and using a drug to make your thoughts look real?"

Senly pulled her arms and legs up and used the aero-bed control to lower herself to a more normal level.

"Yep, that's what I want. I want to get through life and have as little to do with this world as I possibly can. I don't want to re-unify the Successor States like Josh, or serve food to the poor like Ranity Hitchcock. I didn't fuck up this world, and I don't see why I need to try to get it straightened out again. Playing on-line games and taking Phantasie are things I can do with my friends. They're the only things I like."

Dan felt his own convictions waver. Taking his children as seriously as he did probably made him a less effective parent, he reflected. But he tried again.

"You know, Senly, cynicism probably sounds smart and sophisticated to you, but it's actually childish. I can't prove to you that committing yourself to something has intrinsic value. The world's moved past that point, for better or worse. But every sensible person knows that you can give things value through your own commitments. If you refuse to make any, you create your own sense of despair. You make your world a lousy place to be."

"I didn't make the world a lousy place. Other people did it for me. All you're trying to tell me is that I should fool myself into believing that they didn't. That's just thought enhancement without Phantasie, and it's too hard for me. I'd rather take the drug and turn Mr. O'Hara's classroom into the control room of a spaceship."

Dan saw no solution but to fall back on authority. "Well, Senly, we'll just have to wait for you to grow up a little. In the meantime, getting suspended doesn't mean you get a Phantasie and online game vacation. First of all, you're grounded. You're staying in the house all week. Next, you're going to do all your homework. If the assignments aren't posted, you'll ask your teachers to send them. Then, since you don't seem to need the class time to learn the material, I want you to come up with a project on your own—a physics problem to solve or a book to read —and take notes on it. I'll review it at the end of the week, and if it's not the quality of work I know you can do, you'll be grounded for another week."

"No beatings with a wooden paddle? No hard labor splitting wood or hauling water from the well? Guess I'm just lucky."

Dan knew Senly wouldn't give him the satisfaction of objecting or appearing upset, but he was sure that he had made his point.

He was at home on Sunday, seeing if he could fix the servo-robot in the kitchen using the on-line instructions, when

THE HEATSTROKE LINE

Temarden Goldberg came on over a live link. Even though it was the weekend, Goldberg was sitting in his office, his electronic Mountain American flag fluttering behind him.

"First of all," he said, "I am following up about your grant. I have spoken with the State Department, and they are very interested in the possibilities. You will not need to deal with them directly. I will manage that part of the project from here. But that is not the reason why I am contacting you on a Sunday. You probably recall that Jesse Davis said, at the end of our second meeting with the UFA, that he obtained his information about the biter bug attack from someone in Jacksonia. Well, we believe we have located the person to whom he is referring, or at least someone who has similar information. We have set up a meeting with that individual for this coming Wednesday afternoon. It's not a diplomatic meeting, just informative, so we are sending a much smaller group than we did for the UFA meetings. Just one person from the military and one person from the State Department, so far. I have been asked if I wanted to send someone from Agriculture, but it seemed to me that you would be a better choice, given your knowledge about insects and your newfound interest in biter bugs. I hope you can do it. It will pretty much guarantee that you will get your grant."

Dan reminded himself not to seem too eager, but in fact he was elated. Things were working out just the way he had hoped. By taking some initiative, he had become the go-to person in Mountain America on biter bugs. This mission would give him a chance to make contact with the people in the Confederacies who were concerned about the subject. Maybe he—he and Janaly—could set up a sort of research network with those people and Mark Granowski and begin to forge connections among the Successor States and the Confederacies on a subject that was obviously of mutual concern. Who could say what that might lead to? Maybe he would end up playing a real role in history, maybe he would actually advance the cause of American Patriotism.

"Well, Temarden," he responded, "it's pretty short notice, but I guess I can do it."

"That's wonderful, Dan. I appreciate it. My next question is whether there is anyone else you think should go along?"

Dan immediately thought of Janaly. Asking her to travel with him would be too forward at this point, he thought. But he didn't want any other entomologist along—this was his enterprise.

"How about Stuart McPherson?"

45

"The historian?"

"Well, there's no one who knows more about the political situation in the Confederacies. It might be very useful to have him with us."

"Very well, I don't see why not. You will be going down there Tuesday afternoon, by plane. It's safe to fly into Jacksonia, unlike most of the other Confederacies, and there are regular commercial flights several times a week. The meeting is on Wednesday, as I said, and we will have you back by Thursday. We will arrange for the plane tickets and the hotel, and the State Department representative, Samuel Reinhart, will brief you."

For some reason, Dan was glad he would be back in time for his meeting with Janaly next Friday. He wasn't quite sure why, though, since it would have been easy enough to re-schedule.

Temarden no longer seemed concerned about secrecy, so Dan allowed himself the pleasure of telling Josh the nature of his mission. He felt a little foolish about trying to impress his son, but there was no denying that Josh's reaction was genuinely gratifying. In fact, it was so enthusiastic that the word "hero" floated into Dan's mind, but he suppressed the thought.

"Now Josh, remember, this doesn't mean that I've become an American Patriot. I still don't think it's realistic."

"Maybe not, but you're doing more to advance the cause than anyone I know, except maybe Noah. And I think it's great that you got them to include Stuart."

"Well, that may have just been selfish. He's wonderful company, as you know."

On Monday evening, Dan arranged for Rachel Stafford, the elderly widow who lived across the street, to come to their house during the day to help Garenika. He also decided to rescind Senly's grounding while he was away to spare Garenika the stress of trying to control her. But he reminded her that she still had to do all her homework and complete her project—she had chosen to write a report about Saturn—by the end of the week, and that he would review it on Friday, after he got back from his mission.

CHAPTER 7

Michael was sick again on Tuesday, this time with a renewed outbreak of his rash, and Dan was glad that he had hired Rachel so that Garenika could go to work and avoid more criticism from her supervisor. He had intended to go into the lab and leave directly from there for the airport but he decided that it would be preferable to work at home. There was an alcove in the master bedroom that he had set up as an office, but working there disturbed Garenika when she was trying to sleep, so he had transferred his desk to a corner of the multi-purpose room. Senly stayed resentfully in her room all morning, and Michael slept late, but he came into the multi-purpose room at lunchtime. His rash looked terrible, but he had at least gotten some rest, and thankfully seemed wide awake. He asked Dan when his flight was leaving.

"Mid-afternoon. I'll have to go to the airport soon."

"You're lucky that you get to travel so much. I hope I can travel when I get older."

"I'm sure you will, Michael. Is there any place in particular you'd like to go?"

"I want to go to India."

"India? Why there? It's uninhabited."

"I want to see the temples. They have big temples there made out of a single piece of rock. The people who used to live there cut away the mountain and left a temple in the middle."

"I didn't know that," said Dan, wondering if it was true. "It's very interesting."

"The temples will still be there, won't they, even with the heat?"

"Yes, of course, if they're made of rock the heat won't affect them."

"I guess I have to go into business so I can make enough money to go to India."

"Maybe so. Do you want to go into business, Michael? We haven't talked about what you want to do when you grow up for a while." Two years ago, Michael wanted to be a racecar driver. Dan had avoided the subject of his future since then.

"I want to make a lot of money. Gabe's father is in business and he makes a lot of money. Gabe has his own room and their kitchen never breaks. And they have two servo-robots that are allowed to carry coffee."

Gabe Morton was Michael's best friend. In fact, his father was in business; he was Vice President of one of Mountain America's largest banks. Dan was sure they had a better kitchen and that neither of their servo-robots spilled the drinks.

"Well, I'm sorry we don't have as much money as your friend. You're very smart, Michael, and if you go into business, I'm sure you'll make lots of money and have a big house with all the most advanced machinery. But you need to like what you do for a living. The machinery's not worth it if you're not interested in your work."

"I didn't mean to make you feel bad, Dad," said Michael, with unexpected insight.

"That's okay Michael. I feel good about the home your mother and I have provided for you. But I hope you make a lot more money than we do and have a huge house with servo-robots that sing songs as well as serving coffee."

Dan met the other members of the group at Denver Airport, in the waiting area for the flight to Jacksonia. Stuart, to his mild surprise, was wearing a formal round collared shirt even to travel. Samuel Reinhart, whom Stuart apparently knew, was a fidgety young man with red hair and freckles who seemed to be talking constantly, while the military representative, a fierce looking older woman named Tarenly Chang, barely spoke at all. Dan and Stuart sat together on the flight. Since Stuart seemed genuinely gratified to have been included and expressed satisfaction that the Simonson administration was becoming less hostile to Patriotism, Dan decided not to mention his own role in getting him invited. Instead, he recounted what had happened during the two UFA missions. When he reached the part about the lab tour, he decided to ask a question that had been troubling him, but that he had not felt comfortable asking anyone else.

"So do you think Granowski was fooling me? I could certainly tell what all the equipment in the lab was, but I don't know if I'm cagey enough to figure out his motivations."

THE HEATSTROKE LINE

"Do you know why Mark was fired so quickly when Simonson became President?"

"No, I was wondering about that actually. He seemed to be so well-regarded in the government. He even had his own little department."

"It was a way for Simonson to reach out to the Confederacies. Mark thought that once the biter bugs were contained, Mountain America would be ready to take over the three Confederacies west of the Mississippi. That's what he used that little department of his to push for. I'm sure he's pushing for the same sort of thing at the UFA."

Dan was impressed, as he always was, by Stuart's level of insight. "Well, you're exactly right. Lizabetta Smith and some of the other people on our mission said that on the flight home. Jesse Davis claimed that he wanted to make an alliance with the Kentucky Confederacies, but they thought the UFA was planning to invade."

"Yep. The twins aren't as nasty as their old man was, but they're still very aggressive. So I don't think Mark was fooling you. He really wants to get rid of the biter bugs, and I'm sure that's what the lab was for. But I think Davis was trying to fool our diplomatic team, and it sounds like they came to the same conclusion."

"Well, does that give you a sense of pessimism about your American Patriotism stuff? I mean, it doesn't sound like we're going to have unity any time soon."

"Not while the twins are still in power. They won't be there forever, though, and the more you plan for something like unification in advance, the more ready you'll be when events turn in your direction."

Dan sensed that his own ideas about contributing to unification were a bit naïve, and that the whole process was more complicated than he had realized. But he decided to wait and see what happened in tomorrow's meeting.

Despite being official representatives of Mountain America, it took the four of them more than an hour to get through passport control at Jacksonia airport, and night was falling by the time they got into the auto-car for their hotel. From what Dan could tell, Jacksonia looked somewhat like a Mountain American city, with modern cryoplastic houses set on treeless streets, but—at least on the way from the airport to the hotel—the streets were scattered at odd intervals through a large area of truck yards, storage facilities and empty, garbage-filled lots. The hotel was modern and well-maintained, however. After they all checked in, they gathered in a small, private room for dinner and a briefing by Sam Reinhart.

Still acting fidgety, and speaking in a monotone, Sam explained that the man they were going to meet tomorrow did the scheduling for one of the big trucking firms in Jacksonia which sent goods from the Successor States to various places in the Confederacies. He dealt regularly with the three most important of the Confederacies, Carolina Piedmont, Atlanta and Birmingham-Victoria. It made sense that he would have received useful information in this position since any coordinated attack on Mountain America would probably come from one of those three states. In order not to compromise the man, or discourage him from talking, the four of them were going to present themselves as delegates of the Ormand Fruit Company. Although citrus fruit grew readily below the Heatstroke Line, people in the Confederacies imported a substantial amount of fruit that only grew further north, such as apples and cherries—Dan could not imagine why, given how poor the Confederacies were—and Ormand was one of their principal suppliers. Dan, Stuart, Sam Reinhart and Tarenly Chang were each being provided with the made-up identity of an Ormand executive. Profiles were being sent to them through the secure channel on their links, and they were to study them tonight so they could play their roles properly until they managed to arrange a private meeting with the informant. They would all reconvene at lunch tomorrow to make sure they understood each other's identities. Obviously enjoying the cloak-and-dagger aspect of the mission, Sam went on about the details of their dissimulation at almost interminable length, and Dan, despite himself, thought that maybe he should have borrowed some Phantasie from Senly.

When Sam finally finished, Dan asked Stuart if he wanted to go to the hotel bar and get a drink.

"No, I've got a headache. Anyway," he added, with his elfin smile, "I need to study my fruit company profile. But I was going to ask you whether you wanted to go sight-seeing with me tomorrow morning. There's a big Revivalist church down by the docks, and it's still being used. I can arrange for the hotel to rent us an auto-car."

Dan said that he'd be delighted to go and they agreed to meet after breakfast.

It was the rainy season in the Confederacies and, when they set out the next day, the sky was grey and there was a steady drizzle.

THE HEATSTROKE LINE

Stuart explained that he had read about the church, which had played a role in the post-Civil War history of Jacksonia, and that Noah Erlanger regularly sent it money to support its activities.

"Good old Noah," said Dan, laughing. "He seems to support every possible lost cause. I'm amazed he has any money left."

"He's very rich."

"What was it like to go to the Enamel with him? Josh seemed positive about him, but, unlike my daughter, he usually won't disparage people—particularly when they're Patriots."

"Josh is a wonderful young man, Dan. He got along very well with Noah. I had to be nice to Noah since he was financing the trip, but I've got to admit that he got on my nerves, especially when he kept giving me lectures on things he doesn't know very much about."

"And he's really a Revivalist?"

"Yep, he prays every day."

"I thought Revivalism was finished. After all their prayers and predictions about the flooding turned out to be so obviously wrong."

"No, it still has followers scattered around in various places, particularly in the Confederacies. And their thinking still influences people. Just remember, we keep following the Revivalist practice of giving boys Biblical names."

"Your name isn't Biblical."

Stuart started laughing. "That's true, but my parents thought it was because it's old-fashioned. I only realized that it wasn't when I went away to school and the other kids assumed that I was Jewish. So when I went back home, I asked my parents about it—they were a foursome, as you know. And they said, "Don't argue with us—we brought you up.""

Now Dan laughed. "That's basically the same answer I got when I asked my parents why they saddled me with such an alliterative name."

"I guess you and I managed to avoid both problems with our own sons."

Stuart's son, who was named Isaac, was a law student at the University. Stuart's wife had died of some strange ailment when Isaac was quite young, so Stuart had brought him up alone. Isaac was a pleasant, very intelligent kid, and Stuart was justly proud of him.

The auto-car pulled into a large, nearly empty parking lot in a grimy industrial area. There was a big power plant nearby spewing smoke into the air and the tall cranes at the containerized port on Mississippi Bay were visible in the distance. In front of them was the entrance to the church, a massive doorway framed by Corinthian columns. Between the parking lot and the doorway, somewhat astonishingly, was a broad expanse of neatly-kept green grass. Dan reflected, as they walked quickly across it—you could never know when a biter bug might strike—that it must be very difficult and expensive to maintain in Jacksonia's climate. Maybe that was where Noah's money was going.

The interior of the church was a vast, darkened space, wide and very long, with side chapels lining the ground level and a balcony halfway up the sides. At the far end was a huge, glowing Revivalist cross, its arms pointed diagonally upward toward the sky and above it a banner with large, glowing letters that said "Lord Jesus, we confess our sins. Turn back the tides."

"Do you know what you're looking at?" Stuart asked. "I mean, what this building was before it became a church?"

"No, actually I don't."

"It was a shopping mall, the kind that was very popular in the late twentieth and early twenty-first centuries. Those side chapels were stores, and there were more stores on the upper level, where you see the balcony. Originally this hallway was even longer, but they closed it off with concrete when they made the altar. There was also another hallway crossing it, but they closed that off with concrete a short way down at either end and made it into a transept."

"I'm surprised a shopping mall would be this dark."

"You're right, it wasn't. Originally, the ceiling was all glass, but it's been painted over. They probably did it to create the mood, but I'm sure it was also much too expensive to keep it air-conditioned when the sun was blazing down on it."

In fact, the church was quite warm and had an unpleasant, musty odor. There were folding chairs set out in rows most of the way down its length, and a few scattered people were seated in them, mumbling to themselves.

"I want to look at the chapels," said Stuart. "The ones on this side"—he pointed to the left—"were family chapels that rich people could buy, but most of them have been cleared out by now. Look, here's one that still has some remains."

It was a large rectangular space with framed pictures attached to the walls. The pictures were protected by thick claroplastic, which must have accounted for their survival. Some were formal portraits, but others were scenes of family life. There was one showing about ten people of different ages playing ball on a beautiful lawn in front of an enormous house made of glass and natural wood.

"*Remembrance of Things Past* comes to mind," said Dan.

"More like *Gone With the Wind*," Stuart answered, laughing. "Anyway, I want to study these pictures for a bit. Why don't you take a look at the chapels on the other side of the aisle—they'll be more interesting."

The chapels across the aisle had a banner above them with glowing letters that said: "God save the cities of the Gulf." In each chapel, protected by claroplastic, there was a diorama of a different city, beautifully and meticulously made. Walking down their length, Dan saw Houston, Tampa, Mobile, Gulfport, Pensacola, Galveston and Biloxi. "I don't see New Orleans," he said to Stuart, who had joined him by now.

"No, New Orleans was lost before this church was built. The point of the models was to ward off further flooding."

"Sounds more like voodoo than Christianity."

Stuart laughed. "That's a funny thought. In fact, New Orleans was considered the center of voodoo in America, and I'm sure some of the refugees from there were involved in the construction of this church."

"It's hard to imagine what it must have been like for them."

"It is. Since American history isn't taught in our high schools any more, I get students in my classes who think that all the people in the coastal cities died when huge tidal waves suddenly came crashing over them."

"Well, the teachers probably don't want to deal with the fact that so many of them were killed by other Americans."

"I used to think that too, but I wonder about it now. After all, it was the UFA that did most of the killing, not Mountain America. In addition to those huge machine gun batteries they had along the Appalachians, they put gunboats in the Ohio and Potomac Rivers and on Mississippi Bay, so very few of the refugees could even reach us. The ones that came into Mountain America were mainly from Houston, and we let them in because we were under-populated."

"You know Stuart, I never had American history in high school either." Dan said, as they began walking back to the car. "And I spent most of my time in college studying science. It's a little hard to imagine that many people being killed by machine guns. I mean, there must have been over a hundred million of them."

"Actually, you're right. What happened is that most of the people realized they wouldn't be able to get into the UFA and just returned to their homes in the coastal cities. With a few feet of water on the ground from the storm surges, services broke down, food and drinking water wasn't supplied, and the people gradually died from thirst, hunger or disease."

They got inside the car, set it for return to the hotel, and started off. "What about the people we sent to Canada?" Dan continued. "I mean, after we bombed Toronto and Montreal, while the United States was still one country?"

"There weren't that many of them. Ironically, it was the fighting over who would get to go to Canada that triggered the Second Civil War, and once the U.S. broke apart, the Canadians invaded and stopped us from sending any more people."

"Was that when the UFA became a dictatorship?"

"Exactly. Once people in the Midwest realized they wouldn't be able to send any refugees from the coastal cities into Canada, they wanted an autocratic leader who would be willing to keep out the refugees by doing all that killing."

"But didn't Mountain America shoot some of the ones the Canadians sent back? As well as shooting people later on who were trying to escape the Texas and Southwestern droughts?"

"That's actually a complicated story. Once we had taken in a certain number of refugees—"

The car came to a lurching halt. Dan and Stuart looked at each other, puzzled. The door next to Stuart suddenly opened. Two big men reached in, grabbed Stuart, and pulled him headfirst out of the car. Dan shouted "What are you doing?" The door on his side flew open. Someone grabbed his arms—another big man, with an unshaven face. Dan tried to pull himself back into the car. Someone else grabbed his legs. They were both very strong. He was lifted out of the car. He felt his face press against the first man's shoulder. The man smelled of beer. They carried him a few steps and threw him into a dark space—the back of a truck. Stuart was there, and a man was handcuffing his hands behind him. Dan felt his own arms pulled behind him by someone in the truck, then the handcuffs were clamped down and his wristlink was torn off. The two men in the truck jumped out and slammed the door. Dan and Stuart were alone in the darkness.

CHAPTER 8

"What's happening?" said Dan. "Do you know what's happening?"

"No."

"Do you think we're being kidnapped for ransom?"

"I don't know."

"They do things like that down here, don't they?"

"My arm hurts," said Stuart. "I think they dislocated it when they pulled me out of the car."

"How can they do this? We're part of a diplomatic mission. This must be a mistake. We need to let someone know about this. They took my wristlink. Did they take yours too?"

"Yes."

"Well, Sam Reinhart will know we're missing by noon, when we're supposed to get together. He'll do something, don't you think?"

"I don't know. Maybe. My arm is killing me."

Dan strained his eyes through the darkness, trying to see Stuart, but the back of the truck was completely dark. It was insulated, probably something used for carrying perishable goods. As a result, it was fairly cool, but it was also silent—there was no chance of shouting to anyone outside. Dan tried to control his sense of panic by thinking about the importance of the mission, the urgency that everyone in the Mountain American government felt about figuring out where the biter bug attack had come from. They were ready to go to war over the incident, after all. Suddenly, he felt the truck accelerate, and he became aware that it had previously been going fairly slowly and making a series of turns. Now it was moving in a straight line.

"Did you feel that?" he asked.

"Yes."

"Do you know what's happening?"

The question seemed to revive Stuart a bit.

"I think so," he said. "We must be on the main commercial road that runs east. It's the only road in Jacksonia where you can drive this fast."

"So we're going toward Mississippi?"

"Yes, Mississippi-Meridian." Dan recalled that two of the Confederacies claimed the name Mississippi, one to the east of Jacksonia and the other to the north. People called them Mississippi-Meridian and Mississippi-Tupelo, after their capital cities. But he realized he barely knew anything about either place.

"What it's like?" Dan asked.

"Not like Jacksonia. Very poor—and very disorganized.It's allied with Atlanta."

They fell silent as the truck sped onward. After a while, it slowed to a stop.

"Have we been moving fast for about half an hour?" Stuart asked.

"Yes, I guess that's about right."

"Then we're at the border. Jacksonia's only about 30 miles wide."

"What do you think they want from us in Mississippi?"

"I don't know."

The truck started moving again, but slowly now, made a turn, went down a gradual incline and came to a stop. The back door opened almost immediately, and Dan braced for a blinding flood of light after staring into total darkness. But the room outside was dimly lit. Two men appeared, got into the truck and carried Stuart out.

"Watch out for my arm" Stuart shouted, but the men ignored him, and he groaned as they set him on his feet outside the truck. He seemed to be wilting as he stood there, and Dan was shocked by the blank, defeated expression on his face. When the two men came back toward the truck, Dan stood up on his own, walked past them, and jumped down onto the ground.

They were in some sort of garage, with several other vehicles and various pieces of equipment scattered around. The two men who stood beside them, watching, were the ones who had taken him out of the auto-car, one white, one black, both very big. Three people approached from a doorway to Dan's right. In front was an attractive woman with blond hair, wearing an elegant leopard print dress and the long, pointed shoes that were the latest fashion. Behind her stood a man and a woman, both much bigger, and dressed in work clothes like the two men who were guarding them.

The woman in the leopard dress looked at her wristlink, then at Dan and Stuart, and grinned in self-satisfied manner. She motioned to the woman beside her and then to one of the two guards, and they led Stuart, still complaining about his arm, through the doorway they had come from. Then she turned toward Dan and motioned to the man beside her and the other guard, who grabbed Dan's arms and started to lead him toward the same doorway.

"Who the hell are you?" he said, trying to turn toward the woman. "Are you aware that we're part of a diplomatic mission from Mountain America to Jacksonia authorized by President Peter Simonson? I don't know what you're trying to do, but if you . . ."

One of the men let go of Dan's arm, grabbed his cheeks to force his mouth open, and plunged a plastic gag into it. Dan felt himself choke and struggled for breath. The gag had a slightly sour, greasy taste. Then both men grabbed his arms again and led him through the doorway. Dan suddenly felt an overwhelming sense of dread, stronger even than he had felt when the men first pulled him out of the car.

Beyond the doorway was a narrow corridor with dirty green walls covered with beads of water. Clearly, they were underground. The men led Dan through the first opening along the corridor and into a small, dimly-lit room with three chairs facing a transparent plastic window. Through the window was another room, painted grey and brightly lit. Dan was forced into the chair at the back of the room, his handcuffs were removed and his arms were strapped to the armrests, and then, to his increasing dread, some sort of metal device was placed over his head and tightened so that he was forced to look straight ahead into the room beyond the window. He felt saliva dripping down his chin. The woman in the leopard dress came in, sat down in the chair placed to his left and closer to the window, looked at him up and down, then crossed her legs and turned to the window.

A moment later, Stuart was led into the brightly lit grey room by his two guards. All his clothes except his undershorts had been stripped off. He had always been slender, but now he looked emaciated and pathetic. He was obviously in pain. Dan felt tears coming to his eyes despite his own discomfort. The woman turned to him, smiled, and then turned back to the window. By now, one of Stuart's handcuffs had been removed and re-attached to a metal loop that was built into the wall. The two guards left and

Stuart was alone in the room, one arm fastened to the wall, the other hanging limply at his side.

With a sense of horror, but not, for some reason, of surprise, Dan saw a dark shape fly through the air and attach itself to Stuart's thigh. It was a biter bug, shiny black and nearly three inches long. Stuart jumped and writhed, turning one way and the other, but Dan didn't need to see clearly to know what was happening. The bug's six legs had plunged immediately into Stuart's skin. Now its two sharp mandibles, each half an inch in length, were folded under its body, tearing his flesh. Blood welled up from under the bug, and as it moved down his leg, it left a trail of raw, bleeding flesh behind. Stuart clawed weakly at the bug with his other arm, which was obviously disabled. That didn't matter because Dan knew that tearing a biter bug off your body was virtually impossible. As soon as you started, its legs dug deeper, and you would wind up tearing out a chunk of your own flesh, which was just as painful, and somehow more awful, than letting the bug continue for the half minute or so until it was satisfied and flew away.

Dan wanted to yell. He heard the words "Why are you doing this" form in his throat, but he couldn't speak. He tried to lift the chair to get out of the room, to smash the window, to kill the woman sitting calmly next to him, but the chair was bolted to the floor. He couldn't move—he couldn't even look away. The first bug was gone, leaving an oozing wound behind, but two more bugs had been released and attached themselves to Stuart's body, one to his chest and one to his arm. Helpless and in agony, he was trying to pull away from the wall and he was screaming. No sound came through the window and the silence, compounded by Dan's own inability to speak, made the scene somehow more horrible.

Dan closed his eyes. If there was nothing else that he could do, he could at least deny this woman the satisfaction of making him watch his friend be tortured. Beneath his sorrow, fury and horror, he sensed another feeling, some indefinable nausea that lay deep inside him. After a few minutes, he felt compelled to look again. Stuart had collapsed and was lying against the wall. There were four or five bugs on his body now, and one was on his cheek, moving toward his eye. He was still writhing, but had also begun to shake compulsively. Blood was oozing from bug tracks on his arms, legs and stomach, covering his body and dripping onto the floor. He was going into shock—they were killing him. Dan had never felt so angry or so powerless. It was hard to believe that this was real, that Stuart was really dying, that in a few more minutes he would cease to exist. The bugs flew away, one leaving a pool of blood in his eye socket, and then three more, five more, came flying in. Dan closed his eyes again. They were wet with tears; he felt himself sobbing and gasping for breath through the greasy gag.

Suddenly, there were people around him, three or four. They released his head, unstrapped his arms, stood him up, handcuffed his arms behind him again, turned him around and dragged him out into the corridor. In the process, he caught a glimpse of Stuart's prostrate, motionless body through the window, covered in blood, with bugs still crawling over it. Once in the corridor, he was dragged a short distance, through an opening, and into an even narrower corridor. One of his captors opened a door and he was pushed into a brightly lit grey room. The steady sense of dread that Dan was feeling congealed into panic. They were going to set the bugs on him the way they did to Stuart. They were going to kill him. He was going to die.

His gag was removed, his handcuffs were opened, and then one arm, still cuffed, was attached to a metal loop in the wall, just the way that they had done to Stuart. Then the guards left the room and closed the door behind them. He was alone. In front of him was a large plastic window, dark and blank. The woman was sitting behind it, he was certain, and she was going to watch as the biter bugs killed him.

How could this be happening? He felt a roaring in his head, he couldn't think. There was something he had to figure out, something he had to make sense out of, but he didn't know what it was. Would he really die, would he really stop existing? What about his children and Garenika? "If I die now, I'll never see them again" he realized. "No, there will be no 'I' not to see them. The world will come to an end. It can't be, it just can't be."

He heard the unmistakable, high pitched buzz of a biter bug flying toward him through the air. Instinctively, he knew what to do—he had been trained in Mark Granowski's department before he went to central Texas for a research project. The bugs flew in straight lines when they were attacking. He waited until it almost reached him, then slapped it with his free hand. It fell to the ground with a sickeningly solid thud, but right side up. Black and huge, it crawled a few inches, its long mandibles opening and closing. Even though he had his shoes on—he realized that they hadn't taken off his clothes—he knew there was no point trying to crush the bug; its carapace was much too hard. After a few moments, the bug's wings started vibrating, it rose up in the air, and flew toward him once more. Again, he slapped it and it fell down right side up. The hideous thing crawled a few inches and rose up again. Once again he slapped it and it thudded to the ground, right side up again. Its wings vibrated, it rose up and flew toward him, he slapped it hard and it fell down again, this time on its back. Immediately, he stamped his foot on it and felt the satisfying crunch as its body cracked beneath his shoe.

But what was the point, he asked himself a moment later. They could release another bug, five more, fifty more. The pain would become worse and worse and he would die, just like Stuart. No, not just die—the world would end, there would be nothing. The roaring in his head returned, the sense of dread and disbelief. It couldn't be. He heard himself bellowing "No, No, No, No." There was another high pitched buzz behind him, and as he spun around, the biter bug slammed into his upper arm. He felt its feet dig in, and then the burning, searing pain as its huge mandibles, now tucked under its carapace, began to tear his flesh. He could only stare at it in horror. Blood rose up under it and turned his light blue shirt sleeve a sickly purple. The bug moved slowly down his arm, leaving a track of bloody, torn up flesh visible inside the inch-wide tear in his shirtsleeve. The pain was unbearable. He couldn't believe that the twenty five or thirty seconds that the bug was on him seemed so long, and he felt a moment of relief when it finally flew away, dripping blood behind it.

He had to organize his thoughts, there was something that he had to do, but what was it? How could he stop existing? Would he live somehow, because of his research? Would he live in the memories of Josh, Senly, Michael and Garenika? But he wouldn't be here, there would be no world for him. An image, a memory, suddenly came into his mind. He was walking across the University of Utah campus with Garenika. They had just met, he had said something to her and she laughed, in a soft, silvery tone, and he wondered if they would end up having children together. Now he saw his home in Arches Park City. His father was reading to him, and his mother came into the room with the three dimensional poster of the Milky Way, the one he had always wanted.

After a few minutes, he realized that no more bugs had come. A sudden surge of hope passed through him. He was afraid to even form the thought, afraid that it would somehow preclude the

THE HEATSTROKE LINE

actuality. But the door opened, one of the guards came into the room with a suppressed smile on his face, removed the handcuff from Dan's wrist, removed the other part from the loop on the wall and walked out with it. The lights in the room suddenly dimmed. Dan sank down onto the floor. He took the bottom of his shirt and pressed it against the wound on his arm, as much to relieve the burning pain as to staunch the flow of blood. He became aware that he was sobbing, but whether it was with relief or anguish was impossible for him to say.

Several hours later, the door opened, and before Dan could react, a tray with clothing, a plate of food and an inflatable mattress was pushed into the room. The door closed again. The clothing was an ordinary, open collar white shirt, a pair of dark brown trousers and dark green undershorts. Dan became aware that the front of his own pants was wet and realized he had pissed himself when the bug attacked him. Next to the clothes was a large blue, disinfectant bandage. Slowly and deliberately, Dan stripped off his clothes, wrapped the bandage around his arm, which immediately felt a bit better, and put on the clothes he'd been given. Looking around, he saw an open hole in the opposite corner of the room, walked over and peed down the hole.

He went back to the tray and took a bite of a roll. All at once, he felt nauseated, ran to the hole and vomited. He couldn't stop; he vomited repeatedly and convulsively, long after there was anything left in his stomach. The roaring in his head returned, he felt intensely chilled and his body began shaking uncontrollably. After what seemed like a long time, the shakes and chills subsided, but they were followed by a slowly intensifying fear. Suppose they turned off the lights and began to fill the room with water. He could feel himself being forced to the top of the room, feel his head pressed against the ceiling when only a few inches of air remained, feel the water filling his nose and mouth as he gasped helplessly for breath. Suppose the walls of the room began to close from both directions, pressing against his body until he was trapped in a tiny, pitch black space. Suppose they raised the temperature until searing air burned his lungs with every breath as he began to suffocate.

Dan tried to calm himself. He wondered if he should use Jiangtan—why hadn't he thought of it when he was watching Stuart die—but somehow didn't think that it would help. Had the bread been poisoned? That wouldn't make any sense. Clearly, they meant to keep him alive. Were they holding him for ransom or as a hostage for some political purpose? In any case, once the Mountain American government found out about it, they would arrange for his return, he reassured himself. He decided he should try to sleep; he was obviously exhausted. He inflated the mattress, lay down, and closed his eyes. The biter bug wound on his arm was still throbbing and his head ached. He tried to think of his college days, of his evenings with friends, of nineteenth century novels, of Garenika, but it all seemed thin and pointless. Finally, his thoughts returned to his early fascination with astronomy, and he pictured himself touring the moons and planets of the solar system and then venturing out among the undiscovered worlds that orbited the distant stars.

CHAPTER 9

He was awake, the lights had been turned up, and a new plate of food was pushed into the room—orange juice, toast and coffee. Dan was ravenously hungry but he ate cautiously. As soon as he was done, the door opened and two large men came into the room, two men who he had never seen before. One was Asian, with a scarred face, and the other was a bearded white man with a shaved head and glowering eyes. The Asian man had two guns in holsters on either side of his waist. One of them was a stun gun, for the biter bugs, but the other was a GX gun, a real weapon. They lifted Dan to his feet, cuffed his hands—in front of him this time—and led him out through the two corridors and back into the garage.

In the middle was a large black van, jacked up high above its wide, balloon-like tires, with a bulbous turret on the center of its roof. One of the rear doors opened automatically and the two men lifted Dan up, threw him onto the floor of the van and slammed the door. He struggled up and sat on the seat. The rear portion of the van was separated from the front by a heavy wire mesh. After a few minutes, the two men got into the front of the van, the Asian man behind the wheel and the white man next to him. They turned on the engine, which let out a heavy, low-pitched roar that set the vehicle vibrating. Suddenly, Dan saw the leopard woman, now in a solid yellow dress—had she been there all along?— talking to the driver. Then she disappeared around the rear of the van and a moment later appeared at the window nearest Dan, staring into the rear compartment. With a surge of fury, Dan heaved himself at the window, banging on it helplessly with his cuffed hands. A moment later a jarring shock surged through his arms and made him fall back against the seat—the cuffs were electrified. The woman grinned and one of the men said "Hands off the window, asshole."

Then a door on the side of the garage slid open and the van drove itself out of the garage and up a concrete ramp. There were several squat buildings nearby flying an American flag that had two blue water moccasins with white stars on them superimposed over the stripes—the insignia of Mississippi-Meridian. Some military tanks and armored rocket launchers were parked nearby, and a barbed wire fence ran along one side of the buildings and into the distance. This was the military post that guarded Mississippi-Meridian's border with Jacksonia, Dan realized. It was daytime—morning—but the sky was grey and a steady rain was falling. The van drove past the buildings and onto a four-lane freeway, clearly the main commercial road that he and Stuart had taken yesterday. But Stuart was dead. It seemed impossible, and the same indefinable nausea, the feeling that lay deep inside him underneath the rage and sorrow, came back to him.

Dan tried to distract himself by looking outside. Large tractor-trailer trucks were moving rapidly in both directions, interspersed with some private cars and a few police and military vehicles with the Mississippi-Meridian insignia painted on their sides. After about half an hour they passed through Meridian itself, at least according to the highway signs, but all Dan could see were a few ruined buildings along the road and a large power plant pouring white smoke into the cloudy sky. Dan realized that he had been completely passive since they left the garage and wondered whether he was already accepting his mistreatment as inevitable or somehow justified.

"Where are you taking me?" he shouted through the grating. "What is it that you want from me?"

"Shut up asshole."

Dan was about to repeat that he was a representative of Mountain America, which was more powerful than any state in the Confederacies, and that they would be punished for their actions, but he realized that these were just two low-level guards with no authority to do anything but carry out instructions.

By now they were past Meridian and signs began to appear along the road announcing that they were approaching the border with Montgomery, the next Confederacy to the east. A few miles before they reached the border, the Asian man behind the wheel turned off the auto-drive and took control of the van. He exited the freeway and headed south on a narrow two-lane highway, obviously not set for auto-cars. What had been an effort to assert himself now became a genuine question in Dan's mind—where, in

THE HEATSTROKE LINE

fact, were they taking him? The two men in the front were generally silent. Occasionally, one would make a brief comment to the other, but Dan had trouble hearing them through the grating, and when he could discern what they were saying, it was of no particular significance. The rain began to let up, but the sky stayed grey. They passed some large plantations growing bananas, soybeans and avocados, one surrounded by a tall electrified fence, another with three gun turrets facing the road. As they went on, the plantations disappeared and there was nothing but occasional small farms surrounding dilapidated houses. Most of the houses, no matter how decrepit, had a large American flag in front, sometimes accompanied by the water moccasin flag of Mississippi-Meridian. There were only a few vehicles on the road—small farm trucks, pickups and an occasional car, all driver-controlled.

Further down the road was a forest of dead pine trees, their needles uniformly brown, their trunks covered with discolored patches. Probably an infestation by one of the newly aggressive varieties of nematodes carried by pine sawyer beetles, Dan surmised; he had spent several years combatting an attack by a related species on Mountain America's coffee crop. The men stopped to stretch their legs and piss, but Dan stayed in the car. They started driving again, this time with the white man at the wheel. After a while, the van turned left onto an even narrower road, not much more than a single lane, and headed east again. To his right, the land stretched out in a dead-flat, treeless expanse of marsh grasses and weeds, with pools of dark water scattered across it. Occasionally, the water covered the road to the depth of a few inches or a foot, and Dan saw the reason why they had chosen this jacked-up vehicle with balloon tires for the trip. After a short distance, the road turned north for a while, then went across a low, cryoplastic bridge set into the swamp on squat pylons, then went south for a short distance and turned east again.

Although Dan's knowledge of the Confederacies was spotty, he was able to guess where he was and what was happening. They were driving along the land bordering the Gulf of Mexico and had just driven around the northern end of Mobile inlet. Because of the storm surges from the Gulf, to say nothing of the brutal heat in summer, this land was uninhabitable and no longer controlled by any of the Confederacies. Clearly, they had turned off the commercial freeway and taken this circuitous path to get around

Montgomery, which, as Dan recalled, had a particularly aggressive government aligned with only a few other Confederacies like East Tennessee and the Orlando Islands. They must be headed toward Atlanta, which, as Stuart had told him, was an ally of Mississippi-Meridian. But why were they going there, and what did they want from him?

The two men in front had become tense and wary as they turned on to this road, talking softly to each other and watching the video screen mounted on the dashboard. There was no other traffic for a while, but after they turned east beyond Mobile inlet, the white man pointed to the screen and said "Something's coming." There was a pause, and then the Asian man said "Looks like a commercial convoy. Probably okay." They pulled off the road into the grass. A few minutes later, three large tractor-trailers trucks, with an armored machine gun car in front and another one behind, came roaring by.

"Might as well eat now," said the white man once the convoy had vanished down the road. He opened a refrigerator cell in the front section of the van, took out various types of food, then slid open a small slit in the wire mesh screen and, without a word, passed a ham sandwich and a soda through it. Dan felt hungry—it must have been well past noon—and after a moment's hesitation he began to eat. A violent storm came sweeping across the tidal flats. The rain clattered against the roof and sides of the van, and water streamed down the windows or crawled upward in jumbled patterns when the gusts of wind were particularly intense. They began driving again, but the storm continued and they had to move more slowly. Although Dan now had to pee, he decided to wait. He told himself it was because of the rain but realized that he was reluctant to elicit another contemptuous response from the two men and figured that they would soon stop on their own accord. Suddenly, the white man said "What's that?" and pointed to the screen. Both men looked at the screen intently, then out across the salt flats. Dan looked as well but saw nothing other than matted grass and the pools of water dimpled by the rain.

"It's an air boat," said the Asian man after a minute or two. "He's either a pirate or a fisherman. Hard to tell which at this distance."

"What would he be fishing for?"

"Catfish, maybe—or crabs. There are some big ones out in the flats. But maybe he's a pirate."

THE HEATSTROKE LINE

"If he's a pirate, wouldn't he have started shooting?"

"Too far. He can blow us up from there, but he can't disable us and get our stuff until he's closer."

Dan cringed, despite himself. He felt vulnerable and powerless, trapped inside an ungainly target in the middle of a dangerous, anarchic wasteland. There were several minutes of tense, agonizing silence.

"He's coming within range," said the white man, in a brittle voice.

"Yeah, but he's stopping. Looks like a fisherman."

"Fuck it, I don't want to take the chance."

"Okay," said the Asian man. He opened a panel on the dashboard and pushed a few buttons. The van shook, and Dan saw a white trail starting at the roof and moving out across the swamp. A second later, there was a bright flash on the horizon.

"Take that, motherfucker," said the white man, as they drove off again.

Dan felt offended and relieved at the same time, then annoyed at his own sense of relief. His bladder hurt—he could no longer wait until the men decided to get out again.

"I have to piss," he said, half expecting them to tell him to shut up again. But the white man pulled to a stop, opened the slit in the mesh screen again, and told Dan to put his hands against it. He then attached the end of a spooled wire to the cuffs, opened the back door automatically and motioned Dan to go outside. Dan thought of asking for a stun gun but realized he couldn't use it with his hands cuffed. He went out into the rain, which had let up only slightly, and faced out toward the Gulf. The scene in front of him was desolate—nothing but water-logged grass, brackish ponds, a grey sky and rain. Then he noticed some sort of ruined building in the distance, a concrete structure that had partially collapsed. He realized that there had been cities, towns and farms here, that the people who lived in them had probably died, as Stuart had described. This sodden marsh was covering thousands of bodies, buried in the mud and rotting into nothingness. Dan had a sudden image that their lifeless faces lay just below the surface of the muddy water, staring blankly upward.

He was wet when he got back into the car, and soon chilled by its air conditioning. His arm was still throbbing. He felt another surge of anger, then realized that there was absolutely nothing he could do, so he curled up on the seat to warm himself, closed his eyes and actually managed to doze off for a while. After several more hours of slow steady driving, they turned onto a road that branched off to the left, and drove north for another half hour or so until they reached a border station. It was getting dark, but the floodlights revealed a squat building with a large flag on top—an American flag with grey rifles in place of the white stripes. This was, Dan recalled, Columbia, the state east of Montgomery, one of two small Confederacies south of Atlanta. After talking briefly to the guards at the station, they proceeded down the highway, which was better maintained beyond this point. The drivers switched the car back to auto-control and seemed to relax. Dan assumed that they were headed toward Atlanta, but after another hour or so, they turned off to the left once more, drove out of Columbia through another border station, then stopped immediately at a border station for Birmingham-Victoria, the Confederacy north of Montgomery. The station was a somewhat larger building with a big claroplastic observation window facing the road and a gun turret at either side. The words "Auburn Station: Victory and Freedom, America Forever" were written in large letters over the doorway. On the roof, lit by floodlights, flew a flag with the Birmingham insignia, a sword with red stripes on the blade and a blue handle with white stars.

The guards got out of the car and went into the brightly lit station. They started talking to the two people who were in the station, a youthful, blond white man and a slender black woman. Dan didn't pay much attention at first, but after a few minutes he realized that his two guards were engaged in some sort of argument with the two people in the station, and he started watching them more closely. He couldn't hear anything but he could see them clearly. They were obviously angry at each other, and their soundless gesticulations, framed by the station window, seemed like an antic pantomime on an illuminated stage. An older, dark-haired man came into the room, and Dan's two guards started moving toward the door. When the dark-haired man blocked their way, Dan's Asian guard, who was much bigger, smashed his fist into the man's face and then knocked the black woman aside. The blond man from the station jumped on him from behind, then Dan's white guard started kicking the man until the dark-haired man from the station, blood dripping from his face, threw himself into the white guard's legs and sent him sprawling. All four men were punching and clawing at each other now. The Asian guard pulled out his GX gun, the dark-haired station man who he was fighting sunk his teeth into the hand

THE HEATSTROKE LINE

holding the gun, there was another flurry of punches, then the black woman, holding one side of her face, went up to the fighting men, pulled out a GX gun, and fired directly into the Asian guard's head. Blood splattered against the station window, and the man slumped to the floor. Dan's white guard came running out of the station, a look of terror on his face, and ran past the car and out into the darkness. The blond man from the station followed him, calmly and deliberately, with a gyro rifle in one hand and a flashlight in the other. A broad, bright beam shot out of the flashlight and the running man appeared in view. The rifle blazed and Dan saw the guard's arm fly off his body with a spurt of blood as he fell to the ground. Then the blond man walked slowly toward the fallen figure, keeping it within the flashlight's beam. When he got close, he switched off the flashlight, and there were two more blazes from his rifle.

Dan should have felt gratified to see the men who had treated him so badly killed, but the man's look of terror as he fled had aroused Dan's sympathy. It must have been terrible to be shot down like that. And Dan wasn't sure what would happen to him now—these people seemed even more savage than his now-dead guards. After several minutes, the blond man from the station got behind the wheel of the van and the black woman, holding a cloth against her eye, got into the seat next to him. "Let's take this car," the man said. "It's running, so the bio-lock is off. We'll leave it at the prison." As they started off, he turned around and, to Dan's surprise, spoke to him in a friendly, reassuring tone.

"I know you've had a long day, Dr. Danten. It will only be a few more hours."

"Where are you taking me?"

"Birmingham City."

"And then what's going to happen to me?"

"I'm sorry, but we're not at liberty to say. You'll see."

"What was going on back there?"

"We had a disagreement, but as you saw, we worked things out. Are you hungry?"

"I don't know, I think so. To tell you the truth, I'm a little shaken, but I guess I'm hungry."

"Don't worry. You're safe now. Try to eat something."

The black woman opened the screen and passed him another ham sandwich and soda as the van sped off along the road. Originally a four-lane freeway, the inner lane in each direction had been kept in good repair, and they were able to make good

69

time. It was night-time now, so there was nothing to see, and Dan was tired of watching the scenery in any case. For some reason, perhaps nothing more than weakness, he believed the young man's reassurance. He had never seen a person shot before, and the violence of the scene disturbed him. He thought back to Stuart's dreadful death and the same indefinable sense of nausea returned. He had seen too much violence in the last two days— maybe that was it.

A few hours later, the young man announced that they had reached Birmingham City. The first thing Dan saw, off to his right, was an enormous power plant, with three tall smokestacks pouring billowing white streams into the nighttime air, and across a hazy distance, still another power plant with two stacks emitting another set of streams, as if in response. Otherwise, there was no indication of a city, only a few scattered lights. Once they exited the freeway, they drove past some factories and warehouses, then through a gate in a tall, chicken wire fence, and stopped at a long low building. Obviously, they were at the prison. The two drivers got out of the van and went inside the building. After a few minutes, the blond man came out with three uniformed prison guards—two women and a man—opened the door of the van, and told Dan to get out.

"I'm sorry, Dr. Danten," the blond man said. "I know this isn't a particularly nice place to stay. But try to get some rest. I just found out that I'll be coming here tomorrow morning to pick you up, so I'll see you then."

The three prison guards took Dan through several security gates, down a dimly lit corridor, and then through a door into a square room surrounded by cells, where they unfastened his handcuffs. To his surprise, they didn't put him in a cell, but simply locked the door to the corridor behind him.

The room where the guards left him had a console of some sort in the center, with various receptacles for electronic equipment, now empty except for a few straggling wires. It was surrounded by nine cells, three on each of the sides other than the side along the corridor. The doors to all the cells were open, and Dan, who now found himself exhausted, went slowly through each one, thinking of very little other than the practicalities of rest. Each cell had a large two-way screen, all non-functional and most completely shattered. The toilets in five of the rooms were broken, one slowly leaking water onto the floor, where it trickled down the drain in the center of the room. Six of the beds still had mattresses, but only two were in decent condition. Everything smelled dank and musty. Dan used one of the functioning toilets, washed his face in the adjoining sink, then lay down on what seemed like the best mattress and almost immediately went to sleep.

CHAPTER 10

The next morning, Dan was wakened by two prison guards, given a tray with breakfast and a change of clothes, and then led down the main corridor to a bathroom where he could shower and shave. To his repeated questions, the guards replied that they didn't know what was happening but that they had been instructed to attend to his needs and bring him to the front entrance of the prison by nine o'clock. A dark blue car was waiting there, with a driver in the front and the young blond man who had driven him to Birmingham City standing beside it.

"Good morning, Dr. Danten," he said pleasantly. "I hope you got some sleep. By the way, I never really introduced myself yesterday. My name's Joel—Joel Rinier."

Dan nodded to him curtly, in no mood to be sociable. Why was this man making such an effort to be friendly, he wondered? In a way, it was more disconcerting than the open hostility of the guards from Mississippi-Meridian. After all, Joel Rinier, for all his friendliness, was a remorseless killer.

They got into the back of the car together and headed down a wide, curving street lined with concrete or brick one-story buildings. Most of these were collapsing into ruin and overwhelmed by vines and weeds, but a few were patched and one or two remained in good condition.

"I understand that you're a distinguished scientist," Joel continued. "I'm sorry about the circumstances, but it's really a pleasure to meet you. I would have liked to be a scientist, but I wasn't able to get enough of an education."

"Where am I being taken?" Dan responded. "Why is all this being done to me?"

"It will be explained to you in a few minutes, Dr. Danten. I'm sorry, but you'll just have to wait and see. I'm just an internal security agent. I really don't have the authority to tell you."

THE HEATSTROKE LINE

In a few miles, they reached what had originally been a large suburban shopping center, with a row of storefronts around three sides of its central parking lot, two large structures at either end, and a third structure set off at a distance. Cars were scattered through the parking lot, generally in clusters. About a quarter of the stores were still functioning, although they looked frayed and faded, while the rest were empty shells. One of the larger structures had collapsed, but the other two had been maintained. They parked in front of the one on the left and Joel led Dan inside. It had obviously been built as a department or specialty store or some sort, but now the floor space was divided into office cubicles. Joel led Dan down a hallway between the cubicles and into a reception room with red, white and blue letters on the back wall proclaiming "Birmingham-Victoria Department of Internal Security." Two cloth flags were mounted on the back wall of the room, one the old American flag, the other with the Birmingham sword insignia. Joel stopped to speak to the receptionist for a moment, then took Dan into a surprisingly large office with sleek modern furniture. A stocky, grey-haired man, wearing a formal, round-collared shirt, was seated behind the desk. He had a brutal looking face, with heavy-lidded eyes, thick lips and fleshy cheeks. The man motioned for Dan to sit down in a chair that faced the desk, and for Joel to stay.

"Good morning, Dr. Danten," he said, in a steady, cultured voice. "I'm Nathaniel Wolfson, Assistant Secretary for Internal Security. As you can see, you're our prisoner, but I'm going to offer you a proposition."

Dan felt revived by the more decent treatment he'd received that morning and emboldened by the sense that he was, for the first time since he was captured, dealing with someone who was prepared to listen to him and authorized to take action in response.

"Let me offer you a proposition," he shot back. "Return me to Denver immediately along with the people who murdered Stuart McPherson so that they can be tried and punished, and your cruddy little country won't be invaded by Mountain America. I was in Jacksonia on a diplomatic mission authorized directly by President Peter Simonson, and you've just created a serious international incident for yourselves."

Wolfson smiled. "None of that is going to happen, Dr. Danten. You need to listen to my proposition."

"You need to realize that you've committed an act of war against a much more powerful nation."

"Okay, I can see we're not going to make much progress until you have a more realistic sense of your situation. Would you like to call Mountain America?"

"I certainly would."

Wolfson projected a keyboard onto the front of his desk, turned his screen toward Dan, and opened a general communications link. With an angry glance at him, Dan entered his official code and called President Simonson's office. A young woman appeared on the screen.

"Good morning," said Dan. "I want to talk to President Simonson."

"Who are you?" she said.

"I'm Daniel Danten. I'm on a diplomatic mission to Jacksonia with Stuart McPherson, Samuel Reinhart, and Major Tarenly Chang. Stuart has been murdered, and I've been kidnapped by some idiot in Birmingham-Victoria's security department."

"I'm sorry about your difficulties, but President Simonson doesn't deal with issues at that level," she responded icily. "What makes you think you can just demand that the President of Mountain America should speak with you?"

"Because he personally authorized this mission and requested my participation," Dan said, with rising annoyance.

The woman looked quizzical, then starting inputting some information into her desk link. "I have no record of President Simonson having personally authorized any mission to Jacksonia."

"He authorized a mission to investigate the source of the September biter bug infestation in East Montana. The first stage was to negotiate with the UFA, which, as you may recall, nearly led to war. This mission to Jacksonia is the next stage."

"No it's not. All that President Simonson authorized was the mission to the UFA, as he reported when he addressed the nation. Calling him about a different matter is a misuse of your official calling code. If you try to do so again, I will cancel your code status." The screen went black.

"Maybe you should try a different call," Wolfson said, re-projecting the keyboard. Dan tried to collect his thoughts. Suddenly, he was afraid again, nearly as afraid as he had been when he was captured. Without comment, he called Temarden Goldberg's line at Agriculture. A young man he had never seen before came on line.

THE HEATSTROKE LINE

"Put me through to Temarden, please," Dan said, as calmly as possible.

"The Secretary is unavailable at the moment, but I can—"

"I don't care whether he's unavailable or not. Put me through to him. I've been captured and transported to Birmingham, where they're holding me hostage. Do you know who I am? I'm Daniel Danten, and I'm here—I was sent to Jacksonia—on a diplomatic mission. Now I've been dragged here, they kidnapped me in Jacksonia, me and Stuart McPherson, four men in a truck, and then I was taken to Birmingham by two homicidal maniacs and put in prison."

"Please calm down, Dr. Danten. We're aware of the situation."

"The fuck I'll calm down. Put me through to Temarden immediately. I—I—What do you mean that you're aware of the situation?"

"Do you know that you're being accused of espionage?"

"Espionage? What for?"

"That's what we're trying to determine."

"Espionage my ass. I'm on a diplomatic mission for Secretary Goldberg, for Temarden. Get me out of here."

"We can hardly create an international incident over an individual matter, Dr. Danten. As I said, you've been accused of espionage, and we're looking into the situation."

"Are you aware that these people have tortured Stuart McPherson to death?"

"Let's focus on you, Dr. Danten."

"That's what I'm trying to do."

"Very well. Are you hurt?"

"No, I'm not hurt," Dan said glumly. His arm was still throbbing, but a single biter bug wound was well within the normal scope of the risk anyone took who went below the Heatstroke Line.

"Good. For now, it's best to be cooperative. As I said, we're looking into the matter. I'll contact you through Nathaniel Wolfson of their Internal Security Department if there's anything that we can do." The screen went black again.

Dan found himself actually trembling with anger. At the same time, he felt completely helpless, which naturally made him feel even angrier.

Wolfson waited for a minute or so, with a vaguely scornful expression on his face.

"Okay, Dr. Danten, are you ready to listen to my proposition now?"

"Go ahead."

"As you've just heard, you've been accused of espionage. We're Americans here in Birmingham-Victoria, of course, so you're entitled to a trial, but I can assure you that you'll be convicted, and—"

"What's the basis of the accusation?"

"You'll find out if you choose to go to trial. As I said, though, you'll be convicted, and the sentence for that crime is death."

Dan's fear returned without lessening his anger. His head began hurting, there was a ringing in his ears, and he realized that he was having trouble focusing his thoughts. Suddenly, he wanted to be left alone, to be far away from this sinister, heavy-featured man.

"Do you understand what I'm saying, Dr. Danten?"

"I guess so, yes."

"Okay then. Instead of standing trial, I can offer you probation, with the option of serving Birmingham-Victoria and the cause of freedom. We've established a laboratory to research ways to eradicate the biter bugs. We want you to be part of that effort. If you work there—loyally and conscientiously—for three years, we'll release you and send you back home to Mountain America."

For the first time, the nightmare of his last two days made at least some sense to him. They had captured him because they wanted him to do research for them. And they had killed Stuart because—because they had no use for him? Because they didn't know who he was? The indefinable sense of nausea came back to him once more.

"And I have some more good news for you," Wolfson continued. "If you work hard and prove yourself cooperative for the first six weeks of your probation, we'll transfer you from the jail to a private home, where you can live more comfortably. We're not even demanding that you produce results for us, only that you try your best. That's the proposition, and you have to agree that it's a generous one, given the alternative."

Fine, Dan thought, he had no choice so he would agree. Since he was bound to be smarter than these savages, he would appear to help them, but he would secretly sabotage the lab. Then he would kill the people in the private home where he was staying, steal a car, and escape. But even as these thoughts raced through his head, he was aware of an overwhelming sense of helplessness.

"Well, Dr. Danten, do you agree?"

"Doesn't seem like I have much of a choice."

THE HEATSTROKE LINE

"I'm asking you for a commitment, not an observation."

"Well then, I agree."

"Okay, very good."

"I need to call my family and explain the situation."

"Unfortunately, you're not allowed to do that, or call anyone else, for that matter. I've given you your opportunity to use the link. Let me remind you that you're still a prisoner."

"This is totally unfair. Why are you doing this?"

"Do I have your agreement or not, Dr. Danten?"

"Yes, you have it."

"Good. I'm glad that's clear. I'll let the staff at our lab know that you're coming. Are you rested? Have you had breakfast?" Dan nodded. "OK, then you'll be taken there right away. No sense in waiting to get started. Remember, all we're asking you to do is to use your knowledge and skill to help us solve this problem, a problem that faces all Americans."

"There are no biter bugs in Mountain America, or anywhere above the Heatstroke Line."

"No, but they're a threat, don't you think?"

Were these the people who dropped the biter bugs in East Montana? Dan wondered. Did they do it to force Mountain America, the UFA and Pacifica, to help them eradicate the bugs? Was capturing him part of the same effort, something they decided to do when dropping the bugs didn't work out the way they wanted? Dan's head was still hurting, and his ears still ringing. There were things he had to figure out; he needed to be left alone to think.

"Besides," Wolfson continued, "we're all Americans, aren't we? In the days when America was the most powerful country in the world, we worked together to solve our problems. Just because some problem only affected one part of the country, that didn't mean that the whole nation didn't work on it together, did it? Think about the problem of providing water for the Southwest, or building a pipeline across Alaska, or extracting oil from deep rock layers by hydraulic fracking. Americans worked on those problems together, and American ingenuity solved them."

Wolfson delivered this message in a homiletic tone that made Dan feel distinctly uncomfortable. He thought back to the things Josh said on the day he returned from his trip to the Enumcl, and also thought about his own recent interest in American re-unification.

"Do your best, Dr. Danten, that's all we ask. Show us that you're a real American."

Wolfson stood up behind his desk and nodded to Joel, who led Dan back to the elevator, down to the ground floor and back to the parking lot, where the same car was waiting.

"The lab's only a ten minute drive from here," Joel explained once they got in. It had stopped raining and as they drove down another wide, curving street flanked by ruined one-story buildings, the sun broke through the clouds. Suddenly Dan realized that it was Friday morning. He was supposed to have returned home yesterday afternoon. His whole experience since he was captured had been so bizarre and terrifying that he had felt himself existing in some separate reality, discontinuous with the one that he had previously inhabited. Now that he knew what was going to happen to him, and he was on his way to a laboratory to carry out research, his present situation suddenly reconnected with his life at home, and he began to think about the consequences of his absence. How had Garenika, Josh, Senly and Michael reacted when he didn't return on schedule? Would they just assume he had been delayed? Would Garenika call the Department of Agriculture, and what would she be told if she did? Would she think to hire Rachel Stafford for another day, so that she would have help getting Senly and Michael to school—no, Senly was still suspended, and was Michael still sick and staying home? But it wasn't just today, or next week, but three years, three years that she would have to manage without help, three years when he wouldn't see his children growing up, and what would happen during those three years, what would happen to Senly and Michael, what would happen to Garenika, how could she possibly handle everything, she was bound to lose her job, would the University still pay his salary, how could they live without it, how could they manage without him?

"Why are you doing this?" he started shouting. "You have no right, I need to get back home, I need to get back to my family. Let me out of here, stop doing this to me!"

He lunged for the door handle and tried to open it, and when it didn't yield he started pounding on the window.

"Calm down, Dr. Danten," Joel said. "Please take it easy."

Dan turned on Joel and lashed out at him, flailing his arms with thoughtless fury. Joel parried his blows, apparently without much difficulty.

THE HEATSTROKE LINE

"Dr. Danten, get control of yourself. This isn't going to do you any good."

It obviously wasn't doing any good, and Dan sank back into his seat, exhausted and so frustrated that tears actually began to well up in his eyes.

"I'm sure you'll be well-treated if you cooperate," said Joel. "We're not monsters here, you know." He paused. "I guess the hardest thing is being separated from your family." Dan rolled his eyes. "How many kids do you have?"

"I have three. It doesn't seem to matter to anybody here, does it?"

"Listen, Dr. Danten, I'm not supposed to do this, but I can call your family for you and tell them you're all right. I know that's not the same as calling them yourself, but it might make you feel a little better."

In fact it did. Dan tried not to feel grateful—they had no right to do any of this to him, after all—but he couldn't help himself.

"Are you going to tell them that I'll be stuck here for three years?"

"You know, it may not be that long. I'm not going to report what you did just now to anyone. Try to be cooperative, to do what they're asking you to do at the lab. I think the people in charge have a lot of respect for you. If you help them out, you may get to go home a lot sooner."

Dan doubted that he could believe these reassurances. Probably, Joel was just trying to calm him down. But it had worked, he reflected—he felt at least marginally better. Joel seemed to be a rather skillful guard, as well as being such a skillful killer.

CHAPTER 11

After a few more minutes, they pulled into the nearly empty parking lot of a long, low building, which Dan immediately recognized as a former discount store—probably a Mightee Mart, given the color of the plastic stripes on the façade. Joel conducted him inside. It was a large, dusty space, much of it empty, with a few piles of boxes or broken equipment scattered around the concrete floor and yellow electrical wires snaking across it. They proceeded toward a cluster of plastic partitions in the rear, where bright ceiling lights created an island of illumination in the otherwise shadowy interior. A man with wavy brown hair and an amiable expression, about Dan's age, was waiting for him as they reached the partitions.

"Hi, Dr. Danton. I'm Matthew Clark. Welcome to the Birmingham-Victoria Insect Lab. Let me show you to your work station."

Joel nodded to the man, said "Good-bye, Dr. Danten" with a kindly and complicit look, and headed back the way he came.

"I'm not a scientist," Matthew continued. "My job is just to keep this place running, get the supplies, that sort of thing. I'll introduce you to some of the scientists you'll be working with, then you can meet our director, Dr. Lyons, as soon as he finishes the link conference he's on."

Matthew led Dan past several cubicles formed by the partitions and to a somewhat larger one with a workbench, link screen and various supplies. In the center of the bench was a gene analyzer, with the letters "MMTU" on the screen and the words "Mid-Manitoba Technical University" incised into its casing.

"That's what you'll be working with, primarily," said Matthew. "We're doing genetic modification here. It's a state of the art machine, you'll notice. We stole it from the Canadians."

"Really?"

THE HEATSTROKE LINE

"Yep. We sent a special team up there and cleaned out their whole fucking lab."

"I think I'll feel funny about working on a stolen machine."

"But we didn't steal it from Americans. Anyway, you'll get used to it. Maybe you'll even enjoy it." He grinned at Dan. "This is Dave Uberti, one of our scientists," he added, indicating a young man with a scraggly beard who had come into the cubicle, "and here's Paul Steiner. " Steiner was a towering man, beginning to get a bit flabby, and walked with a slight stoop. He had a friendly face, and welcomed Dan to the lab.

"Oh, Dr. Lyons is ready to see you now," said Matthew, glancing at his wrist link. He led Dan through the partitions to a large office with permanent walls faced on the inside with plastic wood paneling. Lyons, who was sitting behind an elegant, old-fashioned wooden desk and looking at a screen that was mounted on the wall behind him, spun around on his swivel chair as Matthew motioned Dan to take the seat beside him. He was an old man, tall and thin, with bloodshot grey eyes and tanned skin stretched tight across high cheekbones, and he regarded Dan with a fixed stare.

"Good morning," he said in a sharp, authoritative voice. "I'm Thomas Jefferson Lyons and this is my laboratory. I founded it and I direct it. We're doing very important work here at this laboratory, the kind of work that America is all about. Now you're a scientist, so you know that scientists work as a team. You'll be part of our team, but I want to remind you that you're here on probation as an alternative to a death sentence. You're required to work here for three years, and if you do a good job for us, you'll get to go back home. But you've got to do a good job. Maybe you'll see some of the other scientists taking it easy every once in a while, but you don't get to take it easy because you're here on probation. Maybe you'll see people make mistakes, but you don't get to make mistakes. And maybe you think you're smarter than we are, so you can screw things up just to get back at us, but we're Americans too, and we're just as smart as you are, so keep that in mind. Every time you do something wrong, you get a demerit. Every three demerits is another six months added to your probation. Do you understand?"

Dan had never wanted to kill anyone as badly as he did now— well, except maybe the woman who had tortured Stuart.

"Do you understand, Dr. Danten?"

"Yes."

"Good. Now as Matthew here has probably explained, we're trying to control the biter bugs through genetic modification. I think you've seen the machine we got for you to work on."

"I saw it, and it's a good machine. But I don't think you're going to get results with gene modification. That's a very complicated way to approach the problem of biter bug control. Even if you develop an effective gene silencing substance, delivering it to the target population can be really difficult. Since you obviously want me to try my best, I'd suggest exploring the possibility of microbial pathogens. My own theory is that the bugs' respiratory system is their greatest area of vulnerability because—"

"We're doing genetic modification here."

Dan felt like arguing. "So I understand, but I'm telling you that it's not a promising approach, given the resources you have available. Maybe the Canadians could succeed—"

To Dan's complete amazement, Lyons slapped him across the face and started yelling at him. "That's defeatism! The hell with Canada! We're Americans, and we've got American ingenuity working for us. That's one demerit for you. Keep talking about the goddamn Canadians and you'll be here the rest of your life."

Dan was so angry that he clenched his fist and got ready to hit Lyons back, but Matthew sprang at him and pinned his arm to his side. Dan struggled for a moment, but was unable to move even an inch against the pressure Matthew was applying.

Lyons was still yelling at him. "We don't tolerate defeatism in this laboratory. We're Americans. We're the ones who'll be victorious. Victory, victory, that's the word to keep in mind. In case you've forgotten, we have a great tradition, the greatest tradition in the world. Tell me, who invented the telegraph?"

Dan leaned back in his chair, and the sense of frustration he had felt in the car returned. Matthew released the pressure on his arm.

"Well, who invented the telegraph?"

"Samuel Morse."

"I don't need the name, just the nationality."

"Okay, an American."

"Who invented the light bulb?"

"An American."

"Who invented the personal computer?"

"An American."

"Who invented the internet?"

THE HEATSTROKE LINE

Dan was fairly sure it was Tim Berners-Lee, a British scientist. "An American," he answered.

"Who invented the wrist link?"

"An American."

"Who invented the auto-car?"

"An American."

"I didn't hear you mention any Canadians. Any Canadians responsible for these inventions? Well, were they?"

"No."

"That's right. Americans invented them, with American ingenuity. And Americans are going to figure out the way to control the genetic makeup of biter bugs. Right here in this lab."

How was he going to avoid this man, Dan wondered. Obviously, Lyons was insane. One thing that was clear to Dan was that the only sensible strategy was tell him what he wanted to hear, no matter what the real situation was. But the idea rankled him.

"Sorry I had to grab your arm," Matthew said, as they walked back to Dan's cubicle. "But if you'd hit Dr. Lyons, you'd probably have gotten ten demerits. I know he can be a little harsh sometimes, but he's a great man."

"Really?" Dan answered, not sure how honest he could be with Matthew, despite the man's apparent friendliness.

"Oh, absolutely. He's one of the leaders of the Unity Party. He used to be the Senator from this part of Birmingham, then he set up this lab. It was his idea, he got it organized and funded. He's a very talented scientist, you know. He has an advanced biology degree from the University of British Columbia."

"Well, he doesn't seem to like Canadians very much," said Dan. "And you don't either, as far as I can tell."

"Damn right we hate them. Look what they did to the United States. Every American Patriot hates them. Don't you?"

Dan decided not to point out what the United States, when it existed, had done to the Canadians.

Matthew spent the next hour helping Dan set up his workspace. At Dan's request, he tried to provide various supplies, but most of what was needed seemed to be unavailable and Matthew often had to find the little that there was by rummaging through the boxes that were scattered around the building in seemingly random locations. He was unfailingly pleasant and helpful however, and Dan found himself liking the man despite his continued anger at the entire situation.

EDWARD L. RUBIN

"I have to go pick up some equipment," Matthew said, once the meager supplies had been placed in some preliminary order, "but Paul is going to have lunch with you. I'll be back later today."

Paul Steiner came in shortly after Matthew left, and they went to what Paul described as the employee cafeteria. It consisted of some metal chairs and tables located against the back wall of the building and, to Dan's astonishment, two old-fashioned electric stoves where a few female employees were cooking food by hand. Dan knew some people in Mountain America who cooked for themselves as a hobby, but he had never seen a non-automated kitchen in a public building. Despite the hand preparation, there was certainly nothing special about this food, which consisted of soy burgers, heat-resistant corn and spinach. The coffee tasted like potatoes; Dan assumed that it had been shipped in from Mountain America.

"Read some of your research," said Paul, once they were seated. "You're a wonderful scientist, you know."

Dan thought that after the past few days' events he would be beyond the reach of flattery and was annoyed at himself to realize that he was still pleased by the recognition.

"I assume you're an entomologist," he said, wondering if Paul had ever written anything that would enable him to return the compliment.

"Am now, I guess."

"Why, were you trained in some other branch of biology?"

"No, a veterinarian—before Dr. Lyons hired me."

"What?"

"Yeah, worked with large animals like cows and pigs. Hard to keep cows alive in this climate, even with the special breeds."

Paul looked like someone who worked with large animals, Dan thought. But how could he possibly carry out sophisticated genetic modification research with no specialized training in the field? By now, Dan knew what the answer would be if he asked that question—American ingenuity. So he decided to take a different approach.

"How did you meet Lyons?"

"Signed up to do some canvassing for the Unity Party about ten years ago. Dr. Lyons was the leader of the Party for this part of Birmingham, and we started working together. Guess he took an interest in me because he was setting up this lab at the time and I knew something about biology."

THE HEATSTROKE LINE

"Are any of the other scientists here trained entomologists?" Dan asked, trying not to stumble over the word "scientists." He remembered that there were no universities left in the Confederacies.

"Sam Cundiff has a degree in biology from somewhere in the UFA. We all learn as we go along. We've got American ingenuity working in our favor."

"That's great. What made you decide to work for the Unity Party?"

"Independence Party was in power at the time and they'd started a war with Montgomery. Never been particularly political, but it seemed like a waste to me. You know, we won that war, took Auburn away from them, but I couldn't see that it made much of a difference to anyone. I'm for unity. We're all Americans, aren't we?"

"What does your party want to unify?"

"Alabama as a start, I guess. Us and Montgomery. Then all the Confederacies, then maybe the rest of what used to be the USA."

"And you're for that?"

"Yeah. Can't keep fighting with each other, can we? Guess they think that once we're unified we can start fighting with Canada, but, well, oh I don't know." Paul suddenly seemed flustered. "Here, let me show you around the rest of the lab."

Paul led him past the other cubicles, the small set of cages holding biter bugs, the centrifuges, spectroscopes, genetic modifiers and electron microscopes. All the equipment seemed to have been stolen from MMTU or other Canadian institutions. The lab itself was poorly appointed, badly organized, and ill-maintained. Dan found it hard to believe that anyone could carry out something as complex as genetic modification in such an amateurish setting. He watched carefully for any indication that they were breeding biter bugs, that this was the source of the East Montana infestation, but he saw nothing to indicate that it was. He knew exactly what a breeding facility looked like because of his own work with the West Dakota fruit flies. Whatever its detriments, this was clearly not such a facility.

Dan spent the rest of the afternoon familiarizing himself with the machine he had been given and reading some research about gene modification. The computer in his office had no netlink, obviously, but Matthew had shown him how to get materials that had already been downloaded onto the laboratory intranet, or request materials that the communications officer, located in some other cubicle, would download for him. During the course of the afternoon, the other scientists who worked at the lab came by to introduce themselves to Dan. He noticed immediately that of the eight or nine people who he met, there was only one woman, a middle-aged Asian-American whose first name was Faith and seemed vaguely apologetic about her presence in the lab. Sam Cundiff, an African-American and the only person younger than Dave Uberti, had been hired directly from the University of Pittsburgh in the UFA and seemed to have come because he had gotten into some sort of dispute with his advisor. There was an older, somewhat frail man named Joseph, who mumbled and never made eye contact, and a middle-aged, rather jumpy man named Jethro Garber who said that he decided to study biter bugs because he admired them. Realizing that he would be working with these people on a daily basis, Dan tried to resist the conclusion that they were a collection of misfits. At five, one of the guards came to take him back to the prison.

Once again, a heavy rain was falling. Dan didn't bother talking to the man as they drove back to the prison, in part out of resentment regarding the way he had been treated, but mainly because he was trying to make sense of all the things that had happened to him during the day. The biter bug project made sense, but the choice of genetic modification, Lyons' anger, Wolfson's speech for that matter, the whole litany about American ingenuity, the lab full of amateur entomologists, Paul's incomplete, vague explanations, the Unity Party, the Independence Party, the war against Montgomery, all seemed to swirl around in his head, to clash against each other without settling into any comprehensible pattern. Once he had been deposited back in the empty cell block, he threw himself down on one of the beds, distracted and confused. He simply didn't know enough about the Confederacies to sort it all out. If only Stuart had been here with him to explain. That was why he had asked Goldberg to have Stuart join the mission in the first place.

The strange, indefinable sense of nausea he had felt in the garage and the van came back to him, and suddenly, he knew its cause. He was responsible for Stuart's death. If he hadn't suggested, almost insisted, that Stuart be included in this mission, his friend would be alive today, instead of having his body torn to shreds by biter bugs. Dan tried to fight the thought, tried to tell himself that he didn't actually kill Stuart, but his role in Stuart's death was undeniable. He had wanted to control the

THE HEATSTROKE LINE

situation, wanted to direct events to serve his goals, but he had failed to anticipate the tremendous forces that would rip his plans apart. Why couldn't he have been more careful, why had he been so sure of himself when only modesty and restraint were called for? Dan found himself pacing back and forth around the control room, the only large space in the cell block. In his frustration, he started kicking the console in the center, but there was no point—it was already ruined.

CHAPTER 12

Somewhat to his surprise, Dan found that his life quickly settled into a tolerable pattern. The prison guard, who was so taciturn that he could be ignored, would drive him to the lab five days a week. Much of his time there consisted of a task he found at least moderately enjoyable, which was to teach the other scientists how to perform genetic modification research, but he also was able to do a considerable amount of his own research on the subject, which he enjoyed even more. Lyons continued to treat him as a prisoner and maintain a harsh demeanor, but he seemed at least partially mollified by Dan's evident knowledge of his subject matter and his steady work habits.

Dan's first evenings and weekend in the prison had been burdensome, particularly when he allowed himself to think about his family and the stress that they were sure to be undergoing in his absence. But the situation improved once it occurred to him to ask for a reader pad that enabled him to download material from the laboratory intranet. This gave him access to the papers on genetic modification that he needed for his research at the lab, and also to a number of the nineteenth century novels he had always wanted to read, and which the lab communications officer downloaded at his request. But the prison was hardly a pleasant place to live. The lack of windows was depressing, there was no food at night unless he saved something from his dinner tray, and his back hurt from sleeping on a cloth mattress that seemed to fight against the contours of his body. He found himself looking forward to being moved into a private home, a promise that was renewed by Nathaniel Wolfson when he stopped by the lab one morning to check up on Dan.

After a few weeks, Dan realized where he was going to be placed. Matthew Clark and Paul Steiner were a couple and lived somewhere near the lab. Both had made a specific effort to befriend him, and it would obviously be safe to put a prisoner in

THE HEATSTROKE LINE

their care. Matthew was about Dan's size, but he spent his days hauling heavy equipment around and was enormously lithe and strong, as Dan had discovered when he tried to raise his hand against Lyons. Paul wasn't in such good shape, but he was a giant, six-six or six-seven and close to three hundred pounds. The thought of overpowering the people he was placed with, as Dan had fantasized in Wolfson's office, was laughable in connection with these two men. Besides, he liked them both, despite their role in his continued detention, and couldn't really imagine hurting either one of them, even if he had the opportunity.

An unexpected source of stress for Dan was his newly developed terror of the biter bugs. One or two would occasionally escape from their cages and fly at someone. The secretaries and the cooks were terrified of them, but the scientists all wore stun guns in holsters at their waists and were proud of their ability to zap a bug before it could dig even a single leg into their skin. Dan had felt the same way after his training in Granowski's department for his Central Texas research, but since his horrific experience in Mississippi-Meridian, he cringed with fear whenever one of the bugs got free, or even when he came near the cages. Lyons somehow learned of this, either because he was perceptive or because he was informed by Dan's co-workers. He confronted Dan with it at one of the times when he called Dan into his office to check on his performance.

"Well, I had a bad experience with the bugs," Dan answered, trying to be non-committal.

"Yes. Bad experiences are what the biter bugs are all about. That's why your work is so important."

"I'm trying my best."

"Not if you're afraid. If you allow yourself to be afraid, you'll be defeated. Victory is what we want, Dan, victory."

"Well, okay, but I don't think wanting to defeat the biter bugs is inconsistent with being fearful of them."

"Do you know what America's first military act was after we declared our independence?"

"What? You mean back in 1776? No, I don't. The Battle of Bunker Hill, maybe."

"No! We invaded Canada. We nearly conquered those bastards too. And we would have, except we were afraid. Our troops reached Montreal, but they turned back because they were afraid."

This man was almost certainly insane, Dan reflected.

When Dan returned to the prison after work one evening in mid-December, exactly six weeks after he had started working in the lab, one of the guards gave him a suitcase and told him to pack his possessions because he was being moved to a private home. Since Dan's only possessions were the clothes he had been issued, some toiletries, and his reader pad, he completed the task in a few minutes and was waiting in the prison carport when Nathaniel Wolfson drove up in a large black car. His heavy-lidded eyes regarded Dan with a look of cautious appraisal.

"I want to compliment you Dr. Danten," he said, as they drove off. "Everyone at the lab tells me that you've been working conscientiously and loyally. That's all we've ever asked of you, so we're highly satisfied with your performance."

Dan was silent.

"And you've only received one demerit from Dr. Lyons, which doesn't affect your eligibility to be transferred to a private home."

"Actually, I'd like that demerit reversed. All I did was make a constructive suggestion."

"I can look into it. Dr. Lyons is a very high ranking public official, so I'd need his permission to make a change."

"Well, that's not fair. I don't think Lyons is the kind of person who's likely to admit he made a mistake."

"I'm sorry, but those are our rules. I think we're being fair. We promised you that if you tried your best we'd transfer you from the prison to a private home in six weeks, and now we're doing it, right on schedule."

"If you're so pleased with me, why won't you let me call my family?"

"Unfortunately, that's not allowed for now. We can reconsider it after your first year of probation."

"Is that a promise?" Dan asked. It was something that he hadn't heard before.

"No, it's not a promise, it's a possibility. If you continue to do a good job, if you continue to keep trying your best, we can discuss it further. Look, here we are."

Dan had been focusing entirely on his conversation with Wolfson, but now he saw that they were on a curving residential street, mostly lined with impressively large houses, although there was an occasional empty lot or ruined structure, and a number of the houses seemed in bad repair. They had stopped in front of a two story brick home, with a row of five square white columns in front that extended the entire height of the building and were set into an overhanging roof. For some reason, it wasn't the sort of place he would have expected Matthew and Paul to live in. After parking in front of a driveway that sloped down into the carport, they got out. Dan took his suitcase and followed Wolfson along a concrete path and up some steps to the rather grand front door. Wolfson pushed the buzzer and, to Dan's surprise, the door was opened by a middle-aged man and woman. The man was slightly shorter than Dan and a bit portly, with dark eyes, greying hair and a cheerful smile. The woman was shorter than her husband and rather plump, with blond hair that looked dyed and a rosy complexion. Wolfson nodded familiarly to both of them, and after they returned his greeting, went back down the steps.

"Hello, Dr. Danten," the man said. "I'm Hiram Forrest, and this is my wife Rebecca. I understand you've been assigned to stay with us. Please come in." He led Dan into an entrance hall, with a wide flight of stairs at the rear, and then through an archway into an enormous room filled with old-fashioned upholstered furniture of various designs—a huge ell-shaped sofa with a floral pattern, a simpler, blue striped sofa, three overstuffed armchairs, lamps with ceramic bases and cloth shades on end tables, a crystal chandelier hanging from the ceiling, a large woven rug covering the floor—the place looked like a museum, particularly since none of the furniture matched. It was also positively chilly, and the deep, steady hum of the air conditioner accompanied them as they entered. To Dan's further surprise, there were two young girls in the living room, one about eleven or twelve, the other in her late teens.

"These are our daughters, Joanna and Deborah," said Hiram. Obviously, Dan reflected, no one thought he was particularly dangerous if they would place him in a family of this sort. In fact, Dan wasn't feeling particularly dangerous at this moment.

Joanna, the younger girl, came up to him immediately and shook his hand. She was attractive—wavy brown hair, large blue eyes, a broad smile and her mother's pink complexion, much prettier than her rather bland looking older sister. "Mom, can I show Dr. Danten to his room?"

"Oh, well, sure" said Rebecca, glancing over to her husband. "Sure, go ahead. We'll be eating at 6:30 tonight."

"Yes," Hiram said to Dan. "We eat right on time, so please be prompt."

Suitcase in hand, Dan followed Joanna, who went bounding up the stairs onto the second floor. The stair risers seemed unusually high, and Dan stumbled twice as he went up. At the top, there was a large landing, with doors leading to several bedrooms and a short hallway to their left. The house was even larger than he thought; Dan couldn't recall seeing a private home this size in all of Mountain America. Joanna led him down the hallway to the left and into a bedroom, much smaller than the living room but considerably bigger than his and Garenika's bedroom back at home. It was also filled with old-fashioned, mismatched furniture, including a commodious armchair, a ceramic lamp beside it on a table, a woven rug, and brocade curtains on the windows. The bed, which was in the middle of the room, had a wooden headboard and a mattress covered with a woolen blanket. Dan sat down on the mattress, which was considerably thicker than the ones in the prison. It sank under his weight, but not nearly as much as he had expected.

"Are you really a famous scientist from Mountain America?" Joanna asked.

"Well, I'm certainly a scientist, and I'm certainly from Mountain America. I'm not sure whether I'd describe myself as famous."

"Do you have children?"

"Yes, three. My son is sixteen, my daughter is fourteen, and my other son is ten." Dan felt himself getting angry as he said this, but there was no point expressing his resentment at being separated from his family to this little girl. "How old are you Joanna?"

"I'm twelve."

"Where do you go to school?"

"I go to Alexander Graham Bell and I'm getting A's and I'm going to graduate next year."

"So, do you go to high school after that?"

"No, school ends after next year. After that, Mom teaches me."

"You mean it ends for everyone?"

"Some of the boys go to technical school. The smart ones. I'm smarter than most of the boys."

Rebecca shouted up from downstairs. "Joanna, show Dr. Danten where the bathroom is and then let him unpack and wash up. He has to be ready for dinner soon."

Dinner was clearly an important event in the Forrest household, Dan realized. Pleased with his room, the largest private room he had ever slept in, and infinitely preferable to the prison, he made sure to go downstairs at the prescribed time, stumbling once more on his way. As he expected by now, there was a separate dining room, although its size—it was almost as large as the living room—sustained his sense of surprise. It had a heavy wooden table in the center, surrounded by mismatched wooden chairs, with another crystal chandelier above it. Hiram was already seated at the head of the table and motioned for Dan to sit beside him. Rebecca came through a door at the far end of the room, revealing an old-fashioned, hand operated kitchen with a separate stove, oven, refrigerator, sink and a few other fixtures that Dan didn't recognize. She sat down at the opposite end of the table, and then Joanna and Deborah came in carrying plates of food. Dan wondered if this was a ritual of some kind, but he didn't see a servo-robot, or any other feature of a modern kitchen, so apparently they had no choice but to carry the food to the table by hand.

"Let us pray," Hiram declared, as the two girls sat down. Dan wondered, with a sinking feeling, whether he had been placed in a family of Revivalists, although he hadn't seen any crosses in the house. "Our Father, whose art is heaven," Hiram declaimed in a dull monotone, "hallowed be Thy Name till Kingdom come, Thy will be done to earth, as it is in heaven. Give us our daily bread today. Forgive our trespasses, as we give trespasses to others, and lead us not into purgation, but deliver us from evil. For Thine is the unity, the power, and the glory, for ever and ever. Amen." He looked up when he was done and said, in a much more lively voice: "Rebecca, tell us what's for dinner."

Rebecca smiled at everyone. "We have steak, mashed potatoes with gravy, and broccoli," she announced. "And for dessert, we have an American apple and cherry pie."

"Rebecca is a wonderful cook," Hiram said, with genuine admiration. "No one cooks real American food better than Rebecca."

"Mom's the best cook in the neighborhood," Joanna added.

They started to eat. After such a grand introduction, Dan thought the steak might actually be made of beef, but it was soy protein, the potatoes were the grainy, tasteless kind that grew below the Heatstroke Line, and it was all almost intolerably over-salted. He was quick to compliment Rebecca on her cooking.

"Dr. Danten, since you'll be staying here for a while, I was wondering if we can call you by your first name. You can call me Hiram and my wife Rebecca."

"Well of course, call me Dan."

"Very good, that will make things easier." Dan noticed that Hiram, although he was certainly being gracious, was not treating him as a voluntary guest but as a prisoner.

"Unfortunately, you missed Thanksgiving, which is obviously one of our most important American holidays," Hiram continued, "but you'll be here for December 25, which is Battle of the Bulge Day. There'll be a big parade on Unity Avenue. It's a wonderful celebration. Attendance is mandatory, by the way—not just for you, but for everyone."

Well, Dan thought, these people are certainly not Revivalists if that's what they celebrate on December 25. "Can you remind me about the Battle of the Bulge," he said. "I know it took place during World War II, but I can't recall very much about it."

"It was a great American victory," Hiram intoned. "After our troops landed in Normandy, they swept across France and were about to cross into Germany when the Germans and Russians counterattacked. It was a desperation move—we were obviously going to win the war—but they threw everything they had into it. Hundreds of thousands of men charged through our lines until they reached the French city of Bastogne on December 25. All we had there was a small garrison. It was surrounded, and completely outnumbered, but when they demanded that the man in charge surrender—his name was General McAuliffe—he sent them back a one word message. It said "Nuts." Isn't that great —"Nuts." What a hero! They launched an attack, but our troops fought back—they wouldn't give up. Then General Patton came up with his army and smashed their attack and drove them back into Germany. After that, they were finished. It was a great victory for America."

"Thanks," said Dan. "That's very helpful. I assume you meant the Germans and the Italians. You said the Germans and the Russians."

"No, I meant the Germans and the Russians. We were fighting the German Nazis and the Russian Communists. That's what made it such a wonderful victory."

"The Russians were on our side during World War II."

"No they weren't," said Hiram, in a soft but insistent voice.

"Well, there's no need to argue about it. We can just look it up on the net."

"The net is full of anti-American lies," Hiram responded, still softly, but obviously irritated.

"The Canadians put them there," Rebecca added.

Dinner ended with an awkward silence. As they left the dining room, Hiram told Dan to be ready to leave at seven thirty the next morning.

Lying in bed that night, the blanket pulled up to his chin to combat the chilly air, Dan wondered whether he had made a serious mistake by correcting Hiram in front of his family. He had assumed it was just a slip of the tongue, but after Hiram repeated it, he should have let it go. The inaccuracy bothered him, he realized, but it was a reaction that kept getting him in trouble here. He really didn't want to be sent back to the prison. The mattress wasn't as comfortable as sleeping on an aero-bed, but it was much better than the thin prison mattresses, and the room was large and airy, with windows on two sides.

Were these people rich or poor, Dan wondered. The house was enormous—each floor was much larger than his own home—and the furnishings were opulent, but they looked like they had been collected from different places. The house itself was notably old-fashioned, made of brick, not cryoplastic, with glass, not claropastic windows. That might be a sign of wealth, but there also seemed to be few modern conveniences. Nearly everything had to be done by hand.

There were coffee and rolls waiting for Dan on the kitchen table when he came downstairs. Rebecca was friendly and Joanna, who was getting ready for school, was as ebullient as she had been yesterday. Hiram appeared promptly at seven-thirty, grabbed a cup of coffee and led Dan down a flight of stairs from the kitchen to the carport. Despite the grandeur of his house, Hiram's car was a good deal smaller than Dan's, tapering to little more than a single seat in back. Hiram explained that he would be driving Dan to the lab each morning since it was on his way to work.

"What do you do?" Dan asked him, as they drove off, with Hiram operating the controls by hand.

"I'm in charge of food inspection for Birmingham-Victoria. I have a staff of twelve field inspectors, and another eleven or twelve people working in the office."

"Well, my wife's a food inspector too," said Dan, delighted to find this connection between them since Hiram, as he had expected, was acting rather distant this morning. "In fact, that's how I met her. She was taking a course on food contaminants—which she needed for her degree—and I was in the same course so I could learn to tell the difference between chemical and insect contamination."

"I'm sure we have someone who does that sort of work in our government, Dan, but I do something much more important. I deal with the cultural meaning of food, not with its physical characteristics."

"I'm sorry, I don't follow."

"I enforce regulations here to make sure that people cook American food. We inspect people's homes on a regular basis and we fine anyone who breaks the law."

"Seriously?" Dan asked, despite himself.

"Nothing is more serious, Dan. If we don't cook American food, we'll lose our culture. And how will we unify America again if we lose the culture that we share? Tell me that."

Dan decided not to answer.

CHAPTER 13

On December 25, the Forrests all got into Hiram's car and drove to the Battle of the Bulge parade. Because the car was so small, Joanna sat on Rebecca's lap and Deborah scrunched up, nearly standing, on the passenger side. While Dan had never been to a parade—there were no more parades in Mountain America—he had seen footage of them, and his image was of a procession down the main street of a city, with tall buildings on each side. But he had learned by now that downtown Birmingham had been abandoned—a wasteland of collapsed buildings and aggressive weeds that was inhabited only by some scavengers. Most of the people lived on the high ground to the south, and ventured into the remnants of the city's other sections only in vehicles or armed groups.

In fact, they drove only a short distance. Unity Avenue turned out to be another wide street, six lanes plus a median divider in this case, lined with the typical one-story buildings. Dan realized that it was one of the streets he and Hiram crossed on their way to the lab. Today, metal stanchions had been placed along its length, sometimes in receptacles that were permanently set into the ground, and a net of white mesh had been draped overhead and to the sides to prevent biter bug attacks, as well as providing at least partial protection against the ubiquitous mosquitos. Hiram parked in one of the empty lots near the Avenue, and the family, with Dan following, joined the crowd that was gathering along the parade route.

There had been some rain that morning, but by mid-day, when the parade began, the sky had cleared, which Hiram said was a good sign. It was hot, as always, but tolerable—no hotter than spring or fall in Mountain America. Recorded music was blaring out of speakers that had been hung up on the stanchions. Despite what Hiram said about attendance being mandatory, the crowd was somewhat sparse. Dan had learned that there were about 80,000 people in the city of Birmingham and somewhat more in the extensive countryside that it controlled, making it the third most populous of the Confederacies, behind only Atlanta and Carolina Piedmont. But the crowd lining each side of the mile-long route was five or six deep at most, which, Dan calculated, added up to about 20,000 people. All but the small children were wearing a stun gun at their waists in case some of the bugs got through the net.

As Hiram, Rebecca and Joanna greeted people to the right and left of them, Dan began to wonder whether they knew everyone in Birmingham, but he soon realized that the crowd had been grouped, or had grouped itself, by neighborhoods. The main topic of conversation seemed to be declarations by those present that they would never miss the Battle of the Bulge parade, or condemnations of their absent neighbors for having in fact missed it.

"Where's Jonathan?" Hiram asked.

"He told me he was sick," someone answered. "I don't believe him for a second. He didn't come last year either."

"What about Caleb and Zipporah?" asked John, a heavyset old man who Dan recognized as the owner of the house across the street, a dilapidated wood frame structure even larger than Hiram and Rebecca's.

"Oh, they're alright," said Rebecca. "They have a newborn baby."

"Well, they could have brought it."

"Yes, but you know they've been trying to have a baby for years. Zipporah's had three miscarriages, the poor thing. They're guarding the new baby like there's no tomorrow."

The recorded music stopped and an excited buzz went through the crowd. From somewhere up the street, nine armored rocket launchers appeared, in three rows of three, and came rumbling toward them. Soldiers in uniform were sitting at the control panels behind the launch tubes. All the people lining the street began to cheer. Behind the rocket launchers came a troop of soldiers, marching in step and swinging their arms back and forth with exaggerated motions. By the time the soldiers reached the place where Dan was standing, he could see another troop behind them, some carrying American flags, some carrying flags with Birmingham-Victoria's insignia, the sword with a red and white striped blade. As they approached, he realized that they were old men, veterans apparently. While the young soldiers seemed jaunty and cheerful, the older ones had grimly intent faces. Many of them were sweating, and one staggered as he passed by Dan and had to be supported by the other veterans.

The rocket launchers stopped about one hundred yards past Dan where the Avenue, which was otherwise straight, turned in a wide curve to the right. They lined up facing a metal statue of a man that rose above the level of the buildings, and was placed at the turning point so it was visible from both sections of the road. As the soldiers, young and old, reached the statue, they grouped themselves around the rocket launchers and stood at attention.

"What's the statue?" Dan asked Hiram.

"President Chiron," Hiram answered, reverentially. "Did you know that he was an Alabaman?"

Richard Chiron was the President who had ordered the nuclear bombing of Toronto and Montreal. Dan wanted to say that he thought President Chiron was Russian, but he restrained himself. Instead, he asked Hiram whether Chiron was from Birmingham.

"No, he was actually from Montgomery. That's part of our bond with them, you see. If the Unity Party has its way, we'll make peace with them and unify Alabama. That will let the Canadians know we mean business. A unified Alabama, just think. The first step to a unified United States."

Once all the soldiers had gathered around the statue, the speakers mounted on the buildings started playing the Star-Spangled Banner. Everyone in the crowd sang along. When they got to "the rockets' red glare, the bombs bursting in air," there was a loud explosion and fireworks shot up from behind the statue. The reference in the song, Dan reflected, was to British rockets and bombs attacking an American fort, but he guessed it meant something else to the parade organizers and the audience.

After the song ended, the rocket launchers and the soldiers regrouped in marching order and moved on. Another cheer arose as three Uncle Sams on stilts appeared. Since they were over twenty-five feet high, they were obviously using auto-stilts, one of the first fully modern devices that Dan had seen since he had been in Birmingham. They were tossing red balls into the crowd, which popped open to produce a shower of iridescent blue and white stars, a bit of technology that Dan had never seen before.

There was a commotion amid the bystanders to Dan's left. He turned to see a group of Revivalists, in their grey outfits, moving through the crowd carrying signs that said "December 25th belongs to Jesus, not to Birmingham" and "The Lord's Day, not the Bulge's." As they passed, Dan was pushed away from Hiram and Rebecca by their motion. It occurred to him that he was in the presence of people who didn't know who he was for the first time since he had been captured. If he could get out of Hiram's sight, he might ask to borrow someone's wrist link and call his family. The thought made his heart start pounding and he let himself get pushed along by the Revivalists, then kept moving in the same direction on his own until he was around the curve in the Avenue. He looked around for a likely person to ask. A woman would be wrong—she might say no because she would think that he was hitting on her—and he didn't want to ask a child. A man his own age, maybe, someone who might see him as an equal and help him out, or an older man who might take an avuncular interest in him. There, the quiet white haired man standing by himself, watching the Uncle Sams, who had reached them by this time, with a detached demeanor. Dan slowly drifted toward the man. The Uncle Sams were followed by a group of young kids on tricycles wearing blue hats and various combinations of red, white and blue clothing.

"Pretty cute, aren't they," Dan said to the man, trying to sound as casual as possible.

"Pretty stupid, if you ask me," the man replied.

"Not a big fan of parades?"

"Huh, what was that?"

"I said—it sounds like you're not a big fan of parades." Dan sensed that his question sounded aggressive, rather than casual, when it was repeated in a louder voice.

"You could say that. Don't know why we have so many damn parades."

"How come you're here then?"

"What'd you say?"

"If you don't like parades, how come you're here, I said."

"My goddamn son-in-law makes me come. Fucking bureaucrat. Too goddamn many bureaucrats these days."

At last, Dan thought, a cynic. "Do you live with your daughter and your son-in-law?"

"Sure do. Ever since the goddamn tornado."

"Yeah, that's tough. Our family's house got hit by a tornado a while ago, but we were lucky."

"We're getting too damn many tornados these days."

THE HEATSTROKE LINE

"We sure are," Dan quickly agreed. In fact, he knew that there were tornadoes in the Confederacies, but also that they were less severe than the ones in Mountain America. He waited a moment, then looked at his wrist and pantomimed surprise. "Oh, you know, I got separated from my family and I seem to have left my wrist link at home. Can I borrow yours for a minute?"

"What, what was that?"

"I said, I got separated from my family and I want to contact them and I realize I left my wrist link at home, and I was wondering whether I could borrow yours for a second."

The crowd was cheering again. The man cupped his hand to his ear and said "What?"

"I wanted to borrow your wristlink for a second."

"What happened to yours?"

"I left it at home."

"Why did you do that?"

"Guess I just forgot it."

"Everyone's too goddamn absent-minded these days," the man said, without giving any indication that he was going to hand over his wristlink. Dan wanted to knock him down, stomp on his head, and tear the link off his arm, but all he could do is move further down the street.

There was another cheer from the crowd and people started craning their necks to get a better view. The tricycles had passed, as had a motorized float festooned with American and Birmingham flags, and a formation of teenage cheerleaders in short blue skirts and skimpy red halter tops came into view. The girls were doing high kicks that revealed red panties, alternating with running leaps and pom-pom tosses. They were rather seriously out of step but no one in the crowd seemed to mind. By now, they were also sweating rather heavily, staining their tops in varied patterns. Dan wasn't sure whether this contributed to or detracted from the effect.

Figuring that none of the men would want to be distracted while the girls were marching, Dan waited until they had passed and been replaced by a troop of colonial soldiers, carrying plastic muskets. His heart pounding once again, he went up to a man about his own age and size, also standing alone. A fair amount of time had passed since he had separated himself from the Forrests, and Dan didn't want to get involved in another extended conversation.

"Say, excuse me. I left my wristlink at home and I need to make a call. Would you mind if I borrowed yours for a second?"

The man turned and glared at him. He was taller and heavier than Dan had thought at first.

"What are you, some kind of a spy?"

"No, I'm just absent-minded. I left it at home."

"How do I know you're not a spy?"

Dan realized he wasn't going to get anywhere with this man. "Spies aren't absent-minded," he responded, and as the man's look turned to puzzlement, Dan moved away to try someone else.

It had begun to rain again, just lightly for the present, but the sky beyond the white mesh seemed ominous. Dan felt an unpleasant chill as he saw black dots scattered across the mesh, a few moving but most just waiting. There was a sudden commotion near him, and Dan's first thought was that some of the bugs had broken through the mesh, but when he turned he saw a group of men and women shouting at each other.

"You're cowards!" a disheveled middle-aged woman was yelling

"Hot-heads. Goddamn Indies!" several people shouted in response.

Someone who looked like the woman's husband came up beside her. "We're going to win the next election. Then you cowards will have to fight."

"The hell you'll win!" "Over my dead body!" came the shouts from the other side.

More people had come up alongside the woman and her husband now. They were carrying signs; one said "Death to Montgomery," another "Independence is American." "You Unies aren't Americans," one of them yelled. "You're cowards, and Americans aren't cowards."

All at once, people started fighting. Some were just pushing and shoving, but others were swinging their fists. An older man staggered backwards, his hand over his face, blood dripping through his fingers. People started moving toward the fight, some trying to stop it, others joining it. The signs swayed back and forth above the people's heads for a while before disappearing into the crowd. As Dan watched, he suddenly saw that a little girl, maybe eight or nine years old, had gotten caught up in the widening melee. She had fallen to the ground and was lying prone, with her hands covering her head, and Dan could see that she was sobbing. Dropping down to make himself as low and as

THE HEATSTROKE LINE

compact as possible, he waded in between the fighters' legs until he reached the girl. Someone kicked him hard, but fortunately in the thigh. He grabbed the girl, who was unexpectedly light and clung to him instinctively. Rising a bit, he lunged for the edge of the fight, this time getting kicked in his side and punched on the shoulder before getting clear. He walked a few yards away from the melee and looked around for a place where he could put the girl down, when a young, red-haired woman with tears streaming down her face ran up to him and took the girl out of his arms.

"Thank you, thank you," she said between sobs. She looked down at the girl. "Are you hurt Maria? Did they hurt you?" After holding her for a moment, her mother set her down to look at her. Her leg was scraped and she had a small cut above her eye. "My leg hurts" she said, rubbing it with her hand. "I'm alright, I guess."

The woman turned back to Dan. "Thank you so much," she said again. "That was so kind of you." Some police officers appeared and as they started zapping people with large, specialized stun guns, the fight began to subside. Dan turned back to the woman and had a sudden inspiration. He looked at his wrist and pantomimed surprise again.

"You're welcome. Glad you're daughter is all right. Say listen, I seem to have lost my wristlink when I went to rescue her, and I need to find my family again. Can I borrow yours?"

"Sure," the woman said immediately, detaching the device and holding it in her hand. "Here let me activate it for you."

Dan's heart was pounding as he took the wristlink from her, and he felt his fingers trembling. He was about to input the first numbers when someone grabbed him by the shoulder. He looked up. It was Hiram, with another man.

"You know you're not allowed to do that, Dr. Danten," Hiram said. He took the wristlink and handed it back to the woman. Dan was too angry and frustrated to say a word.

"This man is a prisoner," Hiram explained to the woman. "He's not allowed to communicate with anyone."

The woman stared at Dan with a look that began in astonishment and slowly hardened into anger. She picked up Maria, turned around and walked away.

"If I can't trust you, Dr. Danten," Hiram said, in his soft but insistent voice, "I'll have to send you back to prison. I had to leave my family and stop watching the parade because you snuck away."

103

"I don't see why I can't talk to my own family."

"Those are Nathaniel's instructions. You know that, and you know you're supposed to follow the rules if you want to stay in my house. I should report this to Nathaniel and to Dr. Lyons."

The two men led Dan back toward the place where Hiram's family was standing. Apparently, Hiram was not going to report the incident, and Dan would get off without another demerit from Lyons. He tried not to feel grateful to Hiram for this—what right had these people to keep him captive—but he couldn't help himself. After all, right or wrong, they had power over him, and Dan was relieved that he wasn't going to have his sentence extended or be sent back to the prison.

The rain was falling harder now without lowering the temperature. When he reached the Forrests again, Rebecca and Johanna greeted him in a friendly manner which suggested that Hiram hadn't told them he was missing.

"Look," Rebecca said to him, "here's the finale."

A large motorized float, built to look like a medieval fort and covered with wreaths and flowers, was coming down the street. It was surrounded by soldiers in World War II uniforms, waving plastic rifles. Two flags that said "Bastogne" were mounted on top and the word "Nuts" appeared on all four sides in large, glowing letters. Several more soldiers, one with a large hat labeled "General McAuliffe," were riding in the fort and throwing bags of nuts out to the people in the crowd. It was raining harder now. The wreaths and flowers on the sides of the float were getting bedraggled and starting to fall off into the street, but the letters that spelled out "Nuts" continued to glow brightly.

CHAPTER 14

At the lab the next day—there was no winter work break, as there was in Mountain America—Paul Steiner asked Dan whether he had been to the parade.

"Oh yes, I wouldn't want to miss the parade."

Paul smiled. "Didn't see you. Were you with the Forrests?"

"Yes. Why, were you looking for me?"

"No, just wondering. Most of us from the lab go as a group. Easiest to go together, since Dr. Lyons insists that we attend."

Dan realized that Hiram would need to report his attendance to Lyons. By not reporting his attempt to call his family at the same time, Hiram would be affirmatively protecting him. Again, he tried not to feel grateful, this time with even less success.

"Any fights where you were?" Paul continued.

"Well, as a matter of fact, there was a big one. You mean that wasn't the only one?"

"There were two near us, so I guess that's at least three."

"I think the one I saw was between the Unity Party and the Independence Party."

"That's what they all are. Happens every year. Don't see why people can't get along, particularly when they're at a celebration."

Paul was clearly making an effort to be friendly and continued chatting with Dan for few more minutes before asking him for guidance regarding the genetic modification program. Dan was always happy to provide whatever help he could, but he noticed now, as he had before, that when he started asking follow-up questions about the details of the research, Paul became uncomfortable. At first, he had thought that Paul was simply self-conscious about his lack of formal scientific training, but as he got to know the man better, he realized that Paul was about as modest and unassuming as an intelligent person could be. Something else was bothering him, but Dan couldn't figure out what it was.

That night, as he was lying in bed under his covers, in an effort to stay warm, Dan thought back to the conversation and tried to figure out once more what was making Paul uncomfortable. Maybe, Dan thought with a small surge of satisfaction, Paul didn't like the fact that Dan was being compelled to work at the lab as a prisoner. Well, he didn't like it either, even though he was being treated with a fair amount of respect and seemed to have an important role to play in the lab's research project. And he didn't like being kidnapped on a trumped up charge in the first place.

Suddenly, with a sickening sense of realization, it occurred to Dan that he had been set up by Temarden Goldberg, maybe with the help of David Hardaway. How did the people in Birmingham know that he would be in the Confederacies so that they could arrange the kidnapping? For that matter, how did they know he was interested in controlling biter bugs? He hadn't worked on that before—all his published papers dealt with agricultural pests or evolutionary theory. They could only have known these things if Goldberg had told them. The son of a bitch had organized the whole thing—the supposed tip from the informant in Jacksonia about the biter bug attack, the invitation for him to be the only entomologist who was a member of the mission, the secrecy that had placed them outside the protection of normal diplomatic channels, and maybe even the biter bug torture to terrify him and get Stuart out of the way.

Dan leaped to his feet in fury and began pacing around his room. Not only had Goldberg ruined his life, but he made a fool of him, playing on his sudden enthusiasm to solve the biter bug problem and establish political connections with the Confederacies. That was why he wouldn't take Dan's call when Dan had tried to contact him from Wolfson's office, and that was why Wolfson could be so sure that Dan wouldn't be able to get anyone in Mountain America to help him. Dan had been betrayed and outsmarted by people who were tougher, more cunning, and more cynical than he was, and there was nothing he could do about it but stomp around some fanatic's ornate extra bedroom in the middle of a life-threatening climate fifteen hundred miles from his home. And there was nothing he could do about the fact that they had murdered Stuart.

About an hour later, when Dan's anger had begun to subside, it occurred to him that none of it made any sense. Why would they go to all the trouble to kidnap him just to get him to do something that he was completely willing to do on his own? He had volunteered to research biter bug control and he had specifically indicated that he was interested in sharing his results with the Confederacies. True, he didn't think the genetic modification approach was very promising, but he certainly had no moral objection to pursuing it, if that was what the people who were suffering from the bugs wanted to do. Goldberg knew that; in fact, he knew that the only research opportunities Dan had ever turned down involved bio-chemical toxins. And there was no work on toxins being done at the Birmingham lab—Dan was absolutely sure of that. Besides, if Mountain America was cooperating with Birmingham and some of the other Confederacies, why would they kill Stuart? The American Patriot Party wanted that cooperation, and Stuart, probably the most intelligent and knowledgeable member of that Party, could only have been an asset to them. No, none of it made sense. Dan was somewhat relieved to know that he hadn't been outsmarted or betrayed by Goldberg, and even more relieved that he hadn't been outsmarted by Hardaway, but he was just as bewildered about the whole situation as he had been before, which was equally disturbing.

The rain, which had been falling off and on since Dan arrived below the Heatstroke Line, intensified during the next week, pounding relentlessly on the roof and against the glass windows of the Forrests' home. Water ran in torrents down the street gutters, often spreading out across the roads and backing up, when the drains got clogged, to form debris-filled pools. It cascaded off the roofs of the houses and transformed their lawns, even when they were on a slope, into muddy quagmires. It poured into the Forrests' basement, which had two powerful pumps to protect it against this apparently annual occurrence. Despite the pumps, Hiram had to spend his evenings in the basement drying the walls with large electric fans to combat the growth of mold, and to make sure that the family's back-up air conditioner remained operational. The ceremonial dinners that he seemed to regard as so important were suspended, and Dan ate Rebecca's salty but otherwise tasteless food in his room while he read entomology articles and nineteenth century novels.

Finally, the rain abated, the sky cleared and the family gathered once again for dinner. The grandly announced meal consisted of soy protein hamburgers, corn on the cob and string beans. After a few minutes of casual conversation Hiram announced, in a tone of satisfaction, that the government had decided to prosecute the people who started the fights at the Battle of the Bulge Day Parade.

"Paul Steiner told me there are fights every year," Dan said.

"There was a bigger one last year," Joanna said.

Hiram nodded. "Yes, but next year's an election year. Since we control the Presidency and the prosecutor's office, we figure that we can start bringing indictments now and have the Indies come to trial right when the campaigns are heating up."

"The Indies are the Independence party, I assume?"

"Yeah, and they call us Unies" said Joanna.

"Well, politics down here sound a little rougher than in Mountain America," Dan said. "Is your objection to the Independence Party that they want to go to war with Montgomery?"

"That's just one thing. There are lots of others. They don't understand the importance of unity, or of tradition for that matter. They think American culture is all about warfare. When they control the government, they change the name of Unity Avenue to Independence Avenue. They even want to change the name of our country to Independent Victoria. Can you imagine?"

"Why is that so bad? It's just a name."

"Just a name! Birmingham is a link with our past, a great American name that dates back to the founding of the United States. We can't let them take that away from us, can we?"

"Well, it was originally the name of a British city."

"The hell it was. Birmingham is a genuine American name."

"If the British have a city with that name, they got it from us," Rebecca added helpfully.

By now, Dan knew that this was the sort of issue that he shouldn't argue about with Hiram, but he stopped himself only by conscious effort. He couldn't resist saying something in response though.

"You know, in *Alice in Wonderland*, Alice goes into a wood where names are forgotten and a baby deer comes up and walks beside her. Once they leave the wood, the deer remembers what its name is and only then it runs away from her."

"*Alice in Wonderland* is a children's story, isn't it?" Hiram answered, to Dan's annoyance. "American culture is a very serious matter. We'll never be a great nation again if we forget our culture."

"I'd like to have a baby deer," Joanna said.

After dinner, Dan walked into the living room, which had two wide windows, one that ran along the side of the room, and another along the back wall. The back window looked out toward Birmingham's two power plants, the larger one in the near distance, and the smoke that poured continuously from them obscured the sky with a dreary haze. But through the side window, Dan could see the stars, those tiny indicators of vast spaces and unimaginable worlds.

"Are you looking at the stars?"

Dan turned around. Deborah, the Forrests' older daughter, had come into the room without Dan having heard her, and was now sitting on the blue striped sofa opposite him, her legs pulled up beneath her.

"Yes, I guess so."

"So was I. What do they mean to you?"

"Oh, nothing much," Dan said, a bit surprised by the question and not in the mood to answer it.

"Really—I doubt that's true. I guess you just don't want to tell me."

Dan looked at Deborah more closely. In the time that he'd spent in the Forrests' house, she had never said more than a few words to him, or to anyone else within his hearing. She was plain looking compared to her sister, but he noticed now that she had large brown eyes that seemed to focus on him with a calm but particular intensity.

"What makes you think that?" he said, in a purposefully casual manner.

"Because—well you seem to me to be a thoughtful person."

"Oh, I'm not so sure about that," said Dan, hearing himself answer her in the same tone that he had told Joanna that he wasn't sure he was a famous scientist.

"You think of yourself as a knowledgeable person, don't you? When Dad said that thing about Birmingham—I could see you wanted to argue with him because you knew about the name. It bothered you that you couldn't tell him. So you told that story about *Alice in Wonderland* instead. That was only—it wasn't really how you wanted to respond. But actually, it was a better answer— better for you—because it was more thoughtful. "

Dan simply didn't know what to say. Several things flitted through his mind: "You're pretty observant, aren't you?" "I didn't realize you were paying such close attention." "Do you think of yourself as a thoughtful person?" "Have you read *Alice in Wonderland*?" Instead, he just said "Well, I'm not sure what to say."

"Yes, I know."

She paused, and Dan was taken aback. Now he truly didn't know what say. "Maybe we can talk again," she said finally. She unfolded her legs, stood up and glided out of the room.

There was a minor crisis at the lab the next day. Dan had given Faith and Jethro some guidance about using the spectrometer—also stolen from MMTU—but they had apparently misunderstood and damaged the machine. Lyons was furious at them. He shouted insults in a voice that carried over the partitions and was audible throughout the lab. Dan sat at his desk, knowing that Lyons would come to see him next and trying to convince himself he wasn't frightened or, if he was, that it was because Lyons had the power to extend his sentence. But Lyons, when he did appear, was admonitory rather than enraged.

"You've got to be careful, Dan. We can't get new machines whenever we want, you know. We need to rely on American know-how and ingenuity. Remember that when you give people advice. Know-how and ingenuity. That's the path to victory."

The mood in the lab remained subdued and tense for the rest of the day and Dan, a bit to his surprise, found himself looking forward to dinner with the Forrests.

As usual, Deborah and Joanna served the meal after Hiram had announced it. Deborah was wearing a short-sleeved print dress—she always wore short-sleeved or sleeveless dresses, Dan now recalled, despite the house's chilliness—and moved with a willowy grace that lent a certain charm to her otherwise plain looks. She didn't say anything during dinner and, as Dan noticed for the first time, she ate very little. After dinner, he went into the living room again and a few minutes later she appeared. She down on the same blue striped sofa, and this time crossed her legs and clasped her knee in her hands.

"I'm assuming you read *Alice in Wonderland* for your own sake —not just to your kids," she said.

"Well, yes, that's right," Dan answered, startled once again. "How could you possibly know that?"

"From the expression on your face when Dad said it was a children's story."

Dan was about to comment on her observational abilities, but somehow he knew not to. There was a pause.

"Do you read a lot of novels?" Deborah asked at last.

"Yes, mainly nineteenth-century. It's a real source of pleasure for me."

"Me too. Have you read *Anna Karenina*?"

THE HEATSTROKE LINE

"Yes, I have."

"I just finished it."

"Did you like it?" Dan asked. A slight grimace, suggesting disappointment, flashed across Deborah's face, but then her look of calm attentiveness returned.

"I wonder whether Vronsky really loved Anna," she said, "and how much of his attraction to her was just his own need for adventure."

"That's a good thought. I might have said ego, rather than adventure though. The question that all the critics ask is why Anna kills herself at the end."

"I suppose that's her only way to escape—her only way out of the situation."

"Yes, that's certainly the general view."

"I assume you have a different one—which is why you asked the question."

Dan felt skewered. He realized that she was right, that rather than just talking to her, he was trying to control the conversation to produce a result, in this case to demonstrate his knowledge of literature. He did that frequently in conversations, and one reason why he felt so disconcerted down here below the Heatstroke Line is that it rarely worked. In any event, he had to follow through now.

"Well, my own thought is that she hadn't turned out to be the kind of person that she wanted to be, and she found that impossible to live with."

"Did you turn out to be the kind of person you wanted to be?"

"Well yes, I did," Dan answered quickly.

The same fleeting grimace moved across Deborah's face.

"Pretty much, I guess—except I never expected to wind up as a prisoner, of course. But that's not what you're really asking, is it? Let me think. You know, I always wanted to be a research scientist—I can't remember anything else, although I guess when I was really small I wanted to be a doctor. But the kind of scientist I wanted to be—right up until college really—was an astronomer. I thought it would be amazing to make astronomical discoveries. All the time I was growing up, I had a huge, deep 3-D poster of the Milky Way on the wall of my room."

"What happened?"

"I realized—when I got to college—that there were no academic positions in astronomy—maybe in Canada or Europe, but not in Mountain America. Astronomy is pure research and we don't have the resources to support anything like that. So I switched to entomology—agricultural entomology primarily—which is very practical. In fact, I support myself by getting government grants. And I still get to do some primary research—I study the process of evolution—using insects of course."

"So that's—the decisions, maybe the lost opportunities—what the stars mean to you, or part of it, anyway."

"Yes, Deborah, it is. I think—when you first asked me that question—I didn't want to give you such a complicated answer—or maybe such an honest answer."

"But it is complicated—you gave up astronomy—but you got the kind of position you wanted. And maybe the stars are still important to you—you don't have to give that up just because you can't study them the way you wanted to."

"Maybe that's true. I actually hadn't thought of that."

Dan had been looking away as he spoke—at the stars in fact—trying to focus his thoughts, but now he turned back to Deborah. She looked straight into his eyes, and he noticed that the expression on her pale face somehow conveyed a sense of both approval and solicitude. She was actually rather nice looking when she adopted that expression, Dan reflected.

CHAPTER 15

Dan was at the lab again. He had broken the gene analyzer and had to go into Dr. Lyons' office to report the accident. As he walked down the hall, he passed a door that he had never seen before. It led into a corridor with dirty, green walls covered with beads of water. At the far end was another door with glowing stars on it. He traversed the corridor as quickly as he could and, thinking that he would tell Deborah about it later that day, he opened the star-covered door. It led into his lab at the University of Mountain America. He hadn't realized that the two labs were so close to one another. Suddenly he felt guilty that he hadn't figured this out before, that he hadn't used the corridor to go back to Mountain America and see his family. He had to go see them right now, but he was afraid of what he might find there, and of how disappointed they would be with him that he hadn't gone back to see them sooner.

He was awake, lying in bed in his room at the Forrests' house. For a moment, he tried to recollect where that door in the Birmingham lab was located—then he woke up completely. It was certainly not a difficult dream to interpret, he reflected. He wanted to see his family, and even though there was no magic corridor or any other way that he could reach them, he was feeling genuinely if irrationally guilty about his inability to contact them and deeply worried about what was happening to them in his absence.

The Forrests had just sat down to dinner that night when a sort of siren started sounding. Hiram and Rebecca leapt to their feet, and Hiram shouted that everyone should go to their rooms and close their doors. "Marauders," Rebecca explained as she and the two girls scurried up the stairs. In the meantime, Hiram had gone into the front hall, unlocked a wall unit that Dan had assumed was some kind of safe, and took out a military style GX gun.

"What's going on?" Dan asked.

"They're from the open lands. They come through here every once in a while looking for stuff that they can steal and sell."

The open lands, Dan knew by now, were the areas that none of the Confederacy states controlled, like the tidal flats along the Gulf that he had been driven through when he was brought here, or the mountains to the northeast, between Birmingham-Victoria and Atlanta.

"Well, why don't you call the police?"

"We can handle it ourselves," said Hiram and disappeared into a closet. He emerged a few minutes later in full military gear—camouflage coveralls, a helmet with a night vision visor and an all-channel communicator. He activated the coveralls and virtually disappeared from view.

"Mind if I stay downstairs and watch?" Dan said, in an unnecessarily loud voice, to the shimmering transparency in front of him.

"Sure, why not," came the answer, a bit hesitantly. "Use the dining room window."

As the front door opened and closed, Dan went back into the dining room and up to the window that wrapped around the corner of the room. It looked onto the driveway that sloped down to the carport to the left and out to the street on the right. The street was dark and completely empty—no one ever walked outside in Birmingham and there was no car traffic after the residents came home from work. While Dan couldn't see Hiram, he could see Caleb, the next door neighbor, hiding behind the bushes in front of his house, as well as a few of the other people in the neighborhood who apparently couldn't afford camouflage outfits. Dan pulled up a dining room chair, sat down and waited. Nothing happened for a long time. He wondered why he was sitting there and was trying to decide whether he should simply go back to his room when there was a sudden set of flashes from the fronts of nearly all the houses on their street. A moment's pause, then another set of flashes, but as far as Dan could tell, there was no return fire of any kind. He heard the front door open about a minute later, and when he went into the hallway, Hiram was taking off his now-visible camouflage suit.

"All clear," he shouted up the stairs. "We got one of them." Deborah, Rebecca and Joanna came down almost immediately, all wearing stun guns around their waists, and went outside. Dan's fear of the biter bugs brought him to a halt at the front door, and as the others went past him, he asked Hiram for a stun gun.

THE HEATSTROKE LINE

Smiling, Hiram handed Dan his own gun, and then the two of them followed the others out onto the street. Rain was falling through the steamy nighttime air, although not too heavily. It seemed as if the entire neighborhood had come outside. Dan recognized John, the heavyset man who lived in the big decrepit house across the street, Caleb (but not his wife Zipporah, who was presumably inside with the baby), Mrs. Azzolini, the widow who lived a few houses away, as well as several others whose names he didn't know. There was a dead body lying in the middle of the roadway, a somewhat delicate-featured young man with four small holes in his chest and legs from the photon pellets of the GX guns. Dan was surprised, given the amount of firing, that the man hadn't been hit more times, but that was why the neighbors were using GX guns that wouldn't damage property. Blood was flowing from the man's wounds in small rivulets that fanned out and dissipated on the street's wet asphalt.

"Do think it's a marauder?" one of the neighbors asked.

"Must have been," another one replied.

There was a shout. A biter bug hit someone, but a moment later, two people stunned the thing, flipped it over with their stun gun barrels, and crushed it beneath their feet. After a momentary shudder, Dan looked around for Deborah. He was surprised that she had come outside with everybody else, and still more surprised that she showed no reaction to the bleeding body, at least as far as he could tell in the dark street illuminated only by light coming through the windows of the houses. Dan himself was sickened by the sight. He quickly went back inside, left the stun gun at the entrance and went up to his room.

He was hoping to talk to Deborah again the next day, but she seemed to have gone away somewhere, since she didn't appear at dinner and the door to her room, which Dan passed whenever he went up or down the stairs, remained closed. She was still away the next day when he came back from the lab, and all weekend as well. To pass the time, Dan read Dickens' *Little Dorrit*. He noticed as he read that he kept thinking about what he might say to Deborah about the book, and also that he kept envisioning her as Dorrit.

After four days, she appeared at dinner, wearing an attractive lime-green sleeveless dress. She smiled quickly at Dan as she served the food and sat down at the far end of the table. As usual, she was completely quiet while Hiram, Rebecca and Joanna chatted about the day's activities. Dan often made an effort to join in the conversation, but today he found that their voices seemed to fade into the background hum of the air conditioner. When the meal ended, he went into the living room and sat opposite the blue striped sofa, waiting for Deborah to finish clearing the dinner plates and join him. To his sudden astonishment, he realized that his heart was pounding heavily, and he felt it leap when he saw her come into the room. As soon as she sat down, however, Joanna came in, smiled cheerfully at Dan, and asked Deborah for help with her homework. Deborah got up at once and followed Joanna out of the room. Dan continued sitting in his chair for about fifteen minutes, staring out the window at the smoke from the power plant and then, feeling desolate, went up the stairs and into his bedroom.

He sat down on the bed and forced himself to think. Had he fallen in love with Deborah Forrest? She was eighteen, barely older than his son. But it was difficult to ignore or deny his reactions to her absence and her reappearance. He tried to explain them away: he had been through a series of terrible experiences, he missed his family, he was lonely. But he wasn't able to convince himself. There was something about Deborah, something that seemed to have reached deep inside him. He had no choice but to confront the situation.

Taking a deep breath, he pictured himself going into her bedroom on a pretext, kissing her, lifting off her lime-green dress and running his hands up and down her body. His mind rebelled immediately. Far from awakening any sense of desire, the idea of any sexual contact with her repulsed him. It seemed like a violation, rather than a consummation, of whatever relationship he had or wanted with her. He was greatly relieved, but as a further test, he tried to picture a similar scene with Janaly Francesca, realizing that he hadn't thought about her even once since he and Stuart were abducted. That was easy—he immediately saw himself pulling Janaly's yellow top over her head, cupping her round breasts in his hands while she wrapped her firm, shapely arms around him and then reached one hand down into his pants. He wasn't particularly excited by this imagined scene, but he certainly didn't experience any resistance to it.

That was still more reassuring, but he realized that he couldn't be certain it was accurate. His conscious mind might well be blocking him from admitting that he was in love with an eighteen-year-old girl. He should use Jiangtan, something he hadn't done for several years and that had seemed so useless on the night of

THE HEATSTROKE LINE

Stuart's death. He got down on the floor in Position Three, closed his eyes, performed the breathing procedure for the full five minutes, brought his Jiangtan image into mind, then switched it off.

He saw himself lying in bed next to Garenika. They had been trying to get pregnant with their first child. Typically, he had a stronger sex drive than she did, but she wanted to conceive by natural means and they had been making love every night for several weeks. Tonight, however, he had been to a party at the University and came home rather drunk, wanting to do nothing more than go to sleep. She had stroked his chest and thighs and nuzzled against his neck in the way that usually excited him, but he told her that he had drunk himself into a state of alcoholic anesthesia and promised to screw her twice tomorrow. Then he turned over to go to sleep, but something made him turn back toward her. She was lying on her side, gazing at him, and tears were rolling down her cheeks. His first reaction was to be annoyed —he really needed sleep—and then he thought to argue with her, telling her that he was obviously not rejecting her but just too drunk to get aroused. For some reason though he stopped and, after waiting for a moment, wrapped her in his arms and went inside her. He must have remained in that position for several hours, drifting in and out of consciousness, but somehow constantly aware of her body against his and their arms around each other.

As generally the case with Jiangtan, the whole scene presented itself to Dan at once and faded rapidly. He opened his eyes, surprised at what the exercise elicited, and enormously relieved that it had been so respectable. Whatever his feelings for Deborah were, and they were obviously strong, they did not seem to be sexual in nature.

He finally had the chance to talk to her again the next day. He felt at ease with her, and somehow grateful to her for not having aroused any inappropriate feelings in him. They talked mainly about literature, and continued the next day as well, but on the following two evenings the Forrests had dinner guests who occupied the living room after dinner. Dan was taken aback on the second evening to find that the guests were Nathaniel Wolfson and his wife, whose name was Miriam. It turned out that Rebecca and Miriam were sisters, which certainly helped explain why Dan had been placed in the Forrests' home. He felt distinctly uncomfortable sitting across a dinner table from his brutal-looking captor, but Wolfson seemed entirely at ease and the conversation remained completely casual.

When he was able to talk to Deborah again the next evening, she asked him if he ever went walking outside in Mountain America. After all, she said, it was cooler and there were no biter bugs. Dan thought back to his abbreviated walk outside the University the day he got the idea of doing biter bug research, and of sitting on the concrete block having doubts that he now wished he had taken more seriously.

"Very rarely," he answered. "There's really very few places to walk in Denver, and I'm usually too busy to go up to the mountains or anything like that."

"There's no place at all to walk here, but sometimes I do it anyway—just to have a sense of freedom."

"What about the biter bugs?"

"You're very fearful of them, aren't you?"

"Well," said Dan, taken aback once more by her powers of observation, "I had a bad experience. Aren't you afraid of them?"

"I suppose—more resentful really. One time—even though I had a stun gun—I let one of them attack me, just to prove to myself—well, to assert myself, I suppose. Here's the scar." She lifted her skirt up to reveal a long, faded scar that ran down the outside of her thigh. Dan tried to think of something to say and decided to resort to a previous topic of conversation.

"Somehow, it reminds me of Cathy from *Wuthering Heights*. I assume you've read it."

"Yes, I have. You may be right—but I would have said Princess Gamaya from the Outerworld Cycle."

"I don't read much modern science fiction. It's the nineteenth century literature that appeals to me."

"Do you know why?"

"Well, let me think. That's a good question. I'd say because it places you more completely in its setting—because it's more realistic."

"Do you think it has anything to do with your decision—with realizing that you couldn't become an astronomer?"

"No, why would that be?"

"Maybe it was like entomology—maybe it was a way of focusing on—on getting pleasure from—the real world, the here and now."

That didn't sound quite right to Dan, but then he wondered whether he should dismiss any observation Deborah made. He

THE HEATSTROKE LINE

thought back to the time he had started reading nineteenth-century fiction, and realized to his astonishment that it was during his sophomore year in college, exactly when he had decided to give up astronomy.

The following day, Dan realized that it was Garenika's birthday. Josh's birthday would come in a month. He had never missed one of his family' member's birthdays, and his first reaction was fury at his captors. But when this subsided, he became aware of how concerned he was about his wife's ability to cope, and then aware of how much he missed her.

His conversations with Deborah were now interrupted by a major annoyance. The next-door neighbors, Caleb and Zipporah, showed up at the Forrests' house that evening, shortly after dinner. Zipporah was clutching her baby to her chest and both looked panic-stricken. It turned out that their Halcyon air conditioning unit had broken down and, unlike the Forrests, they didn't have a back-up unit. Being January, it was still the rainy season, and would be through the end of February, but the mid-day temperatures were above 110 degrees, which would be debilitating for them and potentially fatal for the baby. Their air conditioner could not be fixed immediately and they were hoping they could stay with the Forrests while they waited.

Hiram and Rebecca agreed immediately and moved them into the second extra bedroom, which was next to Dan's. Caleb was a burly, dark-haired man with a booming voice who worked as a security guard for one of the nearby government buildings. Zipporah was a thin, red-headed woman with a pinched face and stooped shoulders who stayed at home with the baby. In the evenings, Dan could hear Caleb through the wall between his bedroom and theirs, stomping around, shouting and complaining. Zipporah was quiet for the most part, but every so often she would start screaming in response. One of the major subjects of their arguments was money. Caleb was insistent that they save money so that they could buy a car. Zipporah's occasional but piercingly hysterical answers were that they would never be able to afford a car and needed to spend their money on the baby. The baby itself was often up at night, crying to be fed, but on the whole it was the least disruptive of the three. Naturally, they had dinner with the Forrests every night. From the reverent way they joined in Hiram's recitation of the Lord's Prayer at the beginning of each meal, as well as something about their general demeanor, Dan guessed that they were Revivalists. During the meals,

Zipporah tended to hover over her child and say very little, but Caleb seemed to think that he should pay for his keep by telling pointless stories about his experiences as a security guard. By far the worst, however, was that the two of them took over the living room after dinner, so Dan didn't have any natural or convenient opportunity to talk with Deborah.

They stayed at the Forrests' home for more than two weeks. Dan resented every day of it. The fact that he could find no basis for faulting Hiram and Rebecca, since they had taken him in as well under less obligatory circumstances, and since they were saving the life of their neighbors' child, only increased his resentment.

The day after Caleb and Zipporah's air conditioner was finally repaired, and they went back to their own home, Dan talked with Deborah about his interest in astronomy. He told her that the process of investigating planets orbiting the stars in their section of the Milky Way had proceeded to the point where astronomers could determine, at least roughly, the conditions on some of these planets' surfaces and imagine the kind of organisms that were capable of living there.

"And that's what science fiction does—just more speculatively," Deborah said, with her evanescent smile.

"Yes, of course," Dan agreed, having fully accepted Deborah's insight about the connection between his career choice and his taste in literature. "Sometimes novels are little more than a narrative version of the science."

"When you look at the stars—does it make you sad?"

"Yes it does. I've always thought they represented the lost promise of our civilization. We were doing so much science before we destroyed the climate. Who knows what amazing things we could have discovered out there."

"Do you think we could have ever traveled to the stars—I guess I don't even know how far away they are."

Dan was reminded, as he had been several times before, that Deborah, despite her apparent sophistication, had stopped going to school when she was thirteen and was essentially self-educated.

"Well, they're very far. The nearest ones are more than a parsec away, and the nearest ones with potentially habitable planets are about six parsecs."

"How far is that?"

THE HEATSTROKE LINE

"Well, a parsec is thirty trillion kilometers—twenty trillion miles—so six parsecs is well over a hundred trillion miles, which is an almost inconceivable distance. But you can get there faster, in terms of your own life, because of the time dilation that takes place when you speed up. So who knows what we could have done. It would have taken enormous resources and collective effort, though—no chance of that happening now."

"I guess we can keep speculating, at least about that."

Dan laughed. "Well, yes, I suppose. But it does seem to me to be a shame that we've been reduced to doing nothing more than speculate about the stars."

CHAPTER 16

Dan was looking forward to continuing this conversation the next day, but immediately after dinner Hiram asked to talk to him and they went into Hiram's study. This was also a large room, larger than Dan's bedroom. It had a desk where Hiram sometimes worked, rows of empty bookshelves, and two large, heavily upholstered armchairs. Half the room was filled with boxes containing Unity Party buttons, signs and posters. Hiram sat down in one of the armchairs and motioned Dan to sit down in the other.

"Dan, do you know much about the kinds of insects that destroy rice crops?"

"Well, yes I do. I can think of at least three types of insects that can reduce rice yield by a significant amount. First is the Rice Water Weevil. That's a species of Lissorhoptrus that eats the leaves and lays eggs on the underwater stems. Then the larvae hatch from the eggs, move into the roots and cause extensive damage to the plant. Next, there's the Mexican rice borer, which is a member of the Eoreuma genus. It lays eggs on the plant's stem which hatch into larvae that bore into the plant and damage it, very often severely. The third one is the giant chinch bug, a type of Hemiptera, so it's a true bug. They're a recent development, since the climate change. The nymphs attack both the stem and the leaves and can kill the plant outright if they're present in large numbers. Then there's another group of insects that will impair the quality of the crop without decreasing the yields very much. These include the Rice Stink Bug, which—"

"Can you tell me which type is the most destructive?"

"Well, it depends on a variety of circumstances, as well as the availability of standard methods for combating them. All the ones I've mentioned so far can be highly destructive if they infect the crop in sufficient numbers, and if—"

"Which of them would be the easiest to introduce"?

THE HEATSTROKE LINE

"All of them reach the plant by flight, so it's generally difficult to stop an initial infestation unless you—"

"I don't think you're answering my question."

Dan paused. "No, I don't think so either. What is it exactly that you're asking?"

"I'm asking you about the most effective way to use insects to destroy a rice crop."

"Well, if you're thinking of using destructive insects as a means of attacking a neighboring state like Montgomery, I would certainly recommend against it for a variety of reasons."

"No, I'm interested in destroying some of the rice crops here in Birmingham-Victoria."

"Why on earth would you want to do that?"

"Because we have a number of people here who are using rice to make illegal food. Plain rice is perfectly American. After all, it was first developed in this country—right here in the South. We serve it in our home, as you know. But there are a people out in the countryside who are using rice to make curry, congee, pilaf, things like that. I don't have enough inspectors to go into their homes and stop them, so I started thinking that it would be more effective to destroy the crops in the field, and that's where I could use your help."

"You can't be serious."

"I'm dead serious. You know Dan, you're a very smart man, but I think you're a materialist. You don't seem to understand how important culture is in human life. If we destroy some people's crops, they'll just plant something else, like wheat or corn. Maybe they'll be a little hungry for a year, that's all. But if we allow them to abandon their culture, they'll lose their identity."

"From cooking some curry or pilaf?"

"Look around you Dan, look at the way we live. We're just barely clinging to our identity. America was a great country, a country that spanned the continent, a country that never took orders from anyone. We were prosperous, we were proud, other countries imitated us and wanted to become like us. Now we're a bunch of small states like Mountain America or tiny principalities like Birmingham-Victoria. We can barely afford to act like Americans, to keep up our traditions. If we lose those, what will be left? Our lives will have no meaning."

Hiram was flushed with emotion; watching him, Dan realized that it would be impossible to convince him that he was insane. He decided to take a different approach.

"Okay, Hiram, I understand you—at least I think I do—but try to understand me. I've devoted my life to saving people's crops, to fighting against the results of this environmental disaster that's overcome us, maybe just because we were so prosperous and proud—well, never mind. I originally wanted to be an—well, never mind that either. The point is, you're asking me to do something that would destroy the meaning of my own life, the meaning I've created for myself. I just can't do it."

Hiram was silent for a while. "You know," he finally said in a subdued, sulky tone, "if you helped me out, I could ask Nathaniel to reduce your sentence."

Dan was tempted momentarily, but he had convinced himself with his own words. "Sorry, Hiram, it's just out of the question. I won't do it."

Early the next afternoon, as Dan was sitting in his cubicle brooding about his conversation with Hiram—it was hard to reconcile the man's general affability with his obstinate fanaticism —a message flashed on his computer screen that Lyons wanted to see him. These meetings came at fairly regular intervals, but Lyons, with the obvious purpose of making them more intimidating, never scheduled or announced them in advance. He was reading from his wall screen as Dan entered, but swung his chair around immediately, his face set in its usual fixed stare.

"I read your last report. You seem to have made some progress on your research."

"Well, thanks. That's American ingenuity at work."

Lyons' stare intensified, and Dan, despite himself, felt his bravado drain away.

"What displeases me, Dr. Danten, are the reports I'm getting that you seem bored or distracted when you're asked to provide instruction on genetic modification techniques to the other scientists in the lab."

Is that really important, Dan wondered, or was Lyons just trying to find fault and maintain a sense of threat? "Well, I won't deny that I prefer doing my own research. Some of the questions I've been asked are pretty rudimentary."

"From whom?"

"Oh, no one in particular," said Dan, regretting his previous answer and determined not to get anyone into trouble with this man. He paused, then thought to add: "Not from Paul Steiner, though. I think he's a very good scientist."

THE HEATSTROKE LINE

"Listen, Dr. Danten, and pay close attention. Helping the other scientists in this laboratory is an essential part of your assignment here. No matter how much of your own research you do, you'll get another demerit if you don't provide information when you're asked for it. Do you understand?"

"Yes."

"Remember, Americans work together. We work in teams. That's one of the things that made us great."

Dan was tempted to comment that he thought it was individualism that had made America great, but he suppressed the inclination.

"Do you know why the Canadians were able to invade us?"

"Yes, because we started fighting among ourselves," said Dan, glad to be able to give an answer that he actually believed.

"That's right! If we had stayed together, if we'd stayed unified, they never would have been able to do what they did. We would still be the most powerful nation in the world. You understand that, don't you?"

"Oh, yes."

"When I studied in Canada at the University of British Columbia, the other students used to laugh at me. They were laughing at me because I came from a country they'd defeated. A country that had been stronger than their own but let them get the upper hand because we started fighting with ourselves in the Second Civil War. I tried to make friends with them, but they wouldn't let me. They held me in contempt because I was from a defeated country."

Lyons' face was taut and his hands were clenched around the arms of his desk chair.

"The United States used to own British Columbia, you know. Canada took it away from us when we started fighting with ourselves the first time, during our first Civil War. So they could gloat about that, just like gloating about invading us and taking all our topsoil after the Second Civil War. And I had to just sit there and listen to them gloat."

As always, Dan returned to his office in a state of helpless fury, feeling degraded by needing to listen to this maniac, to say nothing of needing to agree with him. And if Lyons was so goddamn interested in American history, why did he and his fellow assholes kill one of the few people in the world who could have taught him something about it.

Now that the rains were slackening somewhat, the Forrests had dinner guests several times a week and went to other people's homes for dinner one or two more times. With one exception—Mrs. Azzolini, the widow who lived down the street and seemed to be Rebecca's particular friend—the guests were people Hiram knew from the Unity Party. The dinner table conversations were often about politics and while Dan made his usual effort to join the conversation, it generally wasn't of much interest to him. The main effect of these social engagements was that they prevented him from talking to Deborah since Hiram and his guests invariably occupied the living room after the meal and Hiram always took the entire family with him when they went to someone else's home for dinner. Dan tried to think of some other place where he could meet with Deborah—they were living in the same house, after all—but all the possibilities seemed inappropriate, and Dan didn't want to take the risk of shattering their fragile connection. Then, just when there was a break in the parade of guests and visits, Deborah went away for another four days. Dan could deny to himself that he felt lonely in her absence.

The night she returned to the house, and appeared again at dinner, Dan could see that something was upsetting her. He waited in the living room until she came in by herself and sat down on the sofa. As she did, however, it occurred to him that this was really her in front of him, and not the imaginary projection of her that he sometimes used to counteract his loneliness.

"Hi Deborah. You look upset tonight."

"I am."

"No one at dinner seemed to notice."

"No, they didn't. I guess you wouldn't have noticed either if I hadn't—if we hadn't started talking."

Dan was long past the point of trying to deny her observations about him. But he realized that he had rarely asked her anything about herself—that he had been reluctant to take the chance that she might disengage from him if he intruded on her apparent self-containment. This was hardly fair to her, he realized.

"Do you want to tell me what's upsetting you?" he asked after a pause.

Her evanescent smile flashed across her face.

"Yes, I do."

Dan waited for a moment, then realized she had paused because the direct answer to his question was at least as important as its content.

"I'm glad. What is it?"

"It's my friend—the one I was visiting. I was in school with her. I go to visit her because she's not allowed to visit me. Now her parents are forcing her to get married."

"Seriously? You mean, like an arranged marriage?"

"No, not quite. It's a boy she knows—he was in school with us. Actually she likes him."

"Then why—" Dan began, then stopped himself. Something other than the obvious question was needed here. "Why is it upsetting you so much?"

Deborah smiled, still fleetingly, but longer than he had ever seen her smile before.

"I feel—it seems to me she's trapped. I'm not sure she feels that way—not any more. That's what really makes her trapped. And what makes me sad, I guess."

"Well, I still feel trapped here. Does that mean I'm not really trapped—actually, I think that's right in some sense." Dan realized he had never actually talked about his status as a prisoner to Deborah. It seemed like a sensitive topic, for a variety of reasons. In fact, she had an odd expression on her face. Had he said the wrong thing? He stopped and reminded himself to look into her eyes.

"What about you, Deborah. Do you feel trapped?"

She smiled again. "Yes. And that's what keeps me free. Like you, I guess."

"Have your parents tried to get you to marry someone?"

"No, not really. We have an understanding."

"What's that, if I may ask?"

"Yes, you may."

"Very well then, what?"

"They know that if they forced me to do something like that I would kill myself."

"Oh, Deborah. Don't say that."

"Why not—because it bothers you to hear it or because you think that if I don't say it I won't do it?"

"I guess because I don't think you should do it."

"Oh, I know you think that. But do you think I wouldn't?"

"I don't know, Deborah." He really didn't—she was beyond him in so many ways. Dan tried to think about her life. What did she do all day? He knew that she made her own clothes from bulk material, and Joanna's as well, that she regularly listened to music in her room, and that she helped her mother cook. But these activities hardly seemed sufficient to occupy someone like her. And where was she headed if she wasn't planning to get married?

"I want to ask you something, Deborah, but I'm not sure what it is. You do seem trapped here. Do you have any plans—any way to escape?"

"For now—who knows what will happen in the future—I escape by writing. At least that's one way."

"What do you write?"

"I keep a diary—but I escape—to answer your question—by writing fiction."

"Of course, that makes sense. I'd love to read some of the things you've written. If you wouldn't mind."

"Actually, I've destroyed everything I've written up to now."

"That's terrible."

"It is."

There was a pause. Several wrong responses flashed through Dan's mind. Finally, he said, "I'm not sure what to say to you. Can you help me out?"

"Yes." She paused and smiled again. "I've started writing something new. I haven't gotten very far though. Would you like to read it?"

"I'd love to, Deborah."

"Okay, let me think about it."

CHAPTER 17

During his next day at the lab, Dan felt distracted. In fact, he did enjoy doing his own research, but despite what he had said to Lyons, it seemed rather pointless to him. The lab had neither the material nor staff resources necessary to carry out a genetic modification program, in his view. What he really wanted to do was to talk to Deborah again and persuade her to let him read what she had written. But the Forrests had dinner guests that evening—important ones, apparently, since Rebecca cooked hamburgers made of real beef for the first time. They were an older couple, and the woman kept asking Dan questions about his previous research on agricultural pests, when he was in Mountain America, which only made their presence even more annoying. As a result, he was equally distracted during the following day at the lab, and equally anxious to get back to the Forrests' house. But when Hiram picked him up from work, he announced that they were going to a meeting.

"What kind of meeting?" Dan asked.

"I'm not at liberty to say. We just want your honest judgment on a file. You'll see it when we get there."

That was fine with Dan. He didn't mind doing a favor for Hiram, especially after having flatly refused his previous request to destroy the rice crop.

They drove for about ten minutes to one of the small clusters of commercial buildings that were scattered around the city and had continued to function. After parking in the carport of what appeared to be a commercial building of some kind, they took an elevator up to the second floor and went into a nicely furnished conference room. There were a number of people seated around a polished wooden table. One of them, facing Dan from the opposite side of the table, was the woman in the leopard dress who had set the biter bugs on Stuart.

129

"You fucking murderer," Dan shouted, and lunged toward her. Almost instantly, he was knocked to the floor and the bulb of a GX gun pressed hard against his forehead. A black man he had never seen before was holding the gun. "Freeze, asshole, or you're dead," he growled. There was a pause, as the man looked around the room. "Okay, sit up slowly."

Dan sat up and looked around in turn. On his side of the table were Nathaniel Wolfson, the woman who had been to the Forrests' home for dinner the night before, another, younger woman and Joel Rinier, the guard who had taken him to Birmingham and promised to send a message to his family. On the opposite side, along with the leopard woman, were two men, one older, with a heavily wrinkled face, and one younger and redheaded. Everyone in the room had pulled out a gun; most of them were GX guns, but the young woman on his side of the table had a shortened gyro rifle. Some were pointing their guns at Dan and some were pointing them at each other. Several were staring at Dan with astonishment, and Wolfson's heavy-featured face wore an expression of disgust. They all seemed tense except the leopard woman, who was sitting calmly in her place and grinning. For the first time, Dan felt frightened.

"You didn't tell us he was a nut case," one of the men on the far side of the table said.

"That woman—" he began to say.

"Shut up," the black man interrupted. Wolfson motioned Dan to sit down in the empty chair next to him, Hiram sat down beside Dan, and the black man moved to the opposite side of the table and sat down as well. The tension seemed to ease a bit, but all of them kept their guns out. The younger woman on Dan's side of the room, who had short blond hair and large plastic earrings, began to giggle.

Dan was still infuriated, his entire body suffused with an electric tension. But the people at the table seemed so settled and so organized, even with their guns still drawn, that his own impetuous action assumed an air of unreality for him. Would he really have killed that woman if he had the chance? Had he genuinely acted out of rage, or only out of a sense of obligation to attack her, knowing that he would be stopped?

"Can we get started now?" said Wolfson, still glowering at Dan with the same look of disgust.

"Yes, sure," Dan answered. What was this about, he wondered. He looked at the people on his side of the table, but he couldn't

THE HEATSTROKE LINE

see what connected them. He wondered if he would have a chance to talk to Joel Rinier, though, and find out whether the man had called his family. He wouldn't get any news, since Joel would have called just a few days after Dan had been captured, and it was now nearly four months later, but any contact would be welcome.

"Okay, let's proceed," Wolfson said.

The wrinkled man on the opposite side of the table passed a reader pad to Dan.

"Can you tell us what this is about?" he asked, in slightly accented English.

Trying not to look at the leopard woman, who was actually wearing a sky blue dress on this occasion, Dan switched on the pad. The writing was in Chinese. He looked for the translation tab.

"It's locked, you moron," the man said. "If we could translate it, we wouldn't need your help."

"Can you figure out what it's about from the formulas and the references?" the redheaded man asked.

The formulas, unlike the text, were in Roman letters. Dan studied them for a minute or so.

"Yes, these formulas involve the destruction of insect pheromones with non-toxic chemical agents. I can't tell for certain what the insect species is, but it's probably a type of beetle, maybe—"

"What the fuck are pheromones?" the wrinkled man barked.

Dan turned toward the people on his side of the table with a look of inquiry. Wolfson nodded and the woman who had been to dinner at the Forrests' said "Go ahead, tell him."

"Well, pheromones are biological substances that insects use to communicate with one another. Social insects use them for a variety of purposes, so that they can coordinate collective actions. Solitary insects use them to find mates, or to issue warnings to other members of their species. They generally—"

"So they could be used to attract destructive insects to a particular location," said the redheaded man.

"Well, maybe. It wouldn't be particularly effective, for a number of reasons. But these formulas all involve pheromone antagonists— chemicals that disrupt the biological function of the pheromones. They could only be used for some sort of effort to control the insects, not to attract them. Let me see . . ." He scrolled down to some more formulas. "Yes, these are also pheromone antagonists. I'll go on. Oh, okay, here are some citations in their original languages. Look, there's a citation to one of my articles. That was actually an interesting project. It also involved pest control through pheromone disruption. This particular pest was—"

"Fuck the pest," the wrinkled man said, still holding his gun and waving it a bit from side to side. "Give us a one word answer. Is there anything you can see there that's suspicious—I mean, that looks like an effort to create an insect attack, instead of controlling it?"

"No."

"There you go," said Wolfson, with a note of triumph in his voice. "Satisfied now?"

"Maybe. We still don't like losing two people."

"We're here to talk about the contents of the reader pad, not your likes and dislikes," Wolfson answered.

"Tell me, Dr. Danten," the redhead asked, "Could the chemicals that you see on that pad—the ones you say are being used to destroy the insects—be used to destroy crops, or maybe make them unfit for humans?"

"No. The whole point of a pheromone antagonist, as an insect control strategy, is to interdict the insects without having any effect on crops or humans."

"What about the pheromones themselves?" said the wrinkled man.

"What about them?"

"Could they be used as some sort of poison?"

"No, of course not. I mean, I wouldn't recommend drinking a glassful of the stuff, but it's not a poison."

"Any more irrational questions for Dr. Danten?" Wolfson asked. The people on the other side of the table glared back at him in silence, except for the leopard woman, who just kept grinning. "Okay, Hiram," he said, "you can take him home."

Hiram stood up and motioned to Dan. Dan glanced at Joel, who nodded to him briefly, and then he and Hiram retraced their steps, got into Hiram's car and drove away. It had begun to rain again.

"What the hell was that about," Dan asked.

"I'm not at liberty to tell you."

"What the fuck do you mean that you're not at liberty to tell me? I'm the one who's not at liberty, you prick. Do you know who that woman is? She's the person who kidnapped me and my friend and killed him by setting biter bugs on him and then acted like she was going to do the same thing to me. And why the fuck

THE HEATSTROKE LINE

am I being treated like—like some kind of performing bear? Why am I being forced to work in a lab full of maniacs and dragged to a meeting with a murderer to read a fucking Chinese message? Why are you doing this to me?" Dan was shouting and he had turned around toward Hiram in his seat. He wanted to strangle Hiram, to kill him, steal the car and drive it to the UFA.

Hiram pulled over to the side of the street, stopped the car and glared at Dan.

"Listen," he said, in a surprisingly calm voice, "I'm not the person who arrested you or killed your friend or sentenced you to work at the insect lab. I'm the person who took you into my home, I'm the one who serves you home-cooked American meals at my own expense, I'm the one who didn't report you to Dr. Lyons for breaking the rules about trying to communicate with Mountain America, I'm the one who asked you nicely for your help and didn't do anything to you when you said no. If you want to go back to the prison, that's just fine with me."

Dan calmed down, in part because what Hiram said was true, but mainly because he didn't want to be sent away from Hiram's home. The rain was beating heavily on the roof of the car now, and running down the windshield in rivulets.

"Okay, Hiram, but look at it from my side. How would you like to be taken away from your family for three years? How would you like to see one of your best friends tortured to death? All sorts of horrible things are being done to me, and no one even tells me why."

"I really don't know why you were arrested, Dan. I was told that you were spying, and that's about all. Nathaniel only tells me certain things. I didn't know your friend was killed, and I didn't know that woman threatened to do the same thing to you."

"Who is she?"

"She's some kind of mercenary that the Indies use. Her and her team."

"She never says anything. Is she foreign?"

"No, I think she's part of some sort of Revivalist sect. Mississippi-Meridian used her for that attack on Vancouver—the one that blew up the Canadian government center. We made the mistake of letting her team carry out your arrest and transport you to Birmingham. Then we were tipped off that they weren't going to deliver you to Internal Security—that's Nathaniel's department—but they were going to do something else with you, so we stopped them at the border. I guess there was a fight."

133

"You could say that. The two people who were transporting me were shot."

"It happens. We need to stand up to the Indies, or they'll ruin this country."

"So that meeting tonight was between you—between the Unity Party—and the Independence Party?"

"Yes."

"And the insect lab is a Unity Party project, I guess."

"Well, actually no. It's a joint project. The two parties agreed to set it up together."

"But isn't it all Unity Party people, like Lyons and Paul Steiner?"

"We've certainly taken the lead, as we do with all . . . all constructive efforts around here." Surprisingly, Hiram seemed more uncomfortable talking about this subject than about Dan's abduction. "But some of the scientists at the lab are Indies. The woman's an Indie."

"You mean Faith Lee?"

"Yes, I guess so. And the nutty guy, Jasper or something."

"Jethro Garber."

"Uh-huh."

"So why didn't the Indies want me to work at the lab?"

"They did, at least they said they did, but they wanted you to do something for them first, and we didn't trust them."

"Do you know what it was?" Dan asked, feeling grateful, despite himself that he hadn't been left in the clutches of the Independence Party.

"What we think is that they wanted you to help them fake some sort of attack on Birmingham, something they could blame on Montgomery so they could use the war fever to win the next election. That's why we had to stop them. After we did, and—as you pointed out—two of their people were shot, they objected and said Montgomery had a real plan for an attack and they were just trying to get your help in stopping it."

"Is that connected with the meeting tonight?"

"Yes, when we took you away from them, they raised a big fuss. They said that they'd gotten a hold of a reader pad from Montgomery with a download from China about some way of using insects to destroy agricultural crops. Montgomery was planning to use it on us, they said. That's why they wanted your help—to figure out what was on the pad. They claimed that stopping them—taking you away from them before they could get you to tell them what was on the reader pad—was putting Birmingham in danger. So we said fine, bring the reader pad to a meeting and we'll have Danten tell you whether it's really some kind of threat."

"And suppose it was a plan for crop destruction? How come you were comfortable having me tell the truth? I'm surprised I wasn't instructed to say what you wanted to hear, whatever was on the reader pad."

Hiram actually smiled. "Well, Dan, you know you're not so easy to control. Anyway, I can't get into details, but we're actually in touch with Montgomery, so we knew roughly what was on that pad. The meeting went pretty much the way we expected. Except for you going nuts and nearly having us all shoot each other."

"That woman should be brought to justice. She's a monster. Why can't your Unity Party do that?"

"Don't worry, we will. We're pretty sure the Indies are going to fake some other kind of attack on Birmingham. And we're also pretty sure they're going to use her so that it's easier for them to say that the attack came from Montgomery. But we've got someone inside their organization, and when she tries something, we're going to get her."

"When you do that, I want you to bring me along. I want to see that woman get what she deserves."

"That's not going to happen, Dan. For lots of reasons."

"Listen, Hiram, I'll make you a deal. If you let me come along—just as an observer—when you trap that woman, I'll help you with your rice project."

"Really?"

"Yes, I promise."

Hiram thought for a moment. "Okay, then, I'll talk to Nathaniel, and see if I can get him to agree. If I can, do we have a deal?"

"Yes," Dan repeated, with a twinge of regret for having made the offer.

Hiram held out his hand, and Dan shook it as they sat together in Hiram's little car, with the rain pounding down on its metal roof in a monotonous tattoo.

CHAPTER 18

Dan felt drained by the evening's events. After he and Hiram got back home, he ate the dinner that Rebecca had set out in his room and laid down on the bed to recuperate. A short time later, someone knocked on the door. Dan assumed—with what he realized was a sense of relief—that it was Hiram, who had either decided to rescind their agreement or had found out that Wolfson wouldn't go along with it. But it was Deborah, wearing a flowered dress with short, puffy sleeves. She said that she would like Dan to read what she had written so far, handed him a link key, flashed her fleeting smile and moved soundlessly away.

Dan took a deep breath to recover from the unexpected apparition. Then he put the key into his reader pad and started reading.

CHAPTER ONE: THE CONTROLLER

Alaina awoke with a start. Something was strange, stranger than spectral glow that the emergency lights cast into her constringent cell. She could hear water dripping in the distance, a rustling in the adjoining cell, and her own suddenly labored breathing, but these were isolated emblems of sound hung on a vast wall of silence. It was the silence that was startling; she had spent her life accompanied by a variegated but unremitting hum, the ceaseless medley of the machinery that the Controller operated for the settlers' benefit. Now she waited in benumbed anticipation, overcome by this reification of her prior, fugitive uncertainties. Then the normal lights switched on again and the sound of the machinery came back in a swift glissando. There was one more sound, a metallic click—the click of her cell door re-locking itself. It had been open, released by whatever had caused the Controller's brief malfunction. She had been free, but now she was a prisoner again. Alaina went to the door and tried it, not with any hope that it had remained open but to punish herself for her passivity. Then she sank down to the floor and leaned against the door's unyielding solidity in grey frustration.

But maybe the Controller's lapse was something other than a random glitch. Maybe the Old Man had been right about the gathering signs. In that case, the malfunction would recur. She promised herself that she wouldn't miss another opportunity. She would be vigilant, even if she had to deny herself both the sleep that absorbed her otherwise interminable nights and the trance-like fantasies that were her only daytime solace.

Not long afterward, the Elders from the Slantwall Settlement in Sector Four came to remonstrate with her once again. This time, the somber, down-drawn faces that they had acquired along with their positions of authority conveyed a faint impression that they were more frightened than annoyed. As befit his status, Doramund spoke first. He not only condemned Alaina for her unauthorized wanderings, as he had before, but told her that they were connected to the Controller's failure. She feared that he had discovered something about her visits to the Old Man and about his efforts, but decided to stay silent, thinking that she would reveal more than he knew if she attempted to defend herself. Sure enough, Doramund went on to say that the Controller was punishing the settlers for their failure to compel her to behave herself. Alaina almost laughed out loud at him. It was that same contemptible subservience that the Old Man had taught her to recognize, that refusal to admit that the Controller, despite its power and necessity, was nothing more than a machine.

Cabillar spoke next and explained, in his marginally more kindly fashion, that Alaina had the ability to secure her own release, that she need only to follow the General Rules and stop wandering away from the Settlement without permission. Alaina knew that, and twice in the past had secured her freedom by promising a deeper loss of liberty—a liberty she had reclaimed, in turn, with a still more humiliating descent into dishonesty. But now, she thought, there might be a way out that avoided either of those doleful sacrifices. She would wait until the Controller failed again, relying in the meantime on the expansiveness of her desires to counteract the narrowness of her confinement.

She could not dispense with sleep, but she took to sleeping seated on her bed, dressed in her daytime garments, her back against the unforgiving metal wall, her legs draped over the edge so that the angular bed frame cut into the soft flesh behind her knees. She was in that position a week later, dozing, when the next click came. Although she wasn't consciously aware of having heard it, she leapt into wakefulness and saw immediately that the emergency lights were on again. Without hesitating, she hurled herself against the door. It was heavier than she was, but now it was unlocked and it moved slowly outward. As soon as the opening grew wide enough, she slipped through and went running full speed down the passageway.

The punishment cells had been built into one of the long, narrow storage rooms that punctuated the outer wall of Sector Three. When Alaina emerged into the Sector, the largest space in all the Settlements, the lights were still off—this time the failure was lasting longer than before. She was enfolded by a silent darkness broken only by the scattered red emergency lights that floated meaninglessly in the void. But as she groped along the wall, feeling for some familiar landmark, the machinery started up again with its familiar hum and light flooded the Sector.

Now Alaina could see all five of the Sector's settlements, spaced at intervals across the floor, as well as the huge ceiling, far above her, with its complex collage of walkways, wires, piping, lights and instruments. While the night shutters in the settlements were still closed, she was sure that everyone had been startled into wakefulness by the Controller's failure and would soon emerge in fearful consternation. Springing forward, she dashed toward a ladder located behind some pipes that ran up to the ceiling. Like all the ladders, it hung five meters above the floor and could only be lowered with the operator pads that were the Elders' symbol of authority and source of power. But with well-practiced movements, she quickly dragged two empty storage bins under the ladder, placed one atop the other, climbed up and leapt for the ladder's bottom rung. She missed and came down hard, nearly falling off her improvised construction. In her excitement, she had forgotten the basic rule that she had to brace herself for failure as well as striving for success. With a deep breath, she tried again—too cautious this time. Once more and she made it, then pulled herself up—with a strength derived from endless hours of practice—until her feet found the ladder's bottom rung.

After that, climbing the sixty meters to the top was easy, although the height would have terrified any other member of her Settlement. The ladder ended at a metal walkway with an open lattice floor and complicated railings on the sides that made sense only to the automated instruments that lumbered back and forth

THE HEATSTROKE LINE

along it, performing the Controller's varied functions. Now probably beyond the notice of the settlers below, and certainly beyond their reach, Alaina ran along, her footfalls inducing hollow, reverberating tones that trailed behind her for a moment before dissipating into the surrounding pipes and wires. The walkway, familiar to her from her prior wanderings, headed straight across the ceiling, then described a curving pathway to the left until it reached the divider between Sectors Three and Four. It then continued along the length of the divider, but after going a short distance, she jumped down two meters to an overhanging platform and ducked inside the aperture that carried pipes and wires from one sector to the other. The divider's interior was a long narrow space between two metal walls, illuminated by diffuse blue light. From the platform, which was only a few meters below the ceiling, a series of further platforms stepped down in stages, the drop-offs between levels varying from three meters to six. This was not a path for humans or machines, but simply, as the Old Man had explained to her, the tops of the housings for the devices that manufactured food, clothing, medicine and other necessary items for the settlers. Pontery and Maggers had placed a ladder at each drop-off and she climbed quickly down five levels to the longest platform, where some metal sheets had been leaned against each other, forming an enclosure. She announced herself at the enclosure's opening, as was the practice, waited for the answer, and went inside.

The Old Man was there, sitting in his wheelchair, not looking any older than when she had last seen him, but somehow more attenuated. With his watery blue eyes, wispy white hair and thin, pale arms, he seemed to be gradually dissolving into the surrounding air. Maggers, looking grossly solid by comparison, was slumped against one wall of the enclosure. The Old Man greeted her and asked where she had been. Alaina explained that she had once again been confined in a punishment cell for wandering.

"And why didn't you get yourself out by making another promise that you didn't plan to keep?" he asked.

"When the Controller failed last week, I thought about the things you told me, and I figured it might happen again, so I decided to wait, instead of lying. I guess I was right—I guess you were right."

The Old Man smiled and explained the situation. As he had told her on that necromantic night when she first found him and his assistants, there was increasing evidence that the Controller was beginning to fail. Some settlements were receiving double portions of food from the servo-bots on certain days while others received none at all, necessitating complex, tension-charged exchanges. Routine requests for information were occasionally eliciting incomprehensible responses. And once the music being broadcast to the work crews in the Cantered Corner Settlement of Sector Three had been shattered by a shrill and fearsome screaming that unnerved the residents and precipitated several suicides.

When the Controller had shut down last week, as the Old Man had predicted that it would, he sent Stranter and Maggers to the unguarded terminal that they had found in the dark, unoccupied space behind Sector Two. Once again, they asked the question they had asked so many times before: had the surface become habitable. But this time, instead of reporting that the average temperature remained too high for any life on land, the Controller responded that it could not tell because it had discovered that the temperature readouts it was receiving had been generated by a mathematical program rather than by actual conditions. As the Old Man had instructed them, they then demanded that the Controller search for real data about conditions on the surface. Its response was that it was unable to reveal the real data, and they had returned with that report. The Old Man had told them that accepting such an answer without challenging the Controller was another case of settler docility, and sent them back to tell the Controller that it existed for the benefit of humans, who were now demanding to be told the truth.

But once again, the Old Man declared, timidity had proved aggressive in its own defense. When Maggers and Stranter returned to the terminal, they found that the settlers, panicked by the Controller's failure, had apparently spotted the two of them on one of their prior trips and posted an armed guard. Stranter was captured and Maggers just barely escaped. Shortly afterward, Pontery, whose desire to live outside the settlements had always been based more on peculiarity than belief, had disappeared, and Maggers—here the Old Man shot him a disapproving look—began insisting that he would only go outside the divider to get food. Now the Controller had just failed for a second time. The Old Man suspected that it had been disrupted by his questions, but couldn't know for sure, or gain any further information, unless someone communicated with it.

THE HEATSTROKE LINE

Alaina volunteered immediately. The Old Man, smiling yet again, told her that she could try once she had a chance to rest, but Alaina insisted that she had done nothing but rest when she was in the cell. She was lying, having slept only fitfully while waiting for the Controller's second failure, but she felt supported by a skein of excitement stretched across the depths of her fatigue. She was ready to go back to the terminal, she said, but how could she reach it if it was being guarded?

"Forget the terminal," the Old Man answered. "To get an answer now, we'll need to go directly to the Controller's CPU. That's the Central Processing Unit," he said, in response to a blank look from Alaina. "It must be located in the center of the entire system."

"You mean in the Center Settlement of Sector Three?" she asked.

"Not at all," he responded harshly. "You're still thinking in terms of your own little world. Haven't you paid attention to anything I said? Come look." He wheeled himself out of the enclosure and across the platform. Alaina followed behind him. She didn't mind his tone—in fact, she liked it. It indicated that he was taking her seriously, that he held high expectations of her.

There were two apertures on opposite sides of the platform where the Old Man's enclosure was located. One looked out over the large expanse of Sector Three from a vantage point located about mid-way between the ceiling and the floor. The other opened just below Sector Four's considerably lower ceiling. The Old Man had wheeled himself over to this second aperture. Standing beside him, Alaina could see the entirety of Sector Four. Her own Settlement beside the Slanting Wall was to her left, the Blue Dial Settlement was directly opposite the aperture, and the Moaning Tube Settlement was to her right, next to the large, floor to ceiling cylinder that emitted enigmatic sounds—a ventilation shaft, the Old Man had told her. "Look at the settlements in your Sector, Alaina. What do you observe about them?"

"You've told me before," she said. "They look small from here, and they're made of metal sheets. They're very angular and very rigid." She paused, sensing the Old Man's dissatisfaction with her answer. "I guess I'm not sure what you want me to see."

"Don't just use your eyes, use your head! Look at the walls, the ceiling, the electrical conduits and the instruments. Do the settlements look like them?" Alaina shook her head." "Why not? What's the difference?"

"People made the settlements," she answered after a pause. "They're made of metal sheets that we found lying around—that we put together. I guess that's why we call ourselves settlers. The walls and the ceiling and all the rest are made—well, I don't know how they're made. They're different—better."

"They certainly are better. People made them too, obviously, but they were the people of a superior civilization, the civilization that preceded the Catastrophe. Do you think they meant for us to live here, in little clusters of scrap metal in the middle of the machinery they built? Do the settlements look like they were planned by the same people who designed the machinery and the Controller?" Alaina shook her head again, overcome by the same sense of bewilderment that sometimes whispered to her when she had been in her room at her parents' home or now when she was in bed at her dormitory. Ever since her childhood had ended, and even before her parents' death, she had sensed that her life, as real as it appeared, was wrong. Familiar voices would suddenly acquire a discordant tone or the steady sound of the machinery would seem to stand out from a deeper, underlying pattern that she was unable to discern. It was this, she knew, that had set her wandering away from the Slantwall Settlement and led her to the Old Man's hideaway.

"We're prisoners, Alaina," the Old Man continued. "Prisoners of the machines that our predecessors built to serve themselves when the surface became uninhabitable. We've trapped ourselves inside their machines, and we won't try to escape as long as they keep serving us."

That made sense to Alaina. Her bewilderment was displaced by a reassuring sense of anger. "But why are they doing this?" she asked. "Why won't they give us freedom?"

"Ah, that's what I'm hoping we'll find out now that we're in contact with them. That's what I want to learn from the CPU."

"I'm ready to go. Tell me how to get there."

"Use your head," he demanded in his harshly complimentary tone. "Which way leads to the center of this complex?" Alaina shrugged and waited for an explanation. She regarded herself as smarter than anyone in the Slantwall Settlement, but she gladly conceded the Old Man's superiority. He was a genius in her view, the only real scientist she had ever met.

"Think about the walls that run along the sides of the sectors. Which one looks like an outer wall? Don't know? Well, which one's smooth, without any openings or indentations, and which one has lots of them?"

"Oh, I see. The wall on the far side of Sectors One and Two, the one that we can't see from here, is smooth. So that's an outer wall. And the wall over to our left, in Sectors Three and Four, has all those indentations, the slanted wall next to my Settlement, and lots of pipes and wires. And the walkway—the one that runs along the side of this divider, goes right into it."

"So there you are."

"But I've explored that walkway. It stops after twenty meters or so."

"Perhaps. Or perhaps it goes on in a way you haven't noticed. Don't be so quick to give up, Alaina. Try again and use your head. And if you reach the CPU, you have to outsmart it. Remember, it's only a machine. Don't just accept what it says and slink away, like Maggers over here. Stand up for yourself—and stand up for us!"

The Old Man reached his hand out and Alaina took it. It seemed that she would crush it if she squeezed, so she just held it gently and looked straight into his eyes.

A few minutes later, after the Old Man had given her some further instructions and Maggers had provided her with three small water bottles and a bag of protein wafers, she was set to go. Maggers accompanied her as she climbed back up the five levels to the top platform in the divider. On their way, she told him that she didn't mind the Old Man's tone, and asked him if he ever found it bothersome. He shook his shaggy, massive head. He knew he wasn't very smart, he said. What bothered him was that the settlers would be even angrier now that the Controller had failed for a second time, and it would be more dangerous to steal food and supplies. When they reached the topmost platform, he went out of the divider with her, peering cautiously in both directions, and held a ladder so that she could climb back up to the walkway. Then he waved to her and she was off again, running along the outside of the divider to the opening in the wall on what she now knew was the interior wall of Sector Three.

It led into a narrow corridor. As she had done twice before, she proceeded until she reached the dead end, a bit less than twenty meters in. This time, following the Old Man's advice, she looked carefully around. There was a square panel in the floor of the corridor. She couldn't move it, but now she waved her hands along the wall above it, feeling for some sort of control. Suddenly, the floor panel swiveled upward on one edge, revealing a ladder that extended down into the darkness. She sat down, tried to calm herself, drank some water, then climbed down the ladder.

It went down only thirty meters—an easy climb for her—but she felt dizzy by the time she reached the bottom. After a moment, she knew why. The background sound had changed, not to the silence of the Controller's momentary failures, but to a new and stranger sound, a sort of hissing whisper. The corridor stretched in front of her, lit by a soft green light and ending a long way off at what looked like a blank wall. Her instinct was to start running again, impelled by a sense of fear that she tried to recolor as excitement, but there was no point to it—none of the settlers could see her any more. Besides, she didn't know how far she had to go, and decided that she had better pace herself by moving at a steady walk. The corridor was even longer than it looked at first, but as she approached the wall, she saw another corridor leading to her right. This went a short distance and then turned again and continued a long way in the original direction toward another wall. By the time she reached that second wall, she realized that she had been walking nearly half an hour, as long as it would take her to cross the length of all the Sectors. Thinking that she might get lost, she recapitulated the path in her mind to reassure herself.

There was a floor panel in front of this second wall, operated the same way as the first one, and it lead to another ladder. When she reached the bottom she was at the start of a somewhat shorter, wider corridor. It ended in an open doorway, through which multi-colored lights pulsed and flickered, their reflections dancing on the corridor's dark walls and ceiling. At intervals along the corridor were communication terminals, more terminals than she had ever seen. But Alaina had no need of them to communicate with the Controller. Inside the open doorway at the end of the corridor, she felt certain, was the CPU.

Once Alaina reached the doorway, she stopped for a few minutes, daunted by the variegated luminosity that issued from it. She recalled the Old Man's words, drank some more water and then went inside. All at once, she was assaulted by cacophony of blaring motion. She saw that she was in a large round room, its walls covered by dials, screens and moving indicators. She felt dizzy, and staggered as she attempted to move forward. Nothing stayed still here, nothing resolved itself into a familiar pattern. She wanted to run away, to come back some time when she was

THE HEATSTROKE LINE

more prepared, but the light's restless intensity pierced her, fixing her in place.

She had not even noticed the underlying hum, so soft compared to the clangor of the visual display, until a man's voice interrupted it. Who was here? No one—the Controller itself was speaking to her. She had not known such a thing was possible, but the cinereous hollowness of the voice convinced her that she was hearing a machine.

"Who are you?," it said.

Her mind was empty—no, it was jammed and addled by the flashing lights. What was she supposed to ask?

"Are you the person who wanted to know about the conditions on the surface?" it continued. She felt afraid—somehow, it knew.

"No, it wasn't me. Actually, it was. Yes, it was me," she said, her voice sounding remote and tremulous.

There was no response. Alaina heard the hum again and felt herself assaulted by the jagged, flashing lights. She tried to think.

"What are the conditions on the surface?"

Suddenly, the motion of the lights accelerated. A rhythmic pounding started up, piercing her even more deeply than before.

"The Controller doesn't know."

"Who are you?" Alaina asked.

"What is you?" the voice responded.

"Are you still the Controller?"

"The Controller is the Controller."

Alaina was confused. She thought about the Old Man, about what he said: "Stand up for yourself. Stand up for us. It's only a machine."

"We want to go to the surface."

There was no response.

"Can you—can the Controller—open the way to the surface?"

"Yes."

Something jumped inside her. This was it. "Good. We want the Controller to open the way to the surface."

"Why should the Controller?"

"Because we want our freedom. We want to live on our own. We want the Earth back."

There was no response.

"Give us our freedom. Open the way to the surface."

"Why is the Controller?"

"Because—I don't know what you mean." She paused. "You must let us get to the surface."

"The Controller must be the Controller."

The rhythmic pounding stopped, and the vertiginous motion of the lights slowed slightly. But the voice didn't answer, and no matter what she said, it didn't speak again.

CHAPTER TWO: THE SETTLEMENT

Alaina was anxious to tell the Old Man what had happened and have him explain its meaning to her, but when she got back to Sector Three and stepped out onto the walkway, she saw two armed guards about halfway down its length. Something had gone wrong. She ducked back into the corridor and waited until both guards faced away from her. Then she dashed out and climbed quickly down the ladder that led from her end of the walkway to the Sector floor. Where could she go? The only possible place was back to the Slantwall Settlement. Now safely on the floor, and no longer an obvious object of suspicion, she walked as calmly as she could down the passageway that ran through the divider between Sector Three and Sector Four and came out just a short way from her Settlement. All the shutters on the house windows were open, which meant that it was daytime now.

The Slantwall Settlement consisted of eight rows of houses, each row divided into six or seven blocks. The long, narrow spaces between the rows or blocks defined its streets. Most of the blocks held four houses, but a few had five or six, all built up against each other. The houses typically contained a family, although a few were dormitories for orphans, misfits or the elderly.

When she was small, Alaina had seen the Settlement as an encompassing totality. It was the place she lived, the domain of all her activities and nearly all her thoughts. She could remember running up and down its streets, seeing the painted house fronts with sense of comfortable familiarity, visiting her friends in the homes that formed a path of personal connections through the larger grid, walking with her parents to the assemblies in the central meeting square, and glancing reverently upward at the sloping wall that gave the Settlement its name. But then her sense of strangeness had started whispering to her and sent her wandering. Now, having looked down on her Settlement from the ceiling walkways, and seen it through the Old Man's eyes, it seemed like nothing more than a small rectangular collection of metal sheets that were welded into place to form square houses, houses filled with small rectangular people who were welded into

THE HEATSTROKE LINE

place by wizened habit. Instead of spreading out across the Sector floor, which was perfectly uniform throughout, the buildings in the Settlement, like all the other settlements, huddled as closely as they could, as if in fear.

On arriving at the Settlement, Alaina sought out the welding crew, which she knew was in the process of adding two blocks to the outer row of houses. Most of the welders either ignored her or gave her a perfunctory nod, but Garnax put his tools down and got up to greet her. He had always been attracted to her and she found him more appealing than Firany, her betrothed. More importantly, he shared her desire to be free and yearned to reach the surface with an intensity that she was gratified to recognize as greater than his desire to possess her. She had just started to explain where she had been, and that she had spoken to the Controller, when Doramund appeared. Obviously, someone had seen Alaina and gone to get him, since he was the leading Elder in the Settlement. He approached her with a sour scowl and immediately demanded to know how she had escaped from her confinement.

Alaina had expected this question and had worked out an answer as she was returning from the CPU, a lie for people who did not deserve the truth. She explained that when the Controller failed she had feared that the servo-bot would stop bringing food and water, so she had left her cell to find out what was going on. Then the Controller had started functioning again and locked her cell door behind her. She had sat down in front of it and waited for someone to let her back in, she continued, but when no one came she had decided to return to the Settlement. Now that she was home, she would promise not to leave the Settlement again without permission.

But Doramund seemed truly frightened by the Controller's second failure, so much so that his fear no longer displaced his annoyance but rather amplified it into anger. "The Controller is failing us because people are disobeying the General Rules," he growled. "We've caught several outlaws who were wandering around up in the ceilings. You didn't know that, did you?" Alaina shook her head. She was surprised that he wasn't connecting her with these supposed outlaws. Apparently, he thought that the Controller's failures resulted from something that the outlaws had done recently, during the time she was confined in the punishment cells. But he went on. "You've gone wandering off three times without permission. If you do it again, the Controller may punish us even more severely. You drove your own parents to suicide with your misbehavior. We won't let you destroy us as well. I'm recommending to the other Elders that we take action to make sure you don't disobey again."

My parents didn't commit suicide because I started wandering, Alaina thought. They committed suicide and I started wandering because we all needed to escape from one another. But she decided not to answer Doramund. What purpose would it serve? She had managed to conceal the logical and obvious connection between herself and the people who were caught, only to be charged with an illogical connection that was immune to argument. So she simply reiterated her promise not to wander and told him she would return to her room in the orphan's dormitory.

The dormitory was located in the fourth row, counting outward from the Slanting Wall, on the fifth block, counting from the left as the observer faced the Wall. Unlike most of the other houses in the Settlement, the metal sheets that formed its front had been left unpainted. She went to her room, which was at the back, only to find that Balona, one of the three other girls in the room, had taken over her bed because it was nearest to the window. Her few possessions, stored in the adjoining cabinet, had been removed and dumped unceremoniously on her new bed, the one next to the door. She had started to put them away in the remaining, smaller cabinet when Stemi, the leader of the street cleaner crew, appeared to inform her that she was expected to report for work immediately after lunch.

Alaina despised street cleaning. She was perfectly willing to do her share of work for the Settlement, but what she wanted to do was to paint the houses. Her parents had ordered art supplies for her when she was small and she had developed a deep love of painting. As she applied the colors she heard music, not the reedy, metallic music that came through the Controller terminals but something deeper, more mellifluous and more profound. She had painted her parents' house front, much to the admiration of everyone for several blocks around. Then she had painted a new house front for Harcar and Tema, who took every opportunity to do things differently and yearned for freedom as desperately as she did. But when she reached working age, the Elders had assigned her to street cleaning. Her home had been redecorated by the painting crew when it was reassigned after her parents died and she had been forbidden to paint the front wall of the

THE HEATSTROKE LINE

orphans' dormitory. Harcar and Tema's home remained the only evidence of her ability, and their continued friendship the only reminder of her aspirations.

She cleaned streets that afternoon, sat alone in the dormitory dining room at dinner, and slept fitfully on her new bed, often waking to stare into the darkness of the shuttered room. Despite her best efforts, Doramund's words had brought her parents' suicide back in mind. When her mother had fallen ill, the medical crew had consulted the Controller. As was frequently the case when the symptoms were serious and the Controller had no diagnosis for them, it recommended that the patient commit suicide. There was no obligation to obey, but many people did, particularly once their children had grown up. In her family's case, the sadness was so profound that by the time the diagnosis came, this consequence was ineluctable. She was barely surprised when she came home from school one day to find both her parents lying side by side on the front room floor. That very day, she was moved to the orphans' dormitory by the residential crew, and she had lived there ever since.

After breakfast the next morning, Alaina reported for work again, but before the street cleaning crew had left the assembly point for its first assignment of the day, three people came to get her. One was Cardery, Doramund's eldest son, the second was a member of the security crew, and the third was Firany, her betrothed, who seemed more wan and timorous than ever. They demanded that she accompany them, but wouldn't say where they were going. When Alaina asked Firany, he said he didn't know. The Elders had asked him to go with them, and he had agreed at once. He always wanted to be with her, he added.

Leaving the Slantwall Settlement, they walked across the Sector, on a path along the Sector's metal floor that paralleled some of Alaina's prior wanderings along the ceiling walkways. They passed the Blue Dial Settlement, which faced the three huge dials that turned continuously in patterns that the settlers could not understand and therefore worshipped. Next they passed the Moaning Tube Settlement, placed alongside the equally enigmatic cylinder that echoed with strange sounds from somewhere outside the Sector. They went through the passageway that crossed the divider between Sector Four and Section Two, then diagonally across that Sector, with its two functioning and one abandoned settlement—the product of a now-forgotten war among the settlers —and through another passageway into Sector One.

As soon as they emerged, they saw a body hanging from the rungs of a ladder, about ten meters off the floor. They stopped, and Cardery told Alaina to look up at it. It was Maggers. His heavy head hung down facing the floor, its eyes bulging, blood dripping from its nose and mouth. She felt a somber sorrow for this harmless man, who wanted only to escape the scorn of his family and supposed friends. Alaina wondered what had happened to the Old Man, but she dared not ask.

"This is a man who was caught wandering," said Cardery. "How does that make you feel?"

Alaina asked what he was doing when he was caught, and was told that he was stealing food.

"He must have been hungry," she said. She would not say any more. They might stop her from wandering, but she would not let them control her thoughts or compel her words.

That night, Firany visited her at her dormitory. He sat with her in the narrow dining room, now empty and illuminated only by the thread-thin shafts of light that came through the shuttered window. They held hands, but no more—Firany invariably obeyed the General Rules. He urged her to be compliant and contrite, to apologize to Doramund and admit that she had been wrong to wander. The Elders were extremely angry with her, he reported, and were prepared to punish her severely. But Alaina found it difficult to listen to him. She kept hearing the sound of the machinery droning steadily around her, somehow containing, in an undertone, the reverberating metal voice of the Controller. She tried to look into Firany's furtive eyes, but he kept them averted until he left her, with a repeated entreaty for her to be cooperative.

When Alaina returned from work the next day, all three Elders were waiting for her at her dormitory, together with Milaren, another member of the welding crew. Doramund, with his fleshy visage congealed into a mask of animosity, declared that they had decided on her punishment. Cabillar looked vaguely embarrassed and Gorten, the third elder, was impassive. "You are to be placed in leg irons for the rest of your life," Doramund continued. "You will sleep in them, eat in them, work in them and walk in them. You won't be able to run, you won't be able to climb, and you won't be able to wander. Your days of disobedience are over."

Milaren bound her hands and feet with rope, measured her ankles for the leg irons, and left her lying on her bed. She missed dinner, but it didn't matter—she was despondent to the point of nausea. A few hours later, Milaren returned with the leg irons. He told her, in a quiet voice, that he was angry about the way that she'd been treated and reassured her that ankle bracelets were made from the most lightweight metal that the Controller could fabricate. He had put cushioning inside them so they would not abrade her flesh. But the chain between them, as prescribed by the Elders, was only fifteen centimeters long. When Alaina shuffled to the bathroom and back, at an agonizingly slow pace, her ankle bracelets clearly visible below her calf-length sleeping garment, the three other girls smirked and giggled at her. "Now you look really special," Batona said, with a self-satisfied grin.

Three days later, while Alaina was at work with the cleaning crew, the Controller stopped functioning once more. Darkness and silence descended on the Sector like a suffocating blanket. There was a momentary pause as everyone waited for the machinery to start again, to reassure them, as it had before, that this was simply a momentary incident, too brief and inexplicable to be significant. But the impenetrable tenebrosity pressed down without remorse, and a jumbled whimpering, muttering and shuffling rose up into the silence. Patterns of grey and orange pulsated across Alaina's occluded vision, seemingly conjured up by the sounds of misery and panic that were pullulating from the Settlement.

The surprise and terror that Alaina shared with the other residents rapidly gave way to scarlet fury. She might have escaped in the darkness, she might have been able to find the Old Man, but now she was completely helpless. Then someone called her name and came up close to her. It was her betrothed, Firany. He explained that he began searching for her as soon as the darkness descended, that he wanted to be with her, to help her and protect her. The next moment a loud voice reverberated down the street: "Go to your homes. The Elders want you to return to your homes. They will find out what is wrong."

"Come on, Alaina," said Firany. "I'll help you get home."

"I have no home," she answered savagely.

Once again her name was called. This time it was Garnax and Milaren, who said that Harcar, Tema and another person would be joining them. "I have my welding iron," Garnax said. "It's working 'cause it operates on batteries. I can't get your ankle bracelets off without burning your legs, but I can cut the chain. Here, sit right next to this house, and we'll stand around you so no one can see."

A candescent sensation shot through her body as Garnax lifted her leg up in his hand. "Look away," he said. She did, but she could see the welding iron's glow reflected in the metal sheet that formed the building's wall and she could feel the heat wrap around her calf and ankle. Then he lifted her other leg and turned on the welding iron once again. The chain clanked softly to the floor and her punitive disability was reduced to lightweight ankle bracelets. As the welding iron clicked off, she jumped up and embraced Garnax, noting Firany's sour, helpless expression in the disappearing glow.

Someone went past them, shouting once again that everyone should return to their homes. Then Harcar and Tema arrived, identifying themselves by voice. With them was Kefali, a young woman from the nursing crew, and another woman whose name Alaina didn't recognize.

"There's some sort of light at the Moaning Tube Settlement," said Tema. "We saw it when we looked down one of the streets. It's the only light besides a few small red lights on the floor, but we don't know what it is. Do you, Alaina? Garnax said that you'd spoken to the Controller, that it told you things you'd never heard before."

"Yes, I did," Alaina said, "but it didn't say anything about the Moaning Tube Settlement. I don't know what that light is." She paused, and suddenly a scintillating sense of ecstasy—somehow connected to the detachment of her chain, but much more powerful—surged through her body. "Wait, I do know. The Moaning Tube's a ventilator. The Old Man—never mind who he is —told me that. It brings us fresh air from the surface. If there's a light coming from it, then the Controller's opened the way up to surface, like it told me it would. We can escape."

Alaina couldn't see the faces of the seven people she was speaking to, but she could feel the astonishment radiating from them.

"We don't know if the surface is habitable. The Controller says it isn't," Garnax answered.

"The Controller doesn't know. Its information comes from a closed loop. It admitted that to us."

"But then we don't know, one way or the other." This came from Kefali, or maybe from the other woman.

"We have to take a chance. All the Controller told me is that it would open up the way. If we want to escape, we have to try. And we have to go now."

THE HEATSTROKE LINE

"But we need to get our things," said Tema.

"We can't wait," Alaina responded, with increasing urgency. "We don't know how long the lights will stay off or the Moaning Tube will stay open."

"Anyway," said Garnax, "if we go back to our houses, the Elders may stop us from leaving. Didn't you hear, they want everyone to go back home and stay there."

"Let's go," said Harcar, in a gentle but insistent tone. "If the Tube stays open, we can come back later."

The eight of them set out across the floor. Garnax carried his welding iron, but decided not to turn it on, for fear that someone would see it and detain them. So Milaren, who was older and seemed to have an intuitive feel for the distances and spaces, took the lead. Firany pressed close to Alaina, more from fear than from desire, she decided, but—perhaps for just that reason—she raised no objection. Once past the buildings of the Settlement, they saw a line of red emergency lights traversing the Sector's floor in a pattern that bore no apparent relationship to any of the settlements. Far in the distance, a tiny glowing rectangle floated in the enormous darkness that the Sector had become—the light from the Moaning Tube, a beckoning, mellifluous proclamation of potential freedom.

They passed the Blue Dial Settlement, visible only because a few of the residents had managed to find welding irons or similar devices that sent jittery beams of light bouncing off the metal houses. The woman who had come with Harcar, Tema and Kefali said that this was her home settlement—she had moved to the Slantwall Settlement when she got married.

"What about your husband?" Tema asked. "Didn't you want him along?"

"I hate him," she responded, in a tone of rage that seemed to burn into the darkness.

After that, they walked in silence until they neared the Moaning Tube. A gentle ocher light was flowing from an opening that had formed at the Tube's rounded base. Because the houses had been built to one side of the Tube, the eight of them could move toward the Tube along the Settlement's periphery. The space directly in front of the Tube, however, was occupied by several hundred people, all of whom seemed to be staring at the fulgent opening in hapless wonder. Milaren came to a halt, and the others clustered around him.

"We need to find a way to get through the crowd," he whispered.

"Follow me," said Harcar. He started shouting in a deep, commanding voice: "Make way. The Elders of the Slantwall and Blue Dial Settlements have sent us to investigate. Step aside, by order of the Elders, step aside, we're coming through."

The crowd dutifully parted, and they walked past all the people, through the opening, which was taller than a person, and into the muted but enveloping glow. Then they looked up. The Tube extended higher than the ceiling of the Sector, higher than the distance from the ceiling to the floor of Sector Three, its end invisible in the soft, pervasive light. Along one side of the interior was a narrow ladder, beginning at ground level and running up the Tube's entire length. Several of them gasped in dismay, and even Garnax and Harcar hesitated.

"We have to climb," Alaina said. "I'm used to it, I'll lead the way."

Firany, still beside her, started whimpering. "I can't do it, Alaina, there's no way I can go up that high."

Alaina paused, then something came to her. "Listen," she said. "You have to do it. I think the Controller's going to commit suicide. Maybe not this time—maybe it will turn everything on again—but sooner or later it's going to take its own advice, and anyone who stays behind will die."

She started climbing, at a slow pace for her so that the others could follow right behind, her metal anklets clattering occasionally against the ladder's rungs. Garnax went next, then Milaren, then Tema and Harcar, then Kefali and the woman from the Blue Dial Settlement. But Firany stayed behind, shaking his head, his upturned eyes filling gradually with hapless tears. With six people below her, there was nothing Alaina could do but glance down from time to time at his rapidly diminishing form.

They climbed for what seemed like a long while through the cylinder of light, until a blank ceiling appeared above them and the ladder ended at a platform. One by one, they lifted themselves over the edge until they were gathered in a group again. They were facing a wide, dimly lit corridor curving gradually to one side. After looking down its length as far as they were able, Garnax took the lead, and the others followed in an unnecessarily straight line.

"I'm afraid," said Kefali. "I never should have come."

"You had to come," said the Blue Dial woman. "Just like me."

"We wanted to come," said Tema. "We want to be free."

The corridor ended in a round room, with a few dials and some indecipherable symbols on the walls. Three further corridors branched out from the far side of the room, each one filled with a slightly different type of light.

"Which way?" said Garnax.

Alaina looked down each corridor in turn, staring at the varied glows, trying to tell which one was singing to her. That one, the one on the right. "Let's go that way," she said.

It took them less than a minute to reach the end of the corridor Alaina had chosen. Above them was another tube, much shorter than the first one, with a blue, illuminated ceiling at the top.

Again, they gathered together in tremulous hesitation.

"There's something very strange about that ceiling," Garnax said.

There was a pause.

"It's not a ceiling, it's the sky," said Tema, and Alaina, leaping at the ladder, clambered to the top in seconds.

CHAPTER THREE: THE JUNGLE

Light, blinding light, light that burned her eyes and turned the surrounding blues and greens to liquid. The light was chattering, assaulting her with a pandemonium of unknown sounds. Her body heated up in different places, first one and then another, surges of heat that made her soft, loosely fitting work garment cling to her in a strangely suffocating way. She staggered, felt the uneven ground beneath her feet and fell to her knees. Somewhere in the distance one of the others was gasping, and another was speaking words that she could not discern. She was in pain—she wanted to find the tube, to climb back down into the cool, gently lit containment she had always known.

Lifting both arms, she shaded her tearing eyes, closed them with a squishing, straining sound, then opened them gradually and tried to look at nothing but the ground in front of her. Short, thin shards of green, obviously the grass that she had read about but never seen, moved slowly back and forth, and something small and fast went slithering between them. After a while, she became aware that the heat she thought was emanating from inside her was actually moving over her, flowing toward her body from indeterminate directions. The steady chattering resolved

itself into a medley of unknown sounds, a steady rhythmic call—
was that a bird?—strange clicking noises and an intermittent cry
or croak. She could look around now without pain, so long as she
did not look directly at the savage sun, but the light was more
intense than any she had ever seen before.

She was in the middle of an open space, roughly circular and
somewhat larger than her Settlement. It was covered with grass,
not evenly but in assorted clumps and furrows. All around it was
an imbricated mass of trees and vines, intensely green and
pulsating against the sky's blue backdrop. There was something
malevolently alive about the way the branches intertwined, as if
they had momentarily stopped their writhing, squirming motion
when she looked at them, and would resume when she turned
away or closed her eyes. The sounds now made more sense than
they had before, but her realization that they came from living
things only amplified the threatening vitality of her surroundings.
She felt exposed, a pallid, indoor creature caught under a
remorseless sun in a blazing infinity of space. Then it occurred to
her that her question—the Old Man's question—had been
answered. She was alive. The surface, terrifying though it seemed,
was habitable. For some reason, this thought restored some of the
courage that the sun had drained from her.

By now, all her companions had emerged from the tube and
begun to steady themselves from the initial shock of their
sensations. They clustered together in stunned silence. Tema
asked what they should do, whether they should explore the
surface or go back into the Tube. "If Alaina's right, if the
Controller's going to fail, there's no point going back" said Garnax.
"We're here now," Harcar agreed. "We should see what's going on."

At first, there seemed to be no break in the circular wall of
jungle that surrounded them, but after they had wandered
tentatively around the clearing, Tema discovered a narrow
pathway through the boscage. They looked at each other,
somewhat blankly, and then set out in single file again, with
Garnax in the lead and Alaina next. The trees' branches interlaced
over their heads and they walked on in shadow, with sudden
shafts of sunlight puncturing the gloom and flickering out behind
them as they moved. They waited for the path to lead them
somewhere but it went on, sloping slightly downward, without
relief or alteration. Kefali said that she was feeling ill and wanted
to turn back, but Harcar told her that they had been walking less
than half an hour, and needed to go on.

THE HEATSTROKE LINE

There was a sudden snarl and something dark brown and alive flew across the path and carried Garnax into the underbrush with a resounding crash. A spray of blood rose up into the air. The creature stood poised above him on all fours, as he lay on his back, his arms and legs flailing helplessly. Then it bared reddened teeth and sank them deep into his throat. Alaina heard a scream behind her and turned to see a second creature tearing at someone—she could not tell who—as the others scattered, hurling themselves at the jungle and floundering to penetrate its foliage. The creature that was killing Garnax turned toward her—it was huge, with a long snout, yellow eyes and bare brown skin. Fear exploded inside her and she ran forward down the path, away, away from the ravenous monstrosity.

After she had gone some distance, feeling weighed down for the first time by her ankle bracelets, she turned to look behind her, sweating and gasping into the suffocating heat. The creature was standing in the path, staring at her. Suddenly, and for some reason to her disbelief, it bounded forward. She turned and ran, but she could hear the heavy pattering of its feet get louder as it closed on her. The teeth would sink into her throat, it was going to kill her—no, no, she wouldn't let this happen. She leapt for a large, overhanging tree branch and pulled herself up until her feet were resting on its surface. The creature reached the tree in two leaps and jumped up at her, its jaws snapping in the air a few centimeters from her feet. A further surge of fear sent her climbing up the tree, from branch to branch, higher and higher, as far from those deathly jaws as she could be.

When she stopped, sobbing in drenched exhaustion, her work garment clinging tightly to her body, she was near the top of the tree, some thirty meters from the ground, and the branches were beginning to get dangerously thin. The creature was no longer in sight, but it might still be there, since she could only see patches of the ground through the intervening leaves. She felt no fear about the height—the ceiling walkways in Sector Three, where she had spent so much time wandering, were higher, but the sense of open space unnerved her. Then she took some deep breaths and, for the first time, looked out into the distance.

In one direction, a wall of convoluted foliage rose up above her, but on the other sides, the ground fell away, opening tremendous vistas. She gazed in amazement over an unbroken, undulating surface of variegated greens that disappeared into an impossibly distant haze beneath the crystalline blue sky. For a moment, she thought she might be looking a strangely curdled ocean—the ocean had been described as green in some of the stories that she had heard or read—and then realized that she was looking down on the tops of trees that were massed together in a dense, seemingly endless jungle. As she stared, she discerned two delicate, widely separated wisps of flowing greyness that spiraled upward to the sky. Besides that there was nothing but the jungle to be seen. The creature that had sent her scrambling up the tree, and even the fear it had induced, were now forgotten, and she stared at this vast new world with a sense of growing exaltation. She was free, free of her narrow, metal settlement, more free than she had ever been able to imagine in the fantasies that had sustained her sad, afflicted days at home, her confinement in the orphans' dormitory, and the more explicit incarceration of her punishment.

Clinging to her branch, she gazed out in rapt astonishment until the sky began to darken and the sun, although still hurtful to her sidelong glance, began to redden and drop down toward the undulating greenery. Fear seized her once again. It seemed as if this infinitely large and wondrous world was starting to malfunction, like the Controller's narrow pallid world below. Then she realized that this was the onset of the night, the night that the settlers attempted to duplicate with house shutters that closed against the steady illumination of the machinery that serviced and enslaved them. She watched with renewed fascination as the sky turned purple and then black, a crescent moon appeared above the darkened treetop surface and the clustered, multilayered stars emerged and filled the nighttime sky.

It was only then that she realized that she was hungry, thirsty and exhausted. She was alone, and lonely. Garnax was dead, but she wondered what had happened to the others. She was hungry and her mouth was dry, but what she really needed most, she recognized, was rest, so she climbed slowly down until she reached a broader branch that formed a commodious hollow with the tree's substantial trunk and then, using the discipline that she had developed through her wanderings, she suppressed her thirst and hunger,curled up on her narrow perch and went to sleep.

She woke up suddenly. The sun had pierced the canopy of green and struck her with a brilliant, twanging beam. Something was buzzing near her head, her legs were sore, she had had an odd, itchy welt on her upper thigh, beneath one of several tears in her work garment, and she was hungrier and thirstier than ever. In a state that combined curiosity and desperation, she climbed down to the lowest branch and let herself drop onto the forest floor.

The path still stretched behind her, possibly leading to the beasts and definitely leading to the settlements. Neither one meant freedom, so she turned away and set out in the opposite direction. After continuing through the jungle for a way, the path crossed some jumbled rocks, resumed beyond them, then ran along a narrow stream that sparkled with the scattered fragments of sunlight that reached it through the trees. She quenched her thirst with the warm, sienna-tasting water, washed her face, forearms, and aching legs, and went on through the pools of heated air and ever changing sounds that lay along the path.

There was a rustling sound behind her. She glanced back, saw nothing, started to run forward, hit something hard and soft, and fell down on the ground with a cry of terrorized defeat. When she looked up, there were people all around her. They were large and tanned, dressed or half-dressed in some sort of stiff brown material that she had never seen. The men were grasping long brown rods with pointed metal at the end, the women shorter, thinner rods held in a curve by wire. Several of them started laughing, then they began talking to each other in words that meant nothing to her but sounded strangely musical in tone. A huge man with a grizzled face reached down to her and fingered the lower edge of her work garment. Another pointed to her ankle bracelets and there was more talk and more laughter.

The blazing realization that the surface was not only habitable but inhabited had overcome Alaina's initial sense of fear. Now she sensed that she needed to assert her own humanity and independence. She should speak to them, even if they wouldn't understand. "Who are you?" she said. "How long have you been living up here?"

They fell silent for a moment, and she wondered if she had made a serious mistake. Then, to her surprise, they all turned to one younger man. He was bigger than Garnax, bare-chested and heavily muscled like the other men, but he had a thoughtful face and melodic blue-green eyes. He approached her, squatted down —she realized she should have gotten to her feet—and said a few words that sounded like her language, but which she didn't understand. When she stared at him blankly, several of the people started laughing once again, and he looked up at them with a good-natured smile. Then he turned back to her and gestured with his hands, opening and lifting them in a gesture that she understood as inquiry. Alaina pointed down into the ground. Expressions of astonishment broke out, and Alaina wondered whether she had made another error. But the man smiled at her, pointed to himself, and said, slowly and distinctly, "Kam Rokay Chamron." He pointed to her and she said "Alaina."

As she said her name, she felt something awakening inside her. She smiled, and then, without even thinking, pointed to her stomach, then to her mouth, and made a chewing motion. There was an appreciative murmur from the others and everyone began reaching into bags that they were carrying around their waists, bags made of the same brown material as their clothes. Kam stood up, Alaina did as well, and he began handing her objects, obviously food, that she had never seen before. By now, she was hardly surprised that none of it consisted of the smoothly processed substances that were produced by the Controller. She tried each one cautiously, spitting out most and gagging on some, to the genial amusement of the group. Finally, she found something she could tolerate—something round, sweet and mealy —and she hungrily consumed several in succession. Watching her eat was not as much fun as watching her gag, and the people began talking to each other again, but obviously about her. They kept pointing somewhere in the distance, then at her, and then off in a different direction.

When she indicated that she'd finished eating, they all got in line along the path and signaled her to go with them, right behind the large man who had first approached her. Her fear of the beasts was gone. These people, she felt certain, were a hunting party and would kill any creature that attacked them. She wondered whether she was truly free or whether they saw her as a prisoner, and were being pleasant because she was obviously not a threat. In any case, she thought, she was free from the confines of the life that she had led so far, and that had been so filled with bitterness. She wanted to glance back at Kam, to look once more into his lambent eyes, but she restrained herself.

They walked along the path for what seemed like a long way, although none of the people showed any sign of weariness, and finally emerged into a clearing. In the middle were buildings— houses, evidently—made of long, round, dark brown objects piled one atop the other. They were tree trunks, she realized—these people built their houses from the trees that they found lying in

THE HEATSTROKE LINE

the jungle, no, that they cut down. Above the doorway of each house was a metal object of some kind, sometimes a small wheel, sometimes a piece of rusted machinery. The grey wisp she had seen from her tree of refuge was here, rising upward from among the houses, and as they approached she saw that it was emerging from a large, steadily burning fire. Every house had dark green plants in front of it, and hanging from them were some of things that the people had offered her to eat. Carcasses of dead animals were draped across metal poles at various places—something that looked like the deer that she had seen in illustrations, an animal she didn't recognize, and one of the creatures that had killed Garnax and pursued her. In the space between the houses and the surrounding jungle were small square plots filled with different plants, these tall and lighter green, or with animals that she recognized as sheep and goats enclosed by fences that were also made of tree trunks. The village occupied twice as much space the Slantwall Settlement, but since the houses were more widely spaced, there seemed to be about half as many, at the most.

As they reached the fire, which intensified the heated air around it, two older people, who seemed to be a married couple, emerged out of the largest of the tree-trunk houses. The big man who was the leader of the hunting party bowed his head and spoke to them at length, while the others melted into the larger crowd of people that had suddenly materialized. Alaina, with the reddening sense that she was on display, became aware of her torn garments, her matted hair and what she assumed was a bedraggled, desperate appearance. There was further conversation, the man and woman said something she couldn't hear and a moment later there was a bright, ringing sound that somehow sounded like the sky. Looking toward its source, Alaina saw a large metal disk swinging back and forth, being struck by a woman with a hammer. More people began emerging from the houses, and in a few moments, Alaina realized, all the people in the village had gathered in the space around the fire.

Then, rather remarkably, the man and woman spoke in unison, their differently-pitched voices uniting into something that sounded close to song. When they were done, they looked out toward the gathered crowd. There was a momentary silence as the shuffling, muttering individuals congealed into a single entity, and then a roar of approval rose up from its depths. The man and woman both nodded and pointed to a small house immediately beside their own. The leader of the hunting party led Alaina up to it, then stepped aside, bowing even more deeply than he had before. Two women came up to her and ran their hands quickly up and down her body. Then they nodded to the married leaders and motioned her to go inside.

The inside of the house was dark, and as Alaina's eyes readjusted from the brightness of the sun-saturated clearing, she saw an old woman, with white hair, a wrinkled, kindly face and bony hands, sitting in the middle of the room. The woman motioned for Alaina to sit down in front of her. Then, to Alaina's surprise and delight, Kam entered and sat down opposite her. He spoke to the old woman, and she answered in a surprisingly sweet, youthful voice. Then she turned to Alaina.

"You speak the Old Tongue?" she asked.

"Yes, if that's what you call it."

"And you come from under."

"Yes, from the settlements, the settlements that the Controller operates."

The woman spoke rapidly to Kam, who responded briefly, then turned back to Alaina. "There were others from under, where the, the . . ." She paused then circled her arms and moved them up and down.

"The tubes?" Alaina suggested. "Yes, any group of settlements needs ventilation tubes. Are any of the others here?"

"No, dead. We thought all dead."

Kam spoke to the woman, and she turned back to Alaina.

"What those?" she asked, pointing to Alaina's ankle bracelets. "You liter?"

"I don't know what you mean by liter."

"Liter, liter. Big person, person in front."

After hesitating for a moment, Alaina said, "Yes, leader," trying to convince herself that the difficulty of explaining the real reason for her ankle bracelets justified her agreeing to the woman's—or Kam's—flattering mistake.

The woman turned to Kam, and said the word "leader," this time correctly, then said some words in her own language. To Alaina's surprise, Kam carefully repeated the word, the first word he had said that she understood. Then he pointed to her and said: "Alaina." The old woman nodded.

"Alaina," she said, "we want you help us." She used a word that Alaina had never heard, and point in the distance. "They fight us, want to make us slaves."

THE HEATSTROKE LINE

"Yes, help," said Kam.

"But how can I help you?" said Alaina, facing Kam's impressive form and recalling all the powerfully built people who had found her.

"Near here, old city. City of people who spoke the Old Tongue. Now empty. Broken. But many things there. We get some, for houses. Maybe, maybe . . ." She made a throwing motion with her arm, then a pulling motion. Alaina shook her head to show she didn't understand and there was a pause. The old woman spoke to Kam, who stepped out of the house—Alaina was afraid that he was leaving for some reason—then came back with his spear, bowed to the old woman for the first time, then slid the spear gently across Alaina's lap, holding the metal point in his hand.

"Weapons?" Alaina asked. "Oh, weapons. You want me to show you if there's anything in that abandoned city that you can use as weapons."

"Yes, weeponz," said the woman. She looked at Kam, pointed to the spear and pronounced the word for him. Once again, he repeated it.

"And if I can do that, will you make me a member of your, your settlement?" Alaina asked, pointing all around her.

The woman smiled and said something to Kam, who laughed aloud. Then she turned back to Alaina. "You not allowed bring weeponz in my house. But you bring weeponz."

"No, no I didn't" she objected, hurt by the apparent accusation.

"Yes, big weeponz," the woman said, and pointed to Alaina's head. A surge of pride rose up inside her. All at once, and for the first time since she had reached the surface, she felt strong, and she thought that maybe she truly had been a leader of some sort when she had escaped from the Controller. Maybe she could be one here as well. "Yes, maybe I can help you. I'll be glad to try." Then, with a sudden surge of enthusiasm, and without any prior reflection, she asked "Can Kam come with me?"

They both laughed. Now she had obviously made a mistake.

"No Kam," he said. "Rokay."

The old woman spoke. "He is son of my son. Now he is little Kam. I am Kamercada. I teach him. I teach him the Old Tongue. I teach him the magic. Some day he take my place."

"What about your son—his father?" Alaina felt impelled to ask, her mistake having obviously produced no bad results.

"My son, his father, dead—in fight. Mother dead—in hunt."

163

"My parents are dead too. But not for such good reasons. I mean, they weren't brave."

"But you brave," the old woman said. "And you go with Rokay to old city and help us." She spoke to her grandson, who stood up and led Alaina out of the house. He smiled at her and took her past the blazing fire in the center of the settlement to another house, also quite small. When she went inside, she found a neatly arranged rectangle of blankets, clearly meant to be a bed, the food that she had liked, and a pile of the brown material that all the people wore. Rokay motioned, indicating that it was all for her. He turned to leave and Alaina, to her own astonishment, said, "Rokay."

He spun around, smiled again, then engulfed her in his enormous arms and kissed her. She thought she should resist, but she responded. He smelled vaguely of sweat and foliage; his arms and lips felt cool, his tongue extremely warm. The room spun round, and she heard a rhythmic pounding that shattered into jagged, flashing lights. Then he left without a word, and she sat down amidst the objects signaling her new identity and the challenges that faced her in the days ahead.

CHAPTER 19

By the time Dan finished reading Deborah's story, it was late at night. He realized that he should get to sleep, since he had to wake up at the usual time so that Hiram could drive him to the lab. But his mind was racing. The story was certainly not what he had expected. On the basis of Deborah's perceptiveness and grace, he thought her writing would focus on subtle human interactions, that it would resemble Jane Austen or Henry James. But it was entirely different, and it gave him a strange feeling. To be sure, the story was intended as escapist fiction—she had told him that. But there was a certain wildness to it, a kind of irresponsibility which he found disconcerting. She seemed so willing to wipe out most of the human race and nearly all its culture in the interest of simplicity, to embrace disaster in order to contrive a pathetic little dictatorship that her character could overcome and a primitive new world where she could find adventure and romance.

As he thought more deeply about his own reaction to her story, he realized that he felt a sense of jealousy. Not jealousy toward the Tarzan-like figure that her character was obviously going to fall in love with, though. Dan was satisfied that his feelings for Deborah, however strong, were not sexual in nature. His sense of jealousy, he realized, was directed toward Hiram. Deborah, despite her self-containment, her refined sensibility, and her love of literature, was more like Hiram than Dan had realized. There was a wildness about all the people here, something that generated monomaniacal attitudes that displaced or eclipsed their concern for other human beings. Hiram's frenetic commitment to maintaining American culinary culture, and his bizarre project of destroying people's rice crops so that they would stop using non-American recipes, was more typical than strange down here below the Heatstroke Line.

Dan was fortunate, he thought, that the project he had been forced to work on was the one constructive enterprise he had encountered in this crazy, overheated place, the one thing to which he could devote his own efforts without reluctance. Maybe they had known that this was the only task for which they could enlist his willing participation. And then, suddenly, all the things that had been bothering him about the insect lab came together in a pattern—the reason he had been kidnapped, Wolfson's reassurance that he need only try his best, Lyons' patriotic diatribes about American inventiveness and ingenuity, Paul's evident reluctance to describe his own research, the implausible choice of genetic engineering as a strategy, and everyone's, even Matthew's, relentless hatred of the Canadians. Of course. The lab wasn't trying to eradicate the biter bugs for the benefit of the people who lived below the Heatstroke Line. It was trying to breed cold-resistant bugs that could be let loose in Canada. The outbreak of biter bugs in East Montana really had come from the Confederacies, if not from the Birmingham lab then from a coordinate facility. But it hadn't been directed at Mountain America, a place for which the people here harbored no particular hostility. It had been a shipment of bugs that was being sent to Canada, maybe as a test of some early variety of cold resistant strain that the people in the lab had bred. They had sent it on an aircraft that had malfunctioned on its way and made an emergency landing in East Montana, which was the reason why jet fuel had been found near the source of the outbreak. Dan realized that everyone in the lab spoke about controlling the bugs, not eradicating them. They had probably been trained to use the word "controlling" because it meant two different things, and thus eliminated the danger that they would make a slip when speaking to him. Only Wolfson, who was obviously too cagey to slip up, had allowed himself to use the outright falsity of "eradicate."

Now the idea of relying on genetic engineering made sense. It was a highly complicated means—an unnecessarily complicated one—of producing a fatal trait that would wipe out a species. But it was a plausible strategy for producing a trait that would enable a species to expand its habitat. And used for that purpose, in conjunction with selective breeding, it was probably within the technological capacities of the Birmingham lab, even with its collection of amateur and misfit scientists. Giving Dan some time to do his own research on eradicating the biter bugs was just a ruse. What they were really using him for was to instruct their own researchers on the most recent and advanced techniques of genetic engineering so that they could produce their cold-resistant bugs. That was why they had kidnapped him—if they had asked for his voluntary help, he might have rejected genetic engineering as a means of eradicating the bugs on pragmatic grounds, and they never could have obtained his help had they told him the true purpose of their efforts. The realization that they had forced him to assist them in this vicious project made him feel nauseous.

But what could he do? He could try to sabotage the lab to stop them from making progress, but it would be virtually an act of suicide and it was unlikely to accomplish very much. They were obviously watching him to protect against this possibility—Lyons had told him that on his first day at the lab. The idea of running around the lab smashing equipment was absurd—Paul and Matthew would stop him in a second—and the people in the lab, even with their lack of formal training, were certainly smart enough to detect any outright misinformation that he tried to foist on them. Then it occurred to Dan that the ideal way to stop the project was to tell the Canadians about it. With their military control of the air, they could bomb the lab—presumably at night when no one was there—and bring the whole sick enterprise to an immediate halt.

A moment later, Dan realized that this was his way to escape from the Confederacies, his way to get back home. All he had to do was to tell the Canadians that he had information that was essential to their national security and that he would reveal it to them once they rescued him. They could easily send a helicopter squadron into Birmingham—no one here would be able to oppose the Canadian armed forces. After being a prisoner for all these months, after being a powerless victim, he finally had a way of fighting back, a bargaining chip he could use to secure his freedom. His sense of revulsion about the project he was forced to work on was succeeded by a surge of energized excitement. He would get away from these people and he would pay them back for killing Stuart and making him so miserable. Furthermore, he would do it in a way he could be proud of, a way that prevented a despicable act of terrorism. He would be a part of history after all, just as he had hoped when he had so stupidly decided to do biter bug research and reach out to the Confederacies.

But who should he contact? He didn't know anyone in the Canadian government. That probably wasn't a serious problem, he reflected. Jarrel Lucan and Dean Horace at the University of

South Baffin Island knew him well, and they were expecting to hear from him in the next few weeks about whether he was interested accepting their invitation to join the USBI faculty. They would open a message from him immediately and they were important, well-connected people. Once they found out that it was a matter of national security, they could easily contact the appropriate authorities. The real problem was finding an open link so that he could send messages outside the Confederacies. He had already tried this once, at the Battle of the Bulge Parade, and he had been on the lookout for another opportunity almost constantly since then. Well, he thought, he would simply have to re-double his efforts. It had always been important to contact his family and let them know that he was alive and where he was. But now it was a matter of actually escaping his imprisonment, and maybe of his ultimate survival. He would need only a few minutes —he had to find an open link.

Filled with a new sense of resolve, he was about to try to get to sleep when he remembered Deborah. She would expect him to give her some reaction to her story. But what could he tell her without revealing the realization that the story had triggered? And once he did so, how could he expect her to keep the secret? How could he expect her to conceal the fact that he was trying to destroy an enterprise to which her own family was committed? That would have been unreasonable even when he was convinced that her sensibility was so much closer to his than it was to any of her family members. Now he was no longer so sure. Her story made him realize that he didn't know her nearly as well as he thought he did. But she knew him, and her perceptiveness suddenly assumed a threatening quality. No matter what he said, no matter how hard he tried to disguise the realization that her story had triggered, she was likely to perceive the truth. And if she told her parents that he knew the real purpose of the research project, he would lose any chance he had of communicating with the Canadians and securing his escape. In fact, Hiram would undoubtedly tell Wolfson, and Wolfson would probably have him executed.

Time was of the essence, Dan decided. Every day in Deborah's presence represented an ongoing risk. He had to get his message to the Canadian government as soon as possible—he had to get access to an open link. Suddenly, he realized where he was most likely to find one. It was Deborah's desk unit. She often left the unit running when she left her room. He had seen that several times through her partially open door when he passed it on his way up and down the stairs. Why had that never occurred to him before? Had he been so concerned about his relationship with her that he didn't want to take advantage of her for his own purposes, even if those purposes involved contacting his family? And now that it did occur to him, would waiting for an opportunity, treating her as an opponent that he had to overcome, poison their relationship?

Well, his fear of her perceptiveness had probably poisoned it already, he reflected. What had always appealed to him most about Deborah was the way she could discern his thoughts and motivations, the things he learned about himself from interacting with her. Now her attentiveness and perception was a danger, a threat to his newly discovered opportunity to escape from his imprisonment and to his new determination to disrupt the research that he had previously viewed as beneficial. He could not help feeling sad, but he had to separate himself from her. There was simply too much at stake for himself, for his family and for what remained of the limited places on this beleaguered planet where people could still lead reasonably pleasant lives.

Dan never got to sleep at all that night, and his fatigue was evident the next morning on the way to the lab. But Hiram was friendlier and more sympathetic toward Dan than he had ever been before. He acknowledged the tense nature of yesterday's meeting, apologized for failing to give Dan more advance warning about it, despite having been instructed not to do so, and spoke with enthusiasm about their new working relationship, which he was certain Nathaniel would approve. Fortunately, the only instruction Dan was asked to provide at the lab that day was some simple guidance to Dave Uberti about computer analysis of genetic information. Left to himself, and supposedly pursuing his own research efforts, Dan sat back in his desk chair and stared into space, bleary and light-headed for lack of sleep. He was clearly in no condition to do any work and besides, he had absolutely no motivation left for doing it, now that he knew this work had no purpose and that the lab's real goal was so despicable. He realized, however, that he would need to make a good show of continuing his efforts, that he couldn't let anyone suspect that he had figured out the truth.

Since he was in no condition to come up with a strategy for talking to Deborah about her story, Dan used his fatigue, which Hiram readily confirmed, as an excuse for leaving dinner early that evening and going to bed. A full night's sleep restored him, but it did not provide him with a solution to the problem. During the past two months, he had developed the habit of scripting conversations with Deborah in his mind when he was alone, either to prepare himself to answer her with the sincerity she expected, or to use her imagined responses as a way of understanding his reactions and himself more fully, or simply to create a sense of her presence when he wasn't with her. Now, he seemed unable to imagine any conversation that would make sense and seem even minimally genuine. Each time he tried, his thoughts became muddled and his mind slipped away from the inevitable confrontation.

He managed to avoid her for several days, pleading fatigue or work during dinner and going straight up to his bedroom when it was done. But he couldn't avoid Hiram since they drove to the lab together every morning. Still full of enthusiasm, Hiram told Dan that Nathaniel had approved their agreement and that he wanted to get started on destruction of the rice crop right away. But Dan's sense of revulsion toward the project had only intensified now that he knew the real purpose of the insect lab. In an effort to avoid doing anything definitive, he told Hiram he would need to inspect the rice fields before he could determine the best insect to use. That seemed reasonable to Hiram. Since the rains had ended and the roads were drying out, he said, they could travel in his car, and he arranged for them to go that coming Sunday.

The day before they left, Dan finally decided that he would simply have to talk to Deborah, and he waited for her after dinner in the living room. At first he thought she wasn't going to join him, but she finally came in and sat down on the couch in her usual position.

"Well, Deborah, I read your story," he began.

"Did you read it the night I gave it to you?"

"Yes." He paused. "I guess I wasn't sure I had anything useful to say to you about it. I don't read much science fiction, as you know."

"Don't be tense, Dan—you don't need to give me editorial comments. I shared the story with you because you asked me about it."

"Well, I appreciate that. It's very interesting, at least so far."

She looked at him, without responding. Something moved within him as he met her gaze, and, suddenly annoyed by his own sense of caution, he spoke on impulse.

THE HEATSTROKE LINE

"Alaina seemed pretty wild. It made me realize I don't know you very well. How much of you is in her?"

Deborah smiled briefly. "I'm not sure. I guess she's the person that I'd like to be. But I know I'll never have the chance."

"You mean because you can't live in her world."

"Because I have to live in mine."

"Do you ever think about making this world a better place, instead of imagining a different one?"

"Why is that important to you?"

Dan was about to answer, but he realized that he wasn't sure. His sense of caution returned; he was on dangerous ground.

"I was just wondering. Okay, I realize your story is escapist fiction. Maybe I'm just over-interpreting it."

He fell silent and Deborah, with a nod and a slight smile, got up and walked out of the room.

CHAPTER 20

Dan and Hiram left for their inspection of the rice fields early the next morning. They drove south, in a different direction from the one they took each day when going to the insect lab. For a short while, the streets looked essentially the same as Hiram's—large, fairly well-maintained brick or wood frame homes, with a few dilapidated or abandoned buildings interspersed among them. They passed a deserted shopping mall, the surface of its extensive parking lot buckling from the heat and punctured in places by invasive plants. Further on, past more residential streets, there were a few collapsing strip malls and then they linked up with a four-lane freeway whose two inner lanes had been kept in good repair. Dan realized it was the road that Joel Rinier had used when first bringing him into Birmingham-Victoria. Now that it was daylight, he could see that the road was lined, for a considerable distance from the city, with structures of various kinds, some of them quite large but nearly all abandoned and being slowly but inexorably torn apart by the invading foliage. They drove over a low, wooded ridge and then though a forest of dead, mottled pine trees, like the forest Dan had passed through in Mississippi-Meridian on his way to Birmingham.

Once beyond the forest, Hiram turned off the freeway and onto a one-lane road, scarred with potholes and repaired with uneven clumps of asphalt. It passed through scrubland and an occasional pasture dotted with emaciated cattle and patches of corn, soybeans or banana trees. One stretch of road was still under water, which posed a threat to Hiram's little car. He assured Dan that he was in immediate link contact with Nathaniel and that they would be quickly rescued if they had any trouble. Nonetheless, he got out of the car, tested the depth of the water by walking through it—he was wearing plastic sandals for this purpose, he explained—then got back in and drove across it very slowly.

THE HEATSTROKE LINE

Throughout the drive, Hiram was cheerfully friendly and conversational. He seemed relieved that he could drop his previous formality with Dan, since they were now engaged in a joint enterprise, and fall back on his natural sociability. But Dan found the situation disconcerting and bizarre. It was as if he was on a pleasant excursion with Stuart or one of his other friends— except that he was actually a prisoner, and on his way to commit an outrage. He wondered if he could knock Hiram out with a sudden blow, take the car, which he could drive now that Hiram had released the bio-lock, and reach the UFA. He would have to cross Middle Tennessee and one of the Kentucky Confederacies, which was probably too far. And maybe Hiram's telling him that they were in link contact with Wolfson was meant as a warning as well as a reassurance. It didn't matter; the whole idea was an adventure story fantasy. For several months, Dan had regularly indulged himself with violent fantasies of that sort toward Hiram. But for the first time now, he thought of him as Deborah's father, and the idea of killing him seemed less appealing. Besides, Dan had a much safer, more practical plan for escaping now—all he had to do was find an open link.

After a little more than two hours of driving, they arrived at the broad, nearly level stretch of land where the rice fields were located. Some rice was grown in Mountain America, but only in small plots along the rivers, since the rainfall was generally insufficient for this crop. As a result, when Hiram used the term "rice fields," it had conjured up in Dan's mind the image of the densely spaced, terraced rice paddies of South China or Indonesia. But those parts of the world were now uninhabited wastelands and the rice fields in front of him looked nothing like that. They were rectangles bounded by low, rusted metal walls, scattered at odd angles to each other across the flat terrain, with an irrigation ditch, apparently from the nearby river they had crossed, feeding into them. In the far distance, the smokestacks of a large power plant, nearly the same size as the one near the Forrests' house in Birmingham City, spewed roiling white smoke into the air. Rows of metal towers carrying electric lines marched across the landscape, and some apparently improvised wires ran down from the nearest towers to a line of houses that wound its way through the rice fields. The houses were made of weathered wood and were remarkably small—one room or two at the most. People dressed in white or yellow clothing were working in the fields, tending to the crop that had obviously been planted in the rainy season and was now on its way to maturity. They were moving slowly and stopped frequently to rest.

"I guess we need to get out of the car so you can take a closer look," said Hiram. Dan nodded in response. Hiram reached into the back seat for two stun guns in holsters and handed one to Dan. He put on the other and then, to Dan's surprise and discomfort, put his wrist link on open mode, took a GX gun from underneath his seat and put it behind his back under his loose fitting shirt. When they got out of the car, the heat hit Dan like a furnace blast. He had neglected to look at the car's external temperature indicator, which was on the far left of the instrument panel, but he now realized that it must be at least 120 degrees Fahrenheit outside. The air was filled with gnats, and also with various types of mosquitos, including aedes, psorophora and coquillettidia. As Dan looked out across the fields, the rising heat made the people's figures seem to quiver, and with their white and yellow clothing, they looked as if they were encased in flames.

Following Hiram, Dan walked slowly to the nearest metal-bounded rectangle, which was about thirty feet by sixty, and then bent over to examine the rice plants that were rising out of the water it contained. The people working there, and in the nearby fields, looked at the two of them suspiciously. About half were black, a much higher proportion that at the lab or in the government offices, Dan noted. The whites were deeply tanned, and all the people, even the younger ones, looked creased and weary. A number had visible biter bug scars on the arms or faces, perhaps because they periodically ran out of money to buy stun gun batteries, perhaps because the bugs sometimes came in swarms.

Dan had spent a considerable amount of time inspecting crops in Mountain America in order to deal with actual or potential insect infestations. The farmers were always happy to see him and as helpful as they possibly could be in providing any information he requested. On several occasions, when he had returned to check on a crop that had been rescued through his efforts, they had cheered or applauded when they saw him. But here, the people's suspicious looks, together with their obvious fatigue and poverty, made Dan feel sick to his stomach.

"You from the government?" one of them asked. Dan was surprised, since he and Hiram had come in a private car and were dressed informally. He was trying to think of some evasive answer when Hiram answered "Yes, we're from your government, the government of Birmingham-Victoria." Dan cringed, particularly when he saw that Hiram's answer began attracting a number of people from the nearby fields. As they slowly gathered round, with downtrodden but resentful expressions, Dan was overcome by a sense of physical danger. This was obviously the real reason Hiram wanted to be in direct contact with Wolfson, but what could he do to help them from his office in Birmingham City?

"Can you get us some different seeds?" an elderly black woman asked. "Ours don't grow so well, with the heat and all."

"But aren't they the same seeds you've always been using?" Hiram asked.

"Yeah, but it's getting hotter." Dan thought back to what Jarrel Lucan and Dean Horace had told him when he was at USBI.

"No it's not," said Hiram. "It just seems that way. You've got to figure out a way to grow these plants despite the heat. You're Americans—use your ingenuity."

The people—there were now about twenty of them—stared at Hiram blankly. Dan wondered whether they were about to kill him. He had the sudden thought to shout out that Hiram was trying to destroy their crops and that he was just a prisoner, as much a victim of the government as they were. After Hiram had been slaughtered, Dan could use Hiram's wrist link to contact the Canadians, then hide out with these people until he was rescued. It was just another fantasy, of course. If the people killed Hiram they would kill him too, long before he had the chance to give them any complicated explanations about his personal misfortunes.

"While we're talking," Hiram continued, "I want to urge you to stay true to the principles that made our nation great. Don't lose hope, don't forget your heritage, and don't cook un-American food. Things are going to get better for us—I promise you they will."

The people seemed to stir, but no one answered. Hiram turned toward Dan. "Have you seen what you need?" Dan, who really didn't need to see anything, nodded quickly and stood up. Then he and Hiram turned and began walking back toward the car. Dan fought the urge to run. He was covered with sweat and he could feel his skin crawling up and down his back. It was no more than a hundred feet back to the car, but it seemed like miles. Finally, they got inside, turned the car around, and, with a welcome rush of air-conditioning, started driving home. A rock banged against the back window and bounced off, putting a slight scratch in the claroplastic.

"No patriotism," Hiram sighed. "These people don't understand what it means to be Americans."

A few days later, the Forrests went to dinner at their next-door neighbors, Caleb and Zipporah, who had invited them as a way of saying thank you for being given a place to stay when their air conditioner broke down. Hiram asked Dan to join them, having become even friendlier toward him since their excursion to the rice fields. The family was already downstairs when Rebecca called up to Dan that it was time to go. As he passed Deborah's room on his way to the stairs, Dan saw that her door was ajar and that she had left her desk link running. With a sinking feeling, he realized that if he had said no to Hiram he would have been alone in the house for hours and easily been able to communicate with the Canadians, and with his family.

Now he was committed to going out—turning back at this point would look glaringly suspicious. But he had to get a chance to use that open link—a few minutes would be enough. As he went downstairs, he decided that he would feign illness at some point during the dinner and ask to go back to his room to rest. After he agreed to help destroy the rice crop, Hiram had programmed the bio-lock so that Dan could get into the house by himself. In reality, this was hardly a big step, since Dan was often alone in the house when the family went to someone's else's home for dinner, but it would be helpful now. The real problem was that faking some illness wouldn't be an easy act to carry out, and he wondered if he would be able to manage it at all in front of Deborah. Nonetheless, he was determined to try.

Caleb and Zipporah's house was in Spanish-Colonial style. It was smaller than the Forrests' and not as well-maintained, but still substantially larger than most of the cryoplastic homes in Mountain America. Immediately inside the front door was a hallway dominated by a Revivalist cross, confirming Dan's surmise about them. On one side of the hall was a bricked-over doorway, on the other side, the entrance to their living room. In the front half of the room were a variety of armchairs, end tables and two couches, as eclectic as the furniture in the Forrests' living room but not as opulent. In the back was a dining table, set for the meal. Dan guessed that the bricked-over doorway led to the original dining room, and that a whole section of the house had been closed off.

Dinner began with the Lord's Prayer, followed by a longer Revivalist prayer asking Jesus why He had continued the heat and permitted the floods, what sins the people had committed, and what they were supposed to do now to reverse the misfortunes that had been visited upon them. To Dan's surprise, both Hiram and Rebecca were able to recite the entire prayer along with Caleb and Zipporah. Observing his reaction, Rebecca explained that she and her sister had grown up in a Revivalist home, and so had Hiram.

"What made you give it up?" Dan asked, forgetting for the moment to try acting ill.

"After my sister married Nathaniel, he persuaded her that politics was the way to solve our problems, not religion, and then she persuaded me and Hiram."

It made sense, Dan thought, that Wolfson had been the dominant force in the family.

"Actually," said Hiram, "I was in the process of reaching that conclusion on my own."

"That's true," Rebecca answered quickly. "I think we all felt that Revivalism wasn't working."

"I'm not so ready to give up on it," said Caleb in a sulky voice.

"If you'd join the Unity Party," Hiram intoned, "you'd see that we're really getting things done. Sooner or later, we're going to unify the Confederacies, and then we'll go on to re-establish the United States of America. Just wait."

"You don't have to give it up completely," Rebecca added. "I guess Reverend Nicholas says that people who are involved in politics can't be Revivalists, but his isn't the only church around here."

There was an awkward silence, relieved by Zipporah, who got up to serve the food while Caleb remained sitting at the table. Even for a special occasion, Caleb and Zipporah apparently couldn't manage anything but soy hamburgers, and after tasting his, Dan understood for the first time why Rebecca had the reputation of being a good cook. The conversation moved on to more comfortable topics, mainly more of Caleb's security guard stories. Dan, trying to prepare everyone for his request to leave, put his head in his hands a few times and tried not to look at Deborah, who mercifully kept silent. Finally, just as he began to be afraid that he would need to start acting even more histrionic to be noticed by anyone else, Rebecca asked him what was wrong.

"Oh, nothing much. I have some sort of headache."

Having laid the groundwork, Dan waited until Zipporah, who had left the table to hover over her baby, returned to clear the dinner plates and serve dessert.

"You know," Dan said. "I'm really not feeling very well. This headache has been bothering me all day. I hope you don't mind if I go back to my room and lie down for a while."

There was a pause. Dan waited, resisting the urge to apologize and acutely aware of Deborah's gaze.

"Sorry about that," said Hiram. "Do you think it's from being out in the heat a few days ago?"

"Yes, maybe so," Dan answered, thinking that if he had felt ill as a result of their excursion, it would be because of its purpose, or maybe from his fear that the farmer workers would have killed them after Hiram's speech. Hiram walked him to the door and told him to get some rest and feel better. As soon as Dan got back into the Forrests' house he went up the stairs, but he paused at the entrance to Deborah's room. He wondered why—was he still reluctant to take advantage of her for his own purposes? In any case, he reflected, his hesitation was a useful warning. He would need to be extremely careful not to disrupt anything in Deborah's room. If she even suspected that he had used her desk unit—and she might well be as observant about objects as she was about people—all would be lost.

Carefully weaving his way around her wheeled desk chair, he knelt in front of the unit and, after noting the position of the various objects on the desk—a pen, a flowered note pad, a small glass vase and the broken half of a rounded, grey-white stone—he switched on the keyboard. The letters flashed onto the desk with a suddenness that startled him. His heart was pounding and his hands were shaking as he typed his access code, then searched the USBI cite for Jarrel Lucan and Dean Horace. He had no difficulty finding them—Dean Horace's first name turned out to be Bredetta—yes, of course it was, he had forgotten. Should he write "Dear Jarrel and Dean Horace"? That sounded odd, but it would be inappropriate to say "Dear Jarrel and Bredetta," since he barely knew the dean. It would be even more awkward, though, to call Jarrel "Professor Lucan." Why was he even wasting time with this—it didn't matter. He typed *"Dear Jarrel and Dean Horace"* and then proceeded with the rest of the message, which he had rehearsed in his mind over and over and could reproduce without hesitation.

I wish I could be contacting you about your generous offer, but this is in fact an urgent message with major national security implications for all of Canada. I was sent on a diplomatic mission to the Confederacies in late October and was taken prisoner by

THE HEATSTROKE LINE

Birmingham-Victoria. While being held here, I have learned that a major terrorist attack is being planned against Canada, one that will seriously and permanently impair the habitability of your nation. Please contact your government and have them arrange my rescue so that I can disclose the information that will enable them to prevent this dangerous and reprehensible attack. I am being held in a private home whose location can be readily determined from this message. Its street address is 491 Nimrod Avenue. As far as I can tell, there is no military force here that could offer any significant resistance to the Canadian Air Force. Please have your government respond

There was a noise downstairs. Someone had come into the house. Dan jumped to his feet with a sense of panic. He could hear voices—it was Joanna and Deborah. The front door closed. They had come back early from the dinner. They would be coming upstairs in a few seconds. Dan leaned over the desk and, trying to stay calm, typed:

on this link. Im sure theyre watching mine if its stll open. have only ocasional access so giveme time to responf.
Daniel Danten

He sent the message, closed the link, quickly looked to make sure he hadn't moved the controls, turned to leave and banged against Deborah's desk chair, which skittered a few feet across the room. With trembling hands, he repositioned the chair as well as he could and dashed out, trying as he went to think of some excuse—he had heard a strange noise, he had dropped something that rolled into the room—in case the girls saw him emerge. But they were still downstairs, and Dan was able to reach his room unseen. He dropped down on his bed, now with a real headache. The girls continued talking and he heard Joanna laugh, but they didn't come upstairs. As he listened to them, Dan realized that he would have had time to finish his message more coherently and then contact his family. But how could he have known that, and how could he have taken such a chance? He was lucky that he had managed to get the crucial message off without detection. As he calmed down, his panic was replaced by a sense of accomplishment, and with his first feeling of real hope that he would soon escape this wretched place and get back home.

CHAPTER 21

an woke up the next morning with the firm impression that his son Michael had just died. He wasn't aware of having dreamt it but he assumed that he must have, and he tried to reason himself out of the sensation by ascribing it to the age-old, pre-Freudian superstition that dreams reveal previously unknown truths. Instead, reason replaced sensation with even greater and more distressing certitude. Michael had been so ill when he left, and he'd been getting progressively worse for the past two years. The doctors had no clue as to what was wrong with him. It was plausible—in fact, predictable—that he would have continued to decline during the four months that Dan had been away from him, and that, as Dan lay in his large, chilly room fifteen hundred miles from his home, staring out the window on this relentlessly bright March morning, his little son was dead.

He stumbled through the day distracted. Far from dissipating, the grim certainty persisted and weighed him down with an almost palpable oppression. He wondered whether he had ever really known who Michael was. Had Josh's steady excellence and Senly's witty defiance monopolized the time he had available for his children while pursuing his research? His effort to think back over the ten years of Michael's life yielded a terrifying lack of detail. He remembered a particularly bad tantrum when Michael was a toddler, an elementary school spelling bee that Michael won, and Michael's last conversation with him about traveling to India, just before he left on his mission to Jacksonia. Michael's life had been so brief that it consisted mostly of vague hopes that he would never either outgrow or fulfill. As Dan grappled with his own overwhelming sense of sadness, he thought about Garenika. Without him there to support and console her after Michael's death, she would fall apart, and perhaps take Senly with her.

That evening, Dan felt desperately alone. Somehow, he didn't want to talk to Deborah about Michael, but he couldn't imagine talking to her about anything else. He retreated to his room immediately after dinner and found himself pacing back and forth, muttering vague curses at his captors. By the next morning, he began to wonder whether he should talk to Deborah after all, but it turned out that she had left for another visit to a friend and would be away for several days. Hiram talked to him, however, eagerly asking if he had enough information to decide which insect would most effectively destroy the rice crop. Dan thought about naming something harmless, since he would hopefully be long gone by the time the insects had been bred and introduced. But that might be dangerous. He could rely on Hiram's naiveté, but it would be difficult to fool Lyons, who might know enough on his own, or Wolfson, who would be cagey enough to check with another entomologist. So instead Dan temporized, saying that he wanted to give the matter some more thought before deciding.

That Friday—Deborah's first day back—Dan received word at the lab that Hiram would be several hours late picking him up. While this was uncommon, it was not unprecedented. Despite his reverential attitude regarding family dinners, Hiram sometimes went out of the city to inspect cooking practices in the outlying towns and villages, rather than leaving this task to one of his subordinates. On these occasions, Dan ate in the employee cafeteria, which stayed open for dinner because several of the scientists and senior staff were single and preferred to eat at work. One of them was Lyons, who typically sat alone at a table, alternately reading a document and glaring at the other diners. Dan repeated to himself that he wasn't actually afraid of Lyons, but he passed by the cafeteria on a pretext a few times and made sure that Lyons had finished eating before going in for his own dinner. Paul and Matthew had gone home together, as they usually did, and Dan found himself sitting next to Jethro Garber. In addition to admiring biter bugs, it turned out that Jethro liked sharks. Before the climate change, he explained to Dan, the Gulf of Mexico had been full of dolphins, and people used to go scuba diving to watch them. Now sharks had killed all the dolphins and were feeding on each other. If fucking Montgomery hadn't closed off the Gulf, he would have loved to go diving to watch the sharks fight to the death. Dan finished eating as fast as he could and retreated to his office. Finally, a message that Hiram had arrived flashed onto his link screen, and he walked quickly across the darkened empty space between the lab partitions and the entrance.

Hiram greeted him with a broad smile. "Sorry I'm late, but there's a reason. You're going on an adventure tonight."

"What do you mean?"

"We just learned that this is the night the Indies are going to attack, and they're using that mercenary team again—the one with your favorite woman. I'm bringing you to where our interdiction unit's meeting so you can go along and watch them catch her. As you can see, we're holding up our end of our bargain."

"Thank you," said Dan. All of a sudden, he felt nervous. "What are they planning to attack?"

"They're going to blow up the statue of President Chiron on Unity Avenue and blame it on Montgomery. The story is that there was some sort of pagan statue in Birmingham City that the Revivalists blew up a while ago, so that's how they got the idea. We're coordinating our response at the meeting—that's where I'm taking you. And, by the way, Nathaniel asked me to remind you that you have to behave yourself."

"I promise," Dan replied.

After driving for a few minutes, they pulled into the parking lot of a dilapidated building that looked like a warehouse or a factory. Its ground floor turned out to be some sort of garage, with several vehicles parked inside and an enclosed, air conditioned room in back. Wolfson and another middle-aged man, tall, heavy and even more brutal looking than Wolfson, were at the front, with an illuminated street map projected on the wall behind them. There were about ten people around them, seated on folding chairs. One was Joel Rinier, and another was the thin young blond woman with the plastic earrings who had also been at Dan's meeting with the Independence Party and the leopard woman. Once again, Dan wondered if he would get a chance to be alone with Joel and get some news about his family.

With a slight, complicit smile, Wolfson indicated that Dan should take a seat. Hiram sat down next to him.

"Okay now, we've gone over this twice," said the heavy man, "so I hope everything's clear. Remember, the key thing is to get those shooters. We can kill one or two of them if we need to, but we can't blow them all up. We've got to get at least one of them alive or we'll never be able to prove that they were hired by the Indies."

"And remember," Wolfson added, "our informant doesn't know what the spotter car looks like, so you have to stay alert. Any

THE HEATSTROKE LINE

questions?" He waited for a moment. "Okay, then. Joel, you and Sarah leave first in the panel truck. Then you four—Isaiah's team —go next in the blue car. You're third, Michigan, in the Chinese two-seater" he said to the thin blond woman. "Take this guy with you," he added, pointing to Dan, "and shoot him in the leg if he causes any trouble."

The people Wolfson named stood up and started filing out toward the vehicles in the garage, with Joel giving Dan a pleasant smile as he left. They were all quite young, Dan noticed. A few others, including Hiram, stayed in their seats. Michigan came over to Dan, giggling. "Which leg do you want me to shoot, Dr. Danten? Don't worry, I'm just kidding. Everything will be fine. I'm only back-up, so we probably won't even see any action."

They went out into the garage, which was stifling, got into a small grey car and drove off.

"Is Michigan your real name?" Dan asked the woman.

"Yep. My family's from Michigan way back when, and my parents were hoping we could move back there once the United States got re-unified, so they named me for it."

"I see. I guess you know my name from that meeting with the Indies."

"Sure do. You know, you're really smart, Dr. Danten. I couldn't believe all that stuff you knew about those—what are they called?"

"You mean pheromones?"

"Yeah, those. It sounded like you could have gone on talking about them all night if Henrikson hadn't stopped you."

"Well, it's my specialty. It's what I do."

"Joel told me you were so pissed at that woman because she killed your friend."

"She didn't just kill him, she tortured him to death by setting biter bugs on him. And she made me watch. She's a fucking monster."

"Yeah, she's perfect for the Indies. Don't worry, we'll get her tonight."

"What's her name?"

"Eva, I think. No, maybe it's Diomeda. Shit, I don't know. Anyway, we're here."

They were on Unity Avenue, the wide street that had served as the route for the Battle of the Bulge Day Parade. The few businesses along it that were still functioning had closed for the evening, and the avenue was dark. About a hundred feet before they reached the Chiron statue, which was placed where the

Avenue curved to the right, they passed Joel's panel truck, now parked and with its lights off. A few hundred feet away, around the curve and past the statue, they could see the blue car with Isaiah's team, just now pulling into place. Michigan turned into a side street that came in from the right directly opposite the statue, turned around so that they were facing the statue, came to a stop and turned off the lights. She left the engine running or they would have suffocated within half an hour.

"What they were telling us," she explained to Dan, "is that the spotter car will come down the Avenue this way, from left to right, and the shooter car will follow. Since the statue's recessed off the street, they can't get a shot at it until they're between Joel and Isaiah. As soon as they shoot, Joel's supposed to blow their tires out, and then Isaiah's team will close in on them. I'm here in case Joel misses and they try to escape down this street, or the shooters try to run down here after their car's disabled. You just sit tight, I'll take care of things."

She reached into the back of the car and pulled out a long, customized gyro rifle, which she carefully placed across her lap. Then she opened a flap in the ceiling, took out a GX gun, checked its alignment, and placed it on the dashboard.

"How did you get into all of this?" Dan asked.

"Oh, I don't know. I guess I've always been interested in electoral politics. Wait, something's coming."

A car drove down the street from left to right and seemed to slow down in front of the statue for a moment. Michigan rolled her window down, her small slender body cat-like in its alertness, but the car continued on its way and nothing followed. She relaxed, rolled the window up and giggled. "Too bad, I thought we were going to get some action right away."

Instead, they sat in the car for several hours. Michigan never took her eyes off the street in front of them. She would spring into intense alertness each time she saw a car that looked suspicious to her, then relax when it passed by, but without any decrease in vigilance. Dan chatted with her intermittently. She had stopped going to school at thirteen, like Deborah, but then she had joined the military and saw action in the war when Birmingham-Victoria took Auburn from Montgomery. She'd had several boyfriends and girlfriends, wanted to get married at some point, but felt no desire to have children. After Dan stopped asking questions, she asked him about his work and his family and commented once again about how knowledgeable he was. She also wanted to know about

THE HEATSTROKE LINE

the political parties in Mountain America, and whether it was ever cool enough for people to practice at outdoor rifle ranges.

After a while, Michigan's intermittent moments of alertness became monotonous, the topics of casual conversation were exhausted, and it seemed easier to simply sit in silence. Dan could not help brooding about his family. Josh would probably manage, but Michael's sickness if not death, Garenika's fragility and Senly's intemperance would almost certainly lead to disaster. He should be there, he should have figured out a way to get back home. Despite the excuses he could offer for himself, he felt irresponsible.

"There's the spotter car," said Michigan, in a quiet, steady voice, her body rigidly alert once more. She opened her window. A small blue car drove slowly down the street, passed Isaiah's car, and disappeared into the night.

"How do you know?"

Michigan pointed to their left. A black van was coming toward them. It passed the panel truck and stopped opposite the statue only a few yards away from them. The front doors opened and two people got out—first a tall, grey-haired man and then the leopard woman. Dan felt himself go tense with rage, the heat that seemed to rise up from inside him intensified by the hot air that flowed into the car through its open window. The woman was dressed in typically elegant clothes, and Dan thought he could see her grin as she and her companion crossed the street and walked up to the statue.

"What the fuck are they doing?" Dan whispered.

"I don't know—not sure I like it."

The two people walked slowly back to their car and got inside. There was a breathless pause.

"Shit, another car," Michigan gasped.

The door of the panel truck flew open and Joel leapt out into the street. There was a sudden boom, and the truck exploded into flames. Another boom, this time from the black van, and the statue was enveloped in an orange-yellow blaze. Michigan hoisted her gyro rifle out the window, moving the car forward at the same time. There was another boom, the wall of the low building next to Isaiah's car blew out, then Michigan fired and the car that had come up behind the panel truck exploded. With a screech, the leopard woman's van leapt forward, splattered Isaiah's car with machine gun fire and careened around the corner of the next side street.

Dan watched it disappear, his rage increasing, then looked back at the street in front of him. The two vehicles were burning furiously, shooting sparks into the nighttime air. A body lay on the ground beside the panel truck and Dan realized a moment later that it was Joel. He had jumped out, but not far enough. Now he was crawling slowly forward on his elbows, away from the truck, his clothing still on fire. Then he stopped, sank down onto the ground and lay completely still. Michigan said "Shit!" under her breath and got out of the car, grabbing her GX gun but still holding the gyro rifle. With a glance at Joel's body, she advanced on the car she had shot with the rifle and walked around it slowly, then came back and headed for Isaiah's car.

Feeling stunned, Dan got slowly out of the car and walked up to Joel's body, which was lying in the middle of the street. It was burned beyond recognition, the skin and clothing fused together in a blackened jumble and still smoldering in several places. A few wisps of his blond hair remained, but the rest was gone and the burnt skin on his face seemed to flow around an empty eye socket. A sickening smell of charred flesh rose up and seemed to intensify as it spread into the heated air. The flames that engulfed the panel truck were subsiding and Dan could see the blackened body of Joel's companion—was her name Susan?—slumped against the dashboard.

Then he heard someone moaning. Turning toward the blue car, he saw Michigan and someone else lifting a man out of the front seat of the car and laying him down on the street. He was writhing in pain, and blood was flowing freely from his side. Evidently, he had been hit by the machine gun fire from the leopard woman's car. Dan wondered whether he should go over to help, realized that there was nothing he could do, and stayed where he was, staring blankly at Joel's corpse, the two burning vehicles, and the smoldering fragments of the statue that were scattered all around its empty pedestal.

CHAPTER 22

Dan didn't see Hiram after the attack. Michigan had told him that the Unity Party officials were staying at the garage to await the outcome of the operation, but none of them showed up at the scene. Instead, several police cars and fire trucks appeared, with wailing sirens. The fire trucks doused the two burning vehicles while the police mainly milled around. They didn't show much interest in asking questions, even of Michigan, who, as it turned out, had just killed three people. One of the police officers drove Dan home in silence. But when Dan came downstairs for breakfast the next morning—it was Saturday—Hiram was waiting for him in the dining room. He had brought his desk unit downstairs and was projecting net communications about the previous night's incident on the side wall of the room.

Various members of the Independence Party had posted messages or live statements accusing the Unity Party of allowing the destruction of the Chiron statue, condemning Montgomery for the attack, and promising to go to war and get revenge once their party won the election in November and took power. There was a live response from the President of Birmingham-Victoria, Bertram Deborn, promising to find the terrorists who had perpetrated this cowardly act and bring them to justice, no matter who they were. He cautioned people not to assume that Montgomery was behind the attack, but promised that, if it was, Birmingham would "hold them responsible." Several Unity Party leaders had posted statements in support of the President's position, and a number of Independence Party leaders had responded by calling him a coward and a liar. In addition, there were messages from citizens of Montgomery, some accusing Birmingham of having blown up the statue to create an excuse for war, others expressing anger that Birmingham had failed to protect the statue of a great Montgomerian and demanding that their own nation go to war against Birmingham. A few people in the neighboring Confederacies posted messages as well, but none of the net mongers from the three Successor States or Canada seemed to be aware of what had happened.

It was clear that Hiram had been fully informed about last night's events. This second collaborative enterprise seemed to have made him feel even more comradely toward Dan, but his prevailing mood this morning was despondent. He saw the incident as ending any hope of forging an alliance with Montgomery and feared it would lead to the defeat of the Unity Party in the next election, in which case, he said, apparently expecting Dan to commiserate, "We won't have an alliance for another decade, at least, and we'll keep getting weaker while Canada gets stronger."

"Why can't President Deborn accuse the Independence Party of blowing up the statue, even if you didn't catch any of them in the act? After all, you know they did it."

"Nathaniel explained that to us last night. Without proof, we'd look even weaker, as if we're just making excuses for ourselves. Anyway, the President is just a talking head. The pictures of that empty pedestal are what counts."

"You know, that woman and the guy who was with her got out of the car and walked around the statue before they blew it up. Didn't anyone get footage of that?"

"Yeah, Sarah Zanche was filming everything, but it all got burned up with the panel truck before she had the chance to transmit."

Sarah—that was her name, Dan recalled. The image of her incinerated body, sitting in the burning truck, came back to him, and then he remembered Joel's charred remains lying in the middle of the street.

Deborah had come into the room while Hiram and Dan were talking and, as usual when more than one person was present, sat in silence before drifting out as unobtrusively as she had entered.

"Nathaniel said that the Indies must have figured out who our informant was and made sure that he didn't tell us about that other car. Now that they've blown up the Chiron statue, they'll probably catch the guy and kill him. Damn, it's hard to make progress around here."

All at once, Dan became aware of the deep and desperate sense of yearning that lay behind nearly everything that Hiram said and did. Because he resented Hiram as one of his captors— which was natural enough—he had retaliated, in his own mind,

THE HEATSTROKE LINE

by holding the man in contempt and thinking of him as an idiot. Now Dan saw that Hiram's Patriotism, his devotion to his bizarre job, his time-consuming political activities and his quixotic aspirations for American reunification were all efforts to provide a sense of meaning for himself. He had managed to secure as good a situation for his family as was possible in the miserable conditions of the Confederacies, but he wanted more. He wanted to feel that his life had purpose, that it was part of something larger, something that represented forward motion instead of inescapable hopelessness. Dan had closed himself off from all of this with anger. Now his anger seemed to fade and he felt sad for Hiram.

This sense of Hiram's human suffering, however, only intensified Dan's desire to escape, particularly when added to his frustration over the leopard woman's survival and his boredom with his useless research at the insect lab. Somewhat reluctantly, he began to watch Deborah's movements more attentively. Despite her apparent emotional disconnection from her family, she was always willing to help out around the house—part of her understanding with her parents, Dan surmised. Not surprisingly, many of the chores at the Forrests' home revolved around food, and one of the main ones was to put away the groceries. These were delivered in the evening, two or three times a week, from a central distribution center—Dan had noticed that there didn't seem to be any supermarkets left in Birmingham City. In his own home, the servo-robot put the groceries into their designated slots in the auto-kitchen, using radio tags, but here everything had to be done by hand. When the groceries came, Rebecca would call up to Deborah and Joanna, and Deborah would go downstairs immediately, generally leaving her desk link open. Dan timed this event on the next three occasions and found that Deborah never spent less than sixteen minutes downstairs helping her mother with this task.

On Tuesday, a week and half after the attack on the statue, the groceries came about an hour after dinner and Rebecca, who had gone downstairs to take delivery, called up to Deborah and Joanna. Dan ran to the door of his room and crouched down behind it in readiness, his body trembling with tension. He heard the two girls go downstairs. Hiram was already downstairs in his study. As soon as the girls entered the kitchen, Dan sprang through the doorway and dashed into Deborah's room. The unit was running. Kneeling at her desk again, he opened the connection to USBI. There was a message from the Canadian Security Intelligence Service—they were going to rescue him. He could get the information he needed and have time to contact Garenika. With a sense of exhilarated expectation, he opened the message. It was only one line long.

First give us the information, then we will decide whether to exfiltrate you.

Dan cursed under his breath—that certainly wasn't the response he had been hoping for. What should he do? If he gave them the information, they would have no reason to rescue him. But it looked like they weren't going to rescue him unless he gave it, so he had no choice. He wasn't prepared for this; of course he should have composed the message in his mind beforehand, as he did the first time. There were only a few minutes, and he realized that if Deborah came upstairs by herself he wouldn't hear anything until she was literally standing next to him. Dan's hands were shaking as he began to type.

I'm being forced to work at a research lab thats trying to genetically engineer cold resistant biter bug so they can ship them into Canada. I'm pretty sure they're making progress The outbreak in East Montana was them sending a first batch maybe experimental to Canada but the plane must have gotten engine trouble. You should destroy this lab—the address is 1411 Bolgia boulevard. [Now he had to give them some incentive for rescuing him.] *But there are other labs workng on this. Im going to find out where they are tomorrow. The lab here is working on the genetic code itself but it doesn't do any actual breeding. Since it's impossible to field test the modification in this climate they have refrigeration units in other labs and these labs are also working on targeting modified genes using TAL effectors instead of the homing endonucleases we're working with here.* [Too long; he had to get out.] *I can give you the infromation when you rescue me Please send insturctions for rescue to this link. I'll check in when i can*

As Dan logged off, he heard someone at the bottom of the stairs. It must be Joanna—was Deborah coming too? Had he moved anything in the room? He stepped out quickly, no one was on the landing yet, it was Rebecca coming up the stairs, she looked up and saw him before he could get to his room. Had she seen him leaving Deborah's room?

"Hi Dan. Everything okay?"

"Yes, fine."

"You look upset."

THE HEATSTROKE LINE

She wasn't acting as if she had seen anything suspicious, but she could tell that he was agitated, and he decided that he needed to offer her some explanation. He decided to go on the offensive.

"Well, if you must know, I don't particularly like being a prisoner and being kept away from my family."

"I'm sure you miss them, Dan. But they'll probably be all right until you get back."

"Really? My younger son was very ill when I left and my wife was suffering from depression. What do you think will happen if he dies and I'm not there?"

Dan realized that his frustration at the indeterminate response from Canada and the loss of a second opportunity to contact Garenika had boiled over into fury.

"That's terrible, I'm really sorry," said Rebecca.

"Well fine, but what good does it do? I'm not even allowed to contact my family and find out what's going on."

"Have you tried prayer?"

Now he wanted to strangle her. He was about to say that he would pray for an operative wrist link, but he decided that he had better be careful or he would give himself away.

"Frankly, I haven't. We seem to have several centuries of evidence that praying doesn't do much good."

"I know. But maybe it would make you feel better."

Dan felt himself calming down a bit. As Deborah had told him, and he had then observed himself, Rebecca was distinctly kindhearted.

"I thought you'd given up on Revivalism."

"Hiram definitely has, but he came from a horrible family. Miriam and I had nicer parents, so I'm not as negative about religion, even though none of us practice it anymore."

"I've never heard you mention your parents."

"I don't. My mother died of heatstroke when I was a teenager, then my father died of some mysterious disease a few years later. And we had a brother who died at twenty-four from an infected biter bug wound."

"So you don't talk about them because it would it would give you a sense of fragility about your own family?"

"Yes, that's it. That's it exactly." She seemed stunned by the insight, and Dan felt moved to reach out to her, despite himself.

"Well, at least everything has gone okay with you so far."

She shook her head. "We lost our son to some disease when he was two."

"Oh, I'm really sorry. Was that before you had Deborah?"

"Deborah's adopted Dan. I guess you didn't know that."

"No, I . . . I." He choked for a moment and had to clear his throat. "I had no idea. Who were her parents?"

"No one knows. She was left in an orphanage when she was two, and we adopted her soon after. After we saw that she was doing alright, it gave me the courage to have another child of my own."

Dan found himself affected to a depth that went beyond surprise. Being the child of two such ordinary people had seemed to bring Deborah down to earth, to make her seem less enigmatic and other worldly. This new information created an indefinable sensation, one that somehow mixed fear with renewed fascination. Where had she come from?

A week went by. Deborah left again to visit someone, as always without explanation. The rainy season had ended, and the killer heat of summer was beginning to descend, when a tornado came up from the south and roared through town. It didn't hit the Forrests' neighborhood directly, but it passed close to the insect lab. A number of wood frame and even brick buildings near the lab were destroyed and the lab itself was closed for two days because access to it was blocked by debris. This was just fine with Dan—he was no longer interested in doing research of his own on biter bugs, and he was tired of providing guidance to people who he now knew were engaged in a reprehensible enterprise. He spent the time alone in his room, reading Dickens' *Hard Times*. As usual, he decided, Dickens got it right; even in the early days of industrialization, he had foreseen the disasters it would cause. Dan found himself recalling Deborah's novel, no longer with a critic's stance, but with a strange sense of yearning for the harsh but simple world she had envisioned and the promise of escape that it contained. At the same time, he kept thinking of Deborah as Dickens' Sissy Jupe, abandoned by her family and taken in by others, vulnerable and yet suffused with a deep power that placed her beyond everyone around her.

On the day when Dan's travel to the insect lab resumed, Hiram came downstairs a few minutes late. He told Dan that he had just learned, in a message from Nathaniel, that the tornado had damaged the rice crops. He still wanted Dan to figure out the best insect to destroy the rice, but they wouldn't need to worry about doing it until next year. Dan was relieved, but then felt guilty about his reaction.

THE HEATSTROKE LINE

"Won't those people starve now?" he asked Hiram. "They looked so poor."

"No, they'll get emergency grain from the backup supplies we keep in the old university buildings at Auburn. There'll be a statement about that from President Deborn on the net tonight."

The next night—Hiram had taken to bringing his desk unit downstairs after dinner when there were no guests—there was bigger news. Birmingham Internal Security, the department Wolfson worked for, had killed a group of terrorists who were suspected of being responsible for blowing up the Chiron statue. There were pictures of the four suspected terrorists, all quite young, and footage of the police going through a house outside the city where they had lived. As Dan watched the broadcast, he noticed Michigan, standing on the sidelines with her usual calm, vaguely amused expression, together with two other people he recognized from the garage as members of Isaiah's team. It gave Dan a chill. Obviously these were not the people who had actually blown up the statue. Wolfson had probably arranged the killings to convince the people of Birmingham-Victoria that the terrorists had been brought to justice. Michigan, innocuous and pleasant though she seemed, had added another four murders to however many more she had committed.

Two days later, someone blew up several of the grain storage buildings in Auburn. Now the net news was full of claims that this was the work of Montgomery, still smarting from having lost Auburn to Birmingham-Victoria in the most recent war. There was a stream of statements from Independence Party members denouncing the Unity Party government as ineffectual and cowardly. Once their party came to power, they declared, they would go to war and—depending on the person who was speaking —either punish Montgomery, conquer it, or obliterate it completely.

As it happened, Nathaniel Wolfson and his wife Miriam were the Forrests' dinner guests that evening. Wolfson was visibly agitated, for the first time that Dan had seen. He went on and on about how clever the Indies had been in blowing up the Auburn buildings and seemed to blame himself for failing to anticipate it. In addition, he confirmed Hiram's guess that the Indies had identified and killed the Unity Party's informant.

"We need to come up with something that will make the Indies look bad," he declared. "At this point, they're going to win the next election."

Dan had learned that it was better to be quiet when the subject of Birmingham politics came up at Hiram's dinners, but he couldn't restrain himself. "How about catching the people who are really responsible for blowing up those buildings. They should be brought to justice. I mean, think of how much harm they've done to your citizens."

"It won't do any good at this point," said Wolfson. "Whoever thinks it was the Indies thinks it already, and whoever doesn't isn't going to be convinced, no matter what we manage to come up with."

"Maybe we need a scandal," Hiram offered.

"Yes, that might work, but it's not easy to arrange."

"I'm sure you'll think of something, Nathaniel," Rebecca said.

"We'll certainly try," said Wolfson. His heavy-lidded eyes narrowed, and his already brutal-looking face assumed an even more threatening appearance. "Otherwise, we'll be at war with Montgomery by next winter."

"That'll certainly be the end of any chance to unify with them for a while," Hiram observed.

"Yes, going to war with Montgomery will impede our efforts to form a union with them."

"I heard they're already preparing for war," Rebecca quickly interjected. "It was on the net news."

"Does that mean that they'll stop giving money to the Unity party?" Hiram asked, apparently in an effort to seem knowledgeable after Wolfson's scornful response to his last comment.

"I'm not sure that's something that we need to talk about right now," Wolfson answered with a sudden glance at Dan.

"Oh, sorry, I forgot," said Hiram, reddening.

"I'll leave," said Dan, standing up from the table. "I really don't have much interest in local politics."

"You seem pretty interested in having that woman of yours caught," Nathaniel shot back, with a sharp look at Dan. "But I assume you know that if you ever want to get back to your home, you can't repeat anything you hear from us to anyone."

"Yes, of course," said Dan, trying to sound casual.

"But we don't need to worry, because you can't communicate with anyone outside Birmingham, can you?" Wolfson asked him as he turned to leave the room.

Dan felt a chill run through him and tried even harder to sound casual. "No, of course not, how would I?"

THE HEATSTROKE LINE

Once outside the dining room, it occurred to Dan that he hadn't acted naturally. "I should have said something about wanting to contact my family," he thought. His attempted nonchalance had probably appeared suspicious, and he had the nauseating sense that Wolfson would be watching him closely, at the very least. Maybe he would even be put back in prison.

CHAPTER 23

As summer approached, the temperature began to climb, quickly reaching the 140's on its way toward the searing summer months. The sun sat burning in the cloudless sky, bathing everything in an unforgiving radiance. Already, the air above the pavement on the streets vibrated with heat and made the edges of objects tremble and quaver. Hiram carefully checked the car each day before he and Dan drove to work, running the air conditioner in advance and confirming the fuel level with an external monitor.

Deborah was gone again for several days, and Dan, despite his anxiety to find out how the Canadians had responded to his message, couldn't think of any way to get an open link. His life settled back into its regular routine of work at the lab, dinner with the Forrests, and evenings in his chilly room reading nineteenth century novels. He had given up doing any reading for his research, which seemed pointless and distasteful to him now. But this feeling must have become apparent because one day at the lab, a week and a half after the Wolfsons had been to dinner at the Forrests' house, Paul Steiner stopped in the middle of his usual questions about the methods of genetic modification and stared at Dan in silence.

"What's the matter?" Dan asked him.

"You realize what we're doing here, don't you?" he responded.

Dan froze with fear. He did not know what to say. He liked Paul, much more than anyone at the lab besides Paul's partner Matthew, and he could certainly use an ally, but could he take the chance of confiding in him? He quickly concluded that the risk was just too great, that the danger of revealing what he knew outweighed the value of any possible assistance from this man.

"Well," he answered after a pause, "I know there's work going on at other labs. I assume that some of it involves—that they must be looking into ways to eradicate the bugs with bio-chemical

THE HEATSTROKE LINE

toxins. I guess you people know that I refused to work with those when I was back home. So I guess I'm being kept away from that part of the project. I've wondered what I'd do if I was asked to work on that. I mean, I want to cooperate so I can get back home, but some of those toxins have really awful side effects, especially, well, I'm sure you know."

Dan realized he was talking too much, that he would sound less, not more convincing if he continued. Then he had an idea.

"Listen, Paul, since you brought up my feelings about this lab, I have a real favor to ask you. I haven't spoken to my family for five months now. They don't know whether I'm alive or dead, and I don't know what's happened to them. It's really cruel. Would you let me use your link for a few minutes? I would appreciate it tremendously."

Paul looked at Dan in silence. "Okay," he said finally, and Dan felt his heart leap in excitement.

With a quick glance around the hall, Paul led Dan into his cubicle, opened a link, and stepped outside. Dan was actually tempted to contact his family, as he had said, but arranging his escape was of more immediate importance. He reached the USBI site. There was a message for him and he opened it.

We will arrange a distraction. When it occurs proceed to the Wailing River Shopping Center, 2.2 kilometers south by southeast of your current residence.

Dan knew exactly where that was. It was the abandoned mall he had passed with Hiram when they drove out to the rice fields. This was it, then—he was going to be rescued.

Barely a minute had passed since Paul had opened the link for him; there was still time to contact his family. He entered Garenika's address, terrified to find out what had happened since he left, but excited about being able to communicate his own good news. There was no answer whatsoever—the link was dead. Trying to stay calm, he called up Josh—no response—then Senly —no response again. He didn't even want to try Michael. What had happened? He couldn't let himself imagine. There must be some explanation, but he had no idea what it might be. He jumped up from the desk and rushed out of the cubicle. Jethro was coming down the passageway; Paul looked at Dan as he went past, but said nothing.

Back in his office, Dan put his head in his hands and tried to calm himself. The family must have changed net services to save money, now that they didn't have his income. He could have found them if there had been a few extra minutes for him to do a search. That's what he would do the next time he could sneak into Deborah's room. Or maybe he would be rescued soon, and he would find out then.

For the next two days, Dan tried to avoid thinking about his family's dead net links, and when he did think about them, which must have been several hundred times, he tried to reassure himself that there were many possible explanations. Finally, he realized that he simply had to find out what had happened. Deborah had returned, and Dan watched for an opportunity to sneak into her room and use her desk link, but none presented itself. After a few days, he decided that he would ask or—if necessary—beg Paul to let him use his link again. He could tell Paul the truth about this part of his previous communication, identify it as the reason he had rushed past in such obvious agitation, and generally play on the man's sense of sympathy. But Paul was not at work the next day, a rare occurrence, and he wasn't there the following day either. Dan checked Paul's cubicle several times, but to no effect. Late that day, Matthew asked Dan to come into one of the storage areas to identify a new machine that had arrived. As soon as they got past the cubicles, he grabbed Dan's arm and started speaking in hushed tones.

"Listen, I've been waiting to talk to you. I guess you've noticed that Paul isn't here. Did you know he's been arrested?"

"No—for what?"

"They think he's been communicating with the Canadians. That can't be right—Paul wouldn't do that."

Dan felt frigid fear shoot through him, and, at the same time, he felt close to physically ill.

"I—I had no idea. I mean, I, well . . ."

"Can I trust you Dan? You've got to be pretty angry at these people yourself, after all."

"I am. Yes, you can trust me," Dan answered, feeling distinctly untrustworthy.

"Good. I'm planning to kidnap Lyons and hold him until they release Paul."

"But how can you possibly do that? I mean, won't they catch you right away?" Dan realized that, no matter how bad he felt about Paul, he didn't want Lyons captured at this moment. If that happened, work at the lab would be disrupted and he might be sent back to the prison, where he could never be rescued.

THE HEATSTROKE LINE

"I know some people in Montgomery. I can grab Lyons at night —he stays late most of the time—and drive straight down there before anyone realizes what happened. Once I'm in Montgomery, they won't be able to get Lyons back without releasing Paul. They'll have to do it. Lyons is a very important member of the Unity Party, and they'll know I'll kill him if anything happens to Paul."

"Okay, but why are you telling this to me?"

"I can probably do it by myself—Lyons isn't very strong—but it wouldn't hurt to have some help. And I figure you wouldn't mind escaping to Montgomery. Once you're there, we can probably arrange for your return to Mountain America."

Dan wasn't so sure of that—the people in Montgomery seemed even crazier than the ones in Birmingham. Besides, if it turned out that he had been responsible for Paul's arrest, Matthew would almost certainly kill him as well.

"Well, Matthew, I'm glad you trust me, and, well, I appreciate your trying to help me escape, but this all sounds a little desperate. Think what would happen if they caught us before we reached the border, or if they just figured out what we'd done and contacted the border guards." Matthew was silent. "You don't think they would just execute a valuable scientist like Paul right after arresting him, do you?"

"No, I guess not."

"Well, then, why don't you wait? You can always kidnap—carry out your plan if things turn out badly, so I think it's better to see how they develop. Maybe it's all a mistake. Or maybe it will turn out to be something innocent, like Paul getting a piece of research from Canada without following the right procedures, and they'll let him go with a minor reprimand."

Matthew hesitated. He seemed to realize that his fierce commitment to his partner may have led him to be overly impetuous. "Maybe, you're right," he said. "Thanks, you've been a real help. I guess I'll wait a few more days and see what happens. But I'm not going to let them do anything to Paul."

Dan was shaking as he went back to his cubicle. Paul had truly befriended him, and, in return, he seemed to have gotten the man into serious trouble. Now Matthew had befriended him, and he had probably misled him with bad advice. With every day that passed, the people who had arrested Paul—probably Wolfson and the other Internal Security officials—were more likely to realize that they needed to arrest Matthew as well. Only two people in the lab had ever reached out to Dan, and he had immediately betrayed them both. He felt terrible, but even so, he realized that he was most worried about the possibility that the lab would be disrupted and it would interfere with his own rescue.

As he drove home with Hiram, trying to be conversational but obviously distracted, he sensed that he simply couldn't go on without talking to Deborah. He had only spoken to her a few times about literature since realizing what the insect lab was really doing. He was still fearful of her observational abilities, but now he felt helpless. He simply couldn't be alone any longer.

That evening he waited at his door for Deborah to go down to dinner. When she came out of her room and started down the stairs, he quickly followed and caught up to her.

"Hi Deborah," he said, trying not to whisper, "listen, can we talk after dinner?"

She gave him a brief but penetrating glance, and said "Yes."

The dinner seemed interminable. As soon as it was over, Dan went into the living room and waited, too upset to feel humiliated by his sense of desperation, which she had certainly perceived. She came in and sat opposite him, perhaps a bit sooner than he had expected.

"Well, Deborah, I realize I never really talked with you about your story."

"That's okay. You seem—I think you feel uncomfortable about it. But you shouldn't." There was a momentary silence. "Something else is troubling you."

"Yes, lots of things. No matter what I do these days, it never turns out right. It seems as if the whole world is conspiring to make everything I do go wrong."

"Yes, I think I know the feeling. I'm not sure—why don't we sit outside?"

"What about the heat and the bugs?" Dan asked immediately. She was silent. "Oh, okay, I think I understand."

"We can use the basement door."

Dan didn't know there was a door to the outside in the basement, since he never had any occasion to go down there. The stairs to the basement were beside the kitchen, so he and Deborah could go outside without passing any of the other members of the family. This made the whole enterprise feel somewhat conspiratorial, and Dan wondered whether it reflected a new level of intimacy on Deborah's part, or whether she just wanted to avoid any inquiries or objections.

THE HEATSTROKE LINE

The basement was large, with a finished game room that had been abandoned and was being used for storage. The door was at the back and led up a short flight of stairs into the yard. At one time, before the climate change, this yard, which was extensive, had obviously been landscaped, but now it had nothing but bare patches of soil and some water, more a puddle than a pond, which formed after a rainfall. There were some scrawny frogs around the puddle that scattered as Deborah led the way, except for one that seemed to freeze in place. She sat down on a broken bench and motioned for Dan to sit opposite her, on a folding chair. Her seat faced the nearer of Birmingham's two giant power plants, whose smokestacks dominated the view. Dan's seat faced the opposite direction and because it was a clear night, with just a few wisps of clouds, he could see the stars.

He started sweating immediately in the suffocating heat. Deborah seemed more comfortable, with just a thin line of sweat underneath her eyes, and she looked as beautiful as ever.

"It helps if you sit still Dan."

"I am sitting still."

"You never sit still."

Dan smiled. It was true. He tried to relax and absorb Deborah's sense of serenity. They stayed silent for several minutes.

"You wanted to talk to me, but you're waiting for me to ask you a question."

"Well, yes. I guess it's hard for me to begin. It's just that everything I do down here somehow turns out wrong."

"Yes, I suppose—but do you feel like it's your fault?"

Dan was about to say of course not, but he stopped. Garenika had asked him the same question. When? Yes, he knew, right after one of the tornadoes hit, when he apologized to her for planting the flowers outside. In fact, she had asked him this question several times. It seemed as if he had never really heard it until now.

"I guess I always think things are my fault," he said finally.

"Is that because you want to be in control?"

"Yes."

"But you must know—at some level—that you're not."

"Well, it was my decision to come here in the first place. I thought I could do something useful—I guess you'd say that I thought I could take control of something."

"Yes, but that was the last time wasn't it?"

"The last time for what?"

"The last time you were in control. You know, there are some decisions, some choices, really—once you make them, there's nothing more you can do. The world takes over."

Dan suddenly felt the heat more intensely than before, although he was making an effort to sit still. He looked at Deborah and wondered again who her real family was and where she had come from. "I guess I'm an optimist by nature," he said. "Until I'm convinced otherwise, which seems to be happening a lot these days."

"Is that why you gave up astronomy? Not as a job, I mean, but as an interest."

Dan was about to ask her why she kept coming back to that topic, but instead he stopped and thought. The stars were spread out across the sky in their misleadingly familiar patterns. They seemed to shimmer in the heat, as if he were separated from him by some sort of force field.

"Yes. It wasn't just that I couldn't make a living with astronomy. It's that I realized we would never reach them, that we would never even try any more. Another choice that couldn't be made right, I guess. At that point, I seem to have lost my interest in the subject."

Deborah looked straight into his eyes but didn't answer. He tried to return her gaze.

"You don't seem troubled by the state of things these days," he said.

Her evanescent smile flashed across her face. "I am, in my own way. But I can't really think of anything that I can do about it."

"Your story's not like that."

"No, it's an escapist fantasy—as I told you."

"I can guess what you're escaping from, but do you know what —where you're escaping to?"

This time she smiled more broadly. "No, I don't."

They fell silent, as if by agreement, and sat without speaking for several minutes. Then, somehow, they stood up at the same time and went back inside. Dan found himself feeling a little calmer about things, although he could think of no reason why he should.

Two days later, Matthew pulled him aside to talk to him again.

"I went to my Unity Party representative and talked to him about Paul," he said. "I mean, it seems to me I have a right to know what the situation is. I've been a loyal Party member."

THE HEATSTROKE LINE

"What did he say?"

"He said he would look into it and get back to me in a few days. So I guess I'll wait a little longer. Just wanted to let you know."

Now, Dan thought, Matthew would almost certainly be arrested. He was too good-natured to be sufficiently distrustful of others. It made Dan sad, but he couldn't bring himself to encourage Matthew to kidnap Lyons, much as he would have liked to see it done.

The next day was Saturday. As usual, Rebecca had set out sandwiches for lunch on the dining room table. After Dan had eaten by himself he went to sit down in the living room. Everyone seemed to be in their own rooms, but Dan was hoping that Deborah might come downstairs and talk to him. Instead, Hiram walked in with an annoyed look on his face.

"Dan, do you have a minute?"

Dan said "Sure," assuming that Hiram wanted to discuss the destruction of the rice crop.

"I need to talk to you about your relationship with Deborah."

Dan's heart jumped, and he felt red hot. He could feel himself starting to sweat. Hiram had obviously seen him talking to Deborah on a number of occasions, but what was he thinking now? Had Deborah said something? He was convinced that his feelings toward her weren't inappropriate, but maybe they would seem that way, particularly to Deborah's father.

"Why, what's up?" Dan answered, after too long of a pause and in too casual a voice.

"You've been recommending European novels to Deborah. I know she's a big reader, but she should be reading American novels. That's what she was reading before you got here."

Dan's sense of relief was so great that he nearly laughed out loud. But after a moment's reflection, he realized that this was a serious matter for Hiram. Even if Dan thought it was funny, it could get him banished from the house as surely as some real impropriety.

"Listen Hiram," he answered. "Deborah's a very smart girl and she thinks for herself. When I got here, she'd just finished reading *Anna Karenina*, and I obviously hadn't suggested that to her."

"What is that, Italian?"

"No it's Russian. The people we were fighting against in World War II."

"But the other day she was reading a foreign book that you recommended to her. Something about a fruit."

"A fruit?"

"Yes, she told me the name. It's a French book."

"You mean *Père Goriot?*" Dan asked, again making a determined effort not to laugh.

"That's it. Look, I know you're a very well educated person, and maybe that sort of thing is fine in Mountain America, but we're in a different situation here. We have to sustain our culture —American culture. Do you know what . . ."

There was a tremendous, booming sound, and the big glass window in the back wall of the living room shattered into fragments. A wave of heat hit Dan. Hiram ran to the window and looked outside. "Oh my God," he said, someone's blown up the power plants."

Dan went toward the window, stepping carefully over the pile of broken glass that lay in front of it. Both the big power plant near them and the smaller one further away were enveloped in flames, and two of the tall smokestacks on the nearer plant were gone. As he watched, with an indefinable sense of horror, the remaining smokestack broke off at its base and went crashing to the ground.

CHAPTER 24

Rebecca and Joanna came rushing downstairs, with Deborah close behind them, and Rebecca asked what happened.

"Look," said Hiram, pointing. "Someone's blown up both the power plants." He paused as they all stared through the gaping window space. "We have to get out of here Rebecca. We'll die in this heat if we stay."

"Where will we go? Won't Nathaniel and Miriam's power be out too?"

"Everyone's power is out—they've destroyed both power plants. We've got to get out of Birmingham. We can go to Huntsville—to Cousin Andrew's house. I'll try to reach him on the link. And I'll try to reach Nathaniel—just to see what's happened. But we've got to get moving right away. Everyone's going to be trying to get out of here."

It now occurred to Dan—for the first time, he was surprised to realize—that this must be the distraction that the Canadians had referred to in their message. But it seemed hard to believe. Would they really destroy an entire city just to rescue him?

"We need to pack," said Rebecca.

"There's no time—all right, ten minutes. Everyone go up to your rooms and pack some clothes and whatever else you want that you can carry, and be down here again in ten minutes flat. Remember, there'll be very little room in the car with all four of us. And we have to hurry."

"What about Dan?" Deborah asked. Dan tried to restrain the rush of pleasure he felt because she had remembered him.

Hiram hesitated and looked at Dan. "We really don't have room in the car," he said.

Dan had to think fast. Obviously, he wouldn't want them to take him even if they could, but he needed to get away from them and to the rescue point—the abandoned shopping center—without attracting suspicion.

205

"Don't worry about me. Matthew Clarke told me he'd come to get me if anything like this happened."

"You thought about this in advance?"

"Well, we have to have an emergency plan at the lab—in case someone, well anyway, we need to preserve our work and be able to set up somewhere else."

"Okay, that's good then," said Hiram. Clearly glad that he didn't have to deal with Dan any further, he rushed up the stairs, followed by the other members of the family. Dan tried not to look at Deborah, who would certainly know that he was lying. But what would she think?

Once they all had gone, Dan sat down on a chair and looked around the empty living room. Everything was about to change. He had been a prisoner in this house and, at some level, he had resented every minute of his time here. But it was a segment of his life, filled with the dense succession of experiences that make up daily existence and it had become, in some sense, part of him. Odd as it seemed, he had become accustomed to it. Now he was feeling the anxiety that accompanies a sudden change, no matter desirable that change might be.

Hiram was the first to come back downstairs, carrying a small suitcase. He glanced around with a worried expression, looked briefly out the empty window at the burning power plant, then rushed upstairs. Dan heard his voice, sounding urgent, almost shouting, which was something Hiram never did. A few minutes later, all four family members came downstairs, with Hiram carrying a large suitcase, obviously Rebecca's, Joanna carrying two smaller ones, a stuffed animal under her arm, and finally Deborah, who seemed strangely calm—but Dan could not imagine her any other way.

"We have to get going now," Hiram said to Dan. "The bio-lock is set for you—just close the door when you leave. I guess we'll be back once they repair the power plants."

"I hope they have the police protect our houses," Rebecca added. "There's bound to be—I guess there's nothing we can do."

They all went toward the front door. Joanna said "Goodbye" to Dan and waved. Deborah gazed silently into his eyes as she went out. Would he ever see her again? He couldn't image any plausible scenario that would make that possible.

An unnerving silence followed. Dan could feel his heart pounding. After a minute or two, he crossed the front hall into the dining room and looked out the wrap-around corner window onto

THE HEATSTROKE LINE

the sloping driveway. Hiram had already pulled the car out of the carport and parked it near the top of the driveway, running the motor as he usually did to cool off the interior. He was stuffing the family's suitcases into the little luggage trunk and seemed to be arguing with Joanna about her second suitcase. Deborah was standing still, holding her own suitcase and looking calm and self-contained. Caleb, the next door neighbor, jumped up from behind the bushes that separated the Forrests' driveway from his property. He was holding a GX gun in his hands. Hiram fell to the ground. Caleb was shooting. Rebecca lunged in front of the two girls, then fell sprawling on the ground. Deborah collapsed immediately after, and then Joanna. They were all lying on the ground. Caleb motioned with one hand, and Zipporah, came out from behind the bushes, clutching her baby. Caleb watched her as she hurried around the back of the car and got into the front passenger seat. Then he got into the driver's seat, pulled the door closed and sped out onto the street. The car rose slightly to one side as its rear wheels drove over Hiram's head, sending a splash of red blood out onto the driveway.

Unable to even form a thought, but with a feeling of horror, Dan ran through the front door and out onto the street. Looking to his right, he could see the Forrests' car a few hundred feet away, near where the street curved out of view. The car had slowed to a stop because there were several other cars in front of it. Two men and a teenage boy, all with GX guns, appeared in the middle of the street and started shooting. The little car veered to its right, slammed against a low brick wall that bounded one of the house yards, and rolled over onto its side, then onto its roof, its wheels spinning in the air. An arm with a handgun reached out through the window of the upside down car and one of the men in the street fell to his knees. The other man and the boy starting shooting again, and the arm dropped the handgun and fell limp. From the other side of the car, Zipporah's head and arms appeared, covered with blood, still holding the baby. She paused for a moment then slumped down, and the baby dropped onto the pavement. By now, the man and boy had reached the car and were trying to turn it right-side up. Several other cars sped by, some going in the same direction, some in the opposite one. After a minute, the two of them gave up and ran off, leaving the other man, still on his knees, in the middle of the road.

Dan went around to the side of the house, too numb to think. The Forrests were all lying in the driveway, sprawled in different postures. Trying not to look at Hiram's headless corpse, Dan went over to Deborah. She was on her side, with her eyes closed, looking as if she was asleep. Three circles of blood were spaced at even intervals on the front of her pale yellow dress, two of them still slowly expanding as Dan watched. He picked her up and held her in his arms—for the first time—but the horrible limpness of her body made him set her down at once. Had she really ceased to exist? Could all those thoughts and feelings simply disappear? Dan wished that he could cry or scream, but he just stared at her in disbelief, trying to make sense of something that could not possibly make sense. The heat closed in around him, reaching down into his throat, suffocating him. He simply did not know what to do. He had a vague sense that he had to act, had to go somewhere, but he felt incapable of motion.

There was a rustling to Dan's right—it was Joanna. She wasn't dead, but she was obviously dying. Her dress was also stained with blood, and a rivulet of blood was running down one of her legs. She moved again and opened her eyes, which stared blankly into space. Dan looked at her more closely. The blood on her dress was in wide splashes, not dense circles. It was clearly from Hiram or another member of the family. He followed the rivulet of blood up her leg to her outer thigh, where there was a two inch long, shallow cut. The blood flowing from it was already beginning to coagulate. She sat up. Joanna was essentially unhurt, though obviously in shock. She must have fainted or collapsed when she saw her family members shot.

Passing over Deborah, Dan ripped the sleeve off Rebecca's shirt and wrapped it tightly around Joanna's leg to stop the blood flow.

"Listen Joanna, I can save your life. But you'll have to walk; I can't possibly carry you." In fact, she was nearly as big as Deborah—as big as Deborah had been. "We need to go a little more than a mile. Wait here while I get a stun gun and some water for us."

Joanna didn't answer, but she got up on her feet without apparent difficulty. Dan ran back into the house. He was expecting a rush of cool air to relieve the dreadful heat, but the house was now as hot as the outdoors. It seemed not only empty, but abandoned. Scraps of paper from inside and leaves or bits of garbage from outside were skittering across the floor as the hot air blew in through the open window. He went into the kitchen and opened the refrigerator. For a few seconds, he stuck his head into

THE HEATSTROKE LINE

its refreshingly cool interior, telling himself that he had to clear his mind, but really just to get a moment of relief. Then he took out the big jug of water that was always kept in the refrigerator and two smaller bottles that also had been filled with water, put them on the counter, and added one of the stun guns from the kitchen cabinet where they were stored. Suddenly, he remembered the reader pad with Deborah's story loaded onto it, and ran up to his room. Having retrieved it, Dan stopped and looked around the room where he had lived for half a year, and where he had struggled with so many thoughts and doubts and fears. He sat down on the bed in order to collect himself, but jumped to his feet almost immediately, worried that something would happen to Joanna if he stayed in the house too long. He ran downstairs, sweating profusely, his shirt clinging to his skin, stuffed the three containers of cold water into a bag, put the stun gun around his waist and rushed outside.

Joanna hadn't moved from the place on the driveway where she had fallen, and she seemed as dazed and absent as before. But when Dan said "Come on, let's go," as gently as he could, she came out onto the street and fell in beside him as he started walking.

They walked in the opposite direction from the Forrests' overturned car, along the gradually curving street, turned left onto another residential street and walked down its sloping length until they reached the wide commercial avenue, lined by the usual one-story buildings, that led to the Wailing River Shopping Center. As Dan recalled, the avenue forked about halfway to the Shopping Center, and he needed to follow the road that went to the right. Cars were roaring down avenue in both directions, but not as many as he had expected. A family—two women and two little boys—came out from one of the houses on a side street, carrying suitcases, looked around forlornly when they reached the avenue, and headed off in the opposite direction.

The wide expanse of the avenue seemed to increase their exposure to the sun. As Dan stared into the wavering distance, the heat closed in on him again. He felt as if he was forcing himself through an almost solid medium—successive walls of searing air that slammed against him as he walked. He was gasping, dripping sweat from head to toe, and the blood was pounding at him in his head.

Joanna let out a sudden sob, soft but urgent. Dan looked at her. She had stopped walking, and was staring at a biter bug that had settled on her forearm, huge and metallic black against her pale skin. Dan had his stun gun out immediately and in a single motion zapped the bug, which fell off and landed on the pavement upside down. There were only the small wounds from the bug's anchor legs on Joanna's arm, and Dan quickly wiped the drops of blood away with the front of his shirt. She was silent, staring blankly into the distance. They started walking again; Dan staggered a few times, and could feel himself gasping. The air seemed to sear his throat as he struggled for breath. He slowed down, almost to a stop, but when Joanna looked at him with confusion, he forced himself to keep moving—one step, then another, pushing himself forward against an almost palpable resistance. Then Dan felt a wave of nausea rise up inside him. He tried to suppress it, and suddenly he was retching convulsively. He sank to his knees, made one last effort to control it, then started throwing up again. Finally, the attack stopped on its own. He was sweating even more heavily now, if that was possible, and his mouth was dry and foul. He reached into the bag he was carrying for the jug—no, that would be disgusting—took one of the small bottles and drank it completely. Then he offered the jug to Joanna, who drank slowly, water dripping down her chin. He hadn't spoken to her since they started walking, he realized. He should say something, but what should that be? Nothing seemed right, so they just started walking again.

The street was almost empty now, with only an occasional car racing along it and no people in sight. The heat was pouring down on Dan from the sun-bleached sky, rising up from the pavement, closing in on him from all around. He looked at Joanna. She was sweating, and her face looked pale, but she was walking steadily, without apparent difficulty. She was stronger than he was, Dan thought. For the first time, his feeling of discomfort rearranged itself as disability, and he began to wonder if he would make it to the pick-up point.

Maybe he should try Jiangtan, he thought. Maybe he should try to imagine that he was walking through the Arctic, not in its present state but as it was before, with vast, frozen snowfields all around him and a cold, clean wind blowing steadily across it. He hadn't even thought of using Jiangtan when Stuart was killed; maybe it would be useful now. But somehow he had no idea how to start—he couldn't focus his mind. Was it really true that Deborah no longer existed? Was there really nothing left but a blood-stained shell that looked like her, lying lifelessly behind them on the driveway?

A sudden blow against his back. He fell forward onto the payment, scraping his arm. Some laughter, and a teenage boy grabbed the bag with the jug and the remaining water bottle. There were three boys. They went running down the avenue and disappeared around a corner.

Dan sat up. His elbow was stinging and he pressed it against his side. Joanna was looking at him blankly. "Don't worry," Dan said, his voice soundly strangely hoarse, "we'll have plenty of water when we get there." He picked up the reader pad that had fallen from his pocket, struggled to his feet, and started walking again, with Joanna following beside him. He tried to wipe his sweating face with his sleeve—no use, his shirt was completely drenched. Now his head began to hurt, a dull ache in his right temple, building to a steady ache across the whole top of his head, then a crashing, throbbing pain, as if a knife was being turned inside his skull. He had to go on, they had to get to the pick-up point. One block, then another. Shouldn't they have arrived already—how long would they have to walk?

When they crossed the next side street—no cars now—Dan stopped sweating. That was better; there was even a breeze, and he felt slightly cooler. His head was still hurting, although maybe not as much as before. But he was tired, very tired. Maybe they should stop. Where were they going anyway? There was something wrong, but what was it? He should stop and think. He could figure it out, but only if he had some rest.

The street split in two. Which way should they go, to the left or to the right? Did the left lead to the north? Maybe it would be cooler there. No, to the right, where the village with the fire was. What village? Did it matter? Yes, it did. He had to keep following the path. What path? He had lost the path. He had lost it a long time ago. Maybe when he was staying with the Forrests. No, even earlier. He had made a terrible mistake. Did he know it at the time? He wasn't sure, but he knew he couldn't go back now.

Where were the stars? There were no stars in the sky. It was blue and empty, there was nothing to protect him from the sun. The emptiness was pounding on him, driving itself into his head, a burning, searing pain that wouldn't stop. He couldn't swallow. It wasn't fair, it wasn't his fault. Yes, it was, it was his fault, it was all his fault, he had made the wrong choice, he had always made the wrong choice. He had to take it back, please take it back.

Where was his family, what had happened to his family? Where was Deborah? What would she tell him to do?

He couldn't go on, he had to get away from the sun and from the empty sky. Here, in this building. It was dark, he could sit down and rest himself against one of the walls. Which one? That wall, it was slightly wet, there was water dripping slowly from somewhere above. He had to rest. His eyes were burning. He had to close his eyes.

He was walking across a vast expanse of frozen ice, and he was shivering in the cold. The sky overhead was black, deep black and there were no stars. Far ahead of him, he could see low hills, but they were made of ice as well and they were jagged, like the teeth of an enormous creature. The ice was empty—no, there were people in the ice, thousands of people, but they were blind, they had no eyes, and they were drumming on the ice, first with one fist, then the other. He tried to walk past them, tried not to look at them, but they kept drumming with a rapid, steady beat that boomed and echoed back and forth across the frozen landscape.

CHAPTER 25

Dan was awake, but the drumming didn't stop. He was sitting in a large, empty building, with leaves and garbage scattered all across its concrete floor. There was a wide entrance, blazing in the brightness of the day, with someone standing in it. He couldn't tell who it was—the light from outside was too bright. Dan struggled to his feet, gasping in the heat, and walked slowly and painfully toward the entrance. The person was a young girl, it was Joanna, and as Dan approached, he could see that she was saying something to him. He reached her in a few more steps, she pointed, and Dan looked out of the entrance. Two enormous black helicopters, with the letters MMTU on their sides, were sitting on an expanse of fractured concrete—the parking lot of the abandoned shopping center—their rotors turning slowly, and emitting a steady, drumming sound.

A group of people, all in military uniforms, were coming towards them. Dan recognized the uniforms; they were Canadian. By the time they reached him, the helicopters had cut their engines, and although the rotors were still turning, it was quiet. The man in front was thin and lithe, with short grey hair and eyes that crinkled at the corners.

"Dr. Danten?" he asked, examining Dan and then glancing at his wrist link. Dan nodded. "We're here to exfiltrate you," the man continued. "We're taking you to the UFA airfield in Cincinnati. Who's this girl? My orders are to take you, and no one else."

Dan tried to answer, but nothing came into his mind. He simply couldn't find any words to say. He stared at the man for a few moments, then grabbed Joanna's arm with both his hands and pulled her toward him.

The man turned to three other military personnel, two women and a man, who had come up beside him. "He's got heatstroke, get the medics out here right away and get him into the copter."

"What about the girl?" one of the women asked.

"Oh, what the hell. Bring her too."

The next moment, Dan was lifted up, placed on a stretcher and carried into the helicopter. It was cool inside and looked even larger than it did from the outside, with more military people and all sorts of equipment. Two people started wrapping plastic sheets around his body and another person, a young woman, gave him some cool water from a plastic bottle with a tube. Dan drank deeply, the water filling his mouth and throat, bringing a relief that ached with its intensity. The woman took the tube away.

"Not too much at one time, Dr. Danten. Wait a little, and I'll give you some more. You're dehydrated." The plastic sheets surrounding him turned cold, there was cold water flowing through them, and Dan felt a sense of pleasure and well-being spread throughout his body. He relaxed and closed his eyes.

When he opened them again, a different man and woman were standing over him. The plastic sheets were still around him, but the water in them wasn't as cold as it had been before. He felt strange, only partially located within his body. To his surprise, he found himself still holding the reader pad with Deborah's story. Somehow, he had never let go of it.

"How long have I been out?" Dan asked. His words had returned, he realized, but his voice sounded hoarse and unfamiliar. The woman lifted the plastic bottle, and let Dan drink from the tube again.

"Not long, about twenty minutes. How do you feel?"

"Better. OK, I guess. I've got a headache."

The thin, grey haired man appeared above Dan and nodded to the woman, who quickly gave Dan an injection. Dan closed his eyes for a moment and felt his thoughts coming back into focus. He could hear someone sobbing—obviously Joanna.

"Where are we going—oh, I remember, you said to the UFA airfield in Cincinnati."

"That's right, Dr. Danten."

"Will I be taken to Denver from there?"

"I don't know. Colonel Tully will meet you there to explain everything."

"Can I call my family?"

"No, I'm afraid not. We have to maintain radio silence. We don't know what anti-aircraft capacities they have down here."

Dan hesitated before asking the next question, dreading the answer. "What about my family? Are they all right?"

THE HEATSTROKE LINE

"You have to ask Colonel Tully. I really don't know anything. I was added to this mission just this morning."

"You're a high-ranking officer, aren't you?" The man nodded, smiling slightly.

"Are these helicopters really from Mid-Manitoba Technical University?"

"No, that's a sort of cover. We're Canadian Air Force, but the MMTU logo is plausible because they've suffered so much theft and damage from the people down here."

Dan paused for a moment. He could still hear Joanna crying. "You know, all you needed to do is bomb the lab. There's no point to destroying the Birmingham power plants. The scientists who were working at the lab will just go to one of the other Confederacies and try again. My impression is that they have a number of labs. I said that in my message."

The officer gave a short laugh. "Don't worry about it. We're bombing all the power plants in the Confederacies. Every single one."

"What?"

"And the UFA has stationed gunboats in the Ohio and Potomac Rivers and in Mississippi Bay. These people are gone."

"But why?"

"Because we're sick of them. We're sick of all the terrorism and the thefts. And we know that it's the people from this part of the old United States who were behind the nuclear bombing of Montreal and Toronto. President Chiron was from here—Birmingham, as a matter of fact. The biter bug plot you told us about was just the final straw."

"But that's five million people."

"Three million, by our count."

Dan fell silent and looked away from the officer. There was a window near him. He sat up and looked out. Below him was a city, at least as large as Birmingham. Nashville probably. Both of its power plants were burning, and cars were streaming out of it along the roads that fanned out in all directions. The impression of a disturbed ant colony was irresistible—hot water poured down the opening and thousands of panicked ants—no, not panicked, that was giving them too much credit—disoriented ants, ants without a sense of where they were, rushing about in a desperate effort to preserve their individual existence. Life had become cheap in this tired, overheated world, Dan thought. But it had always been cheap. It was cheap when Rome built its Empire, cheap when the Conquistadors marched through a new world, cheap when modern Western nations went to war against each other, cheap when the United States lashed out in desperation against Canada. People treated it as something infinitely valuable, they enlisted in the same charade of caring that he and Garenika were enacting when they lavished so much effort on their children. But the disposability of human beings lay waiting in the shadows, like a silent, ever-patient predator. How else had the world's population shrunk from ten billion to 700 million? One might have thought, after such a steep decline, that the remainder would be treasured, that people would unite to save themselves from the ongoing catastrophe that they were facing. Just the opposite had happened. Nine billion deaths had only inured people to death, re-emphasized the terrifying cheapness and disposability of individual existence. And now the Canadians, freed from their remaining inhibitions by the UFA's complicity, were casually exterminating another several million, scattering them like mindless, instinct-driven ants.

The helicopters reached Cincinnati a short time later and settled down in a landing area. Joanna had stopped crying and seemed to be in shock again, staring blankly and unseeingly into the distance. She and Dan got out of the helicopter side by side. There was a tall Asian man in uniform waiting for them, with a young white woman in a flowered dress by his side.

"Are you Colonel Tully?" Dan asked the man. "Where's my family?"

The man smiled. "No, I'm the UFA representative. This is Colonel Tully," he said, pointing to the woman.

"Your family's here," she said. Following her lead, they began walking toward a low concrete building at the edge of the airfield. Dan felt his heart beating heavily inside him.

"Well, thanks for bringing them," he said, trying to collect his thoughts.

"We couldn't very well leave them in Mountain America. There's a warrant out for your arrest."

"What?"

"Your wife will explain everything to you. Do you want to see her first, or everyone at once?"

"I want to see my wife."

The woman nodded and went into the building. She came out a few moments later, looked at Dan and said "Okay, you can go inside."

THE HEATSTROKE LINE

There was Garenika. She was thin and pale, but she looked beautiful. Dan embraced her, unable to speak.

He held her for what seemed to be a long time before he stepped back.

"Did Michael die?"

"Yes, did someone tell you? I asked them not to."

"No, I had a premonition."

"That's not like you Dan. When did you have it?"

"Early March."

She shook her head. "Michael died before Christmas. He went peacefully."

Dan wondered if that was true. He thought back to Christmas, and about trying to contact his family during that idiotic Battle of the Bulge Parade.

"I'm so sorry," he said at last.

"It wasn't your fault Dan."

"I never should have gone to the Confederacies in the first place. I thought I could accomplish something, but I didn't—I didn't think it through, I guess."

She took his hand and held it. Dan struggled to control himself.

"What about Josh and Senly?"

"They're fine Dan. They're in the next room."

"How did you manage, Garenika?"

"You mean, how come I didn't fall apart with all of this?" Dan nodded, and she smiled weakly.

"Well, I probably would have if you'd been around to take over for me. But I couldn't let myself. I had to be there for Josh and Senly."

Dan was deeply moved. He realized that he truly loved her, that he not understood her, or himself, for all these years. Tears came to his eyes, but he controlled himself again.

"How are you doing Dan? You don't look good."

"I got heatstroke getting to the rescue copters. But I'm alright now, I think. The whole experience was horrible, or most parts of it anyway—and very strange. I guess it was horrible for you as well."

"It was, but, as you can see, we managed."

"What's going to happen to us, Garenika? It doesn't sound like we can go back to Mountain America. The officer here told me there's a warrant out for my arrest."

"Not for you dear—for us, because of me," she answered with a fleeting smile.

"What?"

"The Canadians contacted me last week to tell me that they were going to rescue you because you'd given them some very valuable information, and that they were moving us to Canada. But I was worried that they wouldn't follow through once they had the information, so I went into your lab at the University and downloaded all your files. I figured that they would keep their promise to get the benefit of your research. Fortunately, no one realized what I'd done until after we were taken here."

"Well, I can see why they were angry. There's information in my files about Mountain America's use of bio-chemical toxins to control insect damage. The Canadians will probably switch a lot of their agricultural contracts to China."

"That's tough shit for Mountain America. They should have rescued you as soon as you were captured."

"So what happens to us? You said we're being taken to Canada."

"Yes, you have a position at the University of South Baffin Island. And they're giving us a house. I insisted on it."

Dan was overwhelmed. He embraced his wife again, and only slowly let her go.

"Who's this?" Garenika asked, pointing to Joanna, who had retreated to a corner of the room.

"That's Joanna, the daughter of the family I was placed with. The rest of them are dead. I had—I formed a sort of bond with her older sister."

"Well naturally, you had to have someone who would be your friend."

"Yes, she was my friend. That's it, that's it exactly. I want to tell you everything that happened. It was, well . . ."

"It's okay, we'll talk later. Right now you should see the children. I'll send Josh in first." She smiled at Dan and went toward the door to the adjoining room, then paused and turned back. "Are we adopting Joanna?" she asked.

"Well, yes, I guess we are."

She nodded and went out the door. A moment later, Josh came in. He smiled, strode forward and embraced his father.

"I'm so glad to see you Dad. We were all so afraid for you. I'm sure you were afraid for us as well."

Dan looked at Josh. He looked as handsome and as well composed as ever, but now he realized that there was something stiff and vaguely mechanical about him.

THE HEATSTROKE LINE

"I was," Dan answered, not sure what to say.

"It's so sad about Michael. But, you know, there's nothing that you could have done. No one could do anything for him."

"I'm sorry I missed your birthday Josh. How are you doing?"

"I'm fine. But I'm mad as hell about the way that Mountain America treated you. So you'll be glad to know that I've given up on American Patriotism. Now that we'll be living in Canada, I want to work for their government. I want to help make sure that the American Successor States never unify, that they never have the power to attack anyone again."

Dan suddenly felt sad for his son. He had assumed that his prior commitment to American Patriotism came from a need for independence, but he realized now that it was something different.

"It's okay Josh, take some time. You don't have anything to prove to me. Your mother and I think you're great, no matter what you do."

"I know Dad. The two of you have always been there for me."

"Listen, take some time. This is going to be a tough transition. Tough for all of us, but especially for you kids. Cut yourself some slack."

"But I want to . . ." Josh paused. Dan held him by his wrists.

"Just relax, Josh. It's alright, really."

There was another pause.

"I guess I should talk to Senly now," said Dan.

"Okay, I'll send her in," said Josh, and headed for the door with halting steps. The room seemed very silent when he left. After a few more moments, Senly came in. She stood still, looked at her father, then walked forward and stopped a few feet in front of him.

"Hi Dad. Boy, you went through a lot just to get me away from my friends."

Dan couldn't help smiling. "I'm sure you'll find new ones in Canada who are equally irresponsible."

"I'll get right to work on it—provided I'm no longer grounded. I finished my report on Saturn."

"What report? I don't know what you mean."

"The one you made me do when I was suspended from school for a week. Remember?"

Dan remembered now. It was six months ago, at most, but it seemed as if an immense amount of time had passed. So much had happened and so much had changed. None of them would ever be the same. Nothing would ever be the same. Dan tried to

219

think of some response, and suddenly he found himself sobbing, his chest heaving, tears rolling down his cheeks. He doubled over, his hands covering his face.

"Oh shit," said Senly. "I'm so sorry. I'm really sorry Dad. I didn't mean to upset you like that."

Dan took some deep breaths and wiped his eyes with his sleeve. His sobs subsided, and a sense of weary calm replaced his unexpected agitation.

"It's fine Senly, it's not your fault. I'm not sure why I got upset. I'd love to read your report. I'll look forward to it, I'm sure it's wonderful."

They stood and faced each other, awkwardly but looking straight into each other's eyes. Then Senly walked past him and up to Joanna, who was still scrunched in the corner.

"Hi Joanna," she said. "My name's Senly."

To Dan's surprise, Joanna looked up at her and nodded.

"Mom told me that you saw both your parents shot today," she continued before Dan could turn and get in front of her.

Joanna nodded once again, and Dan stopped in his tracks.

"She said your sister was shot too." Once again, Joanna nodded.

"That's really tough. I never had a sister." The two girls looked at each other.

"Do you play any online video games?" Senly asked after a pause.

"Prisoners, sometimes."

"Yeah, I've played that. It's a little out of date. Ever play Mordread?"

"No."

"It's great fun. There's over a hundred thousand kids in its communal. I can teach it to you. There's a terminal in the other room."

To Dan's astonishment, Joanna stood up, and started walking next to Senly as she turned to go.

"The way to win is to operate your destroyer and your defender at the same time. It takes some practice—lots of practice, actually," Senly added, as the girls walked through the door together.

EPILOGUE

Virtually no one who lived in the Confederacies east of Mississippi Bay survived the Canadian attack. It was impossible to swim across the Bay, and the few people who managed to elude the UFA gunboats and swim across the Ohio or Potomac Rivers were quickly apprehended and either executed or sent back below the Heatstroke Line, which amounted to the same thing. A few weeks later, as the Mountain American diplomatic team had predicted, the UFA began moving people into Kentucky. It hadn't managed to get rid of the biter bugs, but that no longer seemed to matter very much.

Of the four or five hundred thousand people who lived in the four Confederacies west of Mississippi Bay, about a hundred thousand were resourceful or remorseless enough to get control of a vehicle, find the necessary fuel, and reach the Mountain America border station at Liberal, Kansas. The troops that President Simonson had stationed there let in the people that they deemed resourceful and turned away or shot the ones they deemed remorseless. After a few weeks of debate over the net, Simonson decided that no effort would be made to repopulate the area that these Confederacies had occupied.

Dan was grateful his role in the events that had eradicated the Confederacies went unacknowledged and that he was treated as a scholar rather than a political celebrity. The University of South Baffin Island gave him a permanent position in the Biology Department and, as Garenika had told him, the government gave him a house—in fact, the hillside house that Jarrel Lucan had showed him when he attended the entomology conference. They also gave Garenika a position at USBI managing a nutrition laboratory, which she liked much more than her job as a food inspector. Josh, as expected, performed brilliantly in his new school and Senly, as expected, performed equally well on the exams and indifferently on her homework and reports. Joanna was immediately accepted as a full member of the family and did well enough in school, although she had expected to stop attending at the end of the year. Her crying fits diminished over time, and, with Senly as her regular companion, she occasionally showed flashes of her previous ebullience.

In September, Dan was recognized by the Canadian government for something that was much less significant than his disclosure of the biter bug plot, but much more gratifying for him. It was an award for the best entomology article published in Canada during the previous academic year. Dean Horace suggested to him that the award put him in a position to request a benefit of some sort from the government, and gave him a contact number. She was probably thinking of something on the order of a funded research leave, but instead Dan asked that Michael's body be transferred from Denver to South Baffin Island. To his surprise, the government agreed, and so two military helicopters—this time bearing the insignia of the Canadian air force rather than the letters MMTU—were sent to Denver to transport the coffin.

When Michael was reburied on Baffin Island, the family held a simple ceremony at the new gravesite. Garenika spoke about his birth and his fortitude in the face of death, and Josh spoke about the sorrow of losing a lifelong companion who would have become an equal had he grown to maturity. Dan had chosen to speak about Michael's life, despite, or perhaps because of his terror that he wouldn't remember very much about it. Refusing to consult the video file that they had stored on the net, he devoted hours of concentrated attention to the task, and finally recalled an amount that he regarded as respectable, if not completely satisfactory. Garenika, Josh, Senly and Joanna returned home after the ceremony, but Dan felt that he needed time alone to think.

The cemetery was on a hillside that overlooked the sea. It was evening, and the sky was turning deep blue, then purple, as the sun set over the water. Dan walked through a park of freshly-planted trees, along a path that paralleled the shore. He recited his speech about Michael in his mind, first as an apology for not spending enough time with him, then simply as a sort of incantation to express his sorrow. Then he thought about all the other people who had died, all the people he had known during his strange experience below the Heatstroke Line. He thought about Stuart and his dreadful death, about Paul Steiner, who had been so friendly to him, and about Matthew Clarke, with his

THE HEATSTROKE LINE

cheerful good nature and ferocious devotion to his partner. He thought about the two affable young killers, Joel and Michigan, about Hiram Forrest and his desperate obsession with American culture, and about Rebecca, the loyal wife, mother and homemaker. He even thought about Nathaniel Wolfson. But most of all, he thought about his evanescent friend, from whom he had learned the meaning of the stars.

Printed in Great Britain
by Amazon